only
so many
summers

EVI JAMES

ISBN: 979-8-9911988-7-5 (paperback)

ISBN: 979-8-9911988-6-8 (e-book)

Cover Art and Chapter Heading Art by WTJones

Cover Design by Mel D. Designs

Map by Tylee Hansen, @tyleeplusart

Editing by Mandi Andrejka, Inky Pen Editorial Services

Proofread and Interior Formatting Edits by Andrea Halland

Visit evijamesauthor.com for more information.

Author's Note

Only So Many Summers contains adult themes that may be difficult for some readers.

Please read the content warnings on this website for more information:

evijamesauthor.com

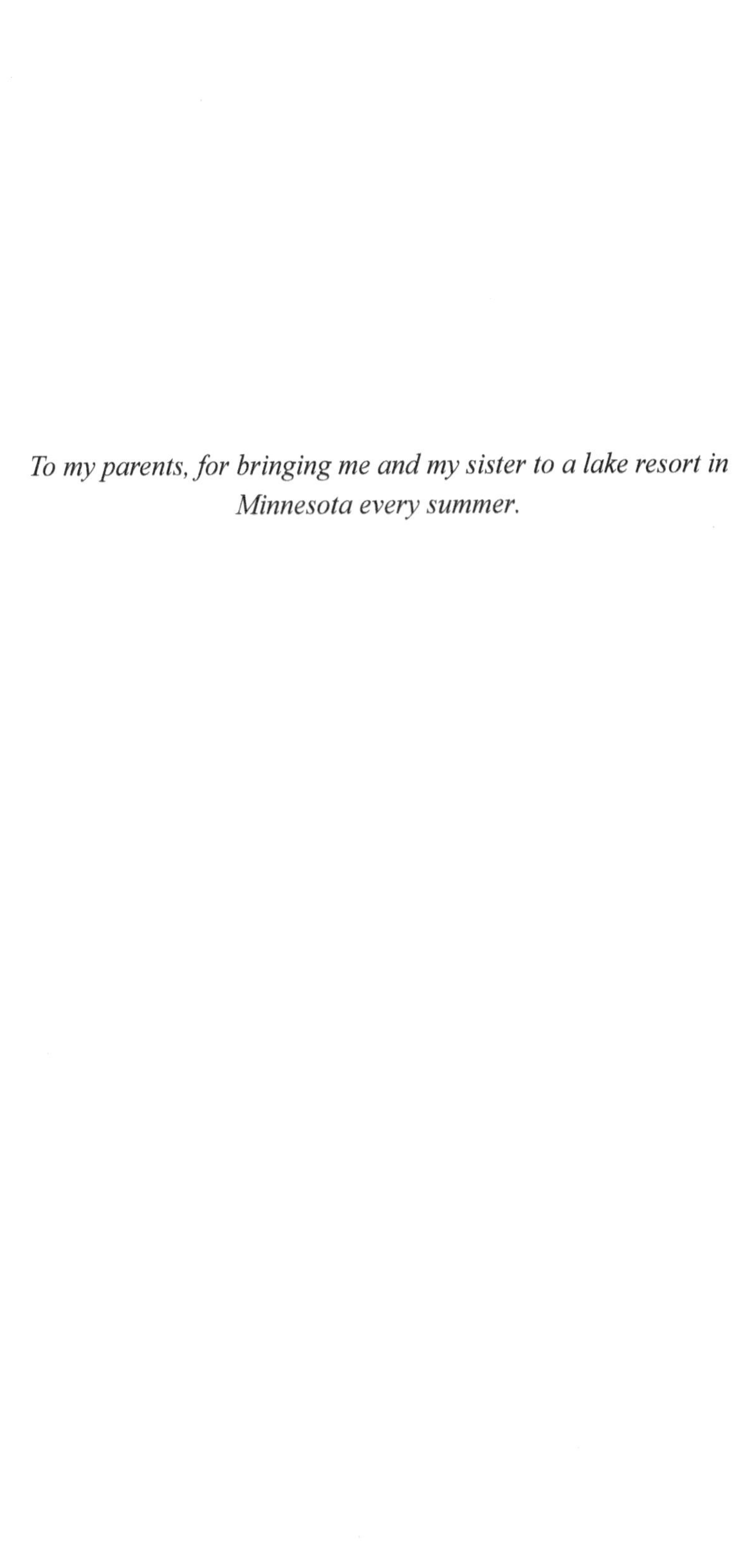

To my parents, for bringing me and my sister to a lake resort in Minnesota every summer.

Agate Harbors
AGATE HARBORS
MIA'S
CHLOE + CALEB'S
LAKESIDE ESTATES
THE LODGE
GILL + BETTY'S
BOWER'S
WATER SKI CLUB
REEL BROS
REEL BROS
BOAT LAUNCH
TIKI BAR
PARTY COVE
PADDLE POINT
ANNIE'S HOUSE
JOJO'S
JOJO'S RESTAURANT
PUBLIC BEACH

AGATE: A FINE GRAINED VARIEGATED, TYPICALLY TRANSLUCENT QUARTZ HAVING ITS COLORS ARRANGED IN STRIPES, BLENDED IN CLOUDS, OR SHOWING MOSSLIKE FORMS. - *MERRIAM-WEBSTER*

Fourteen Years Ago

Chapter One

Mia

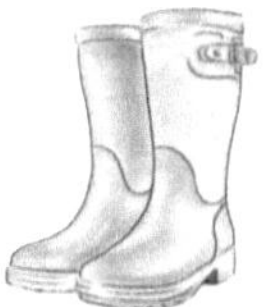

There was something magical about coming to the lake. It was a time capsule my family walked into every summer. We stayed our week, left our dust behind, and took our memories with us.

My sister, Ruby, had beaten me up to our room—the open loft where we slept and shared a bathroom. She always did everything faster, harder, more impulsively. She was older, longer legged, and had fewer bags to carry up the twenty-two stairs into our shared space.

By the time I'd made it to the top, she'd already unpacked her things—shoved shorts and shirts haphazardly into half-closed dresser drawers and scattered her toothbrush and hair ties across the bathroom counter like dice on a craps table.

The quilts covering the identical twin beds had been there since my family had started coming to this cabin at the Agate Harbors lake resort three years ago, when I'd been eight. Each year the fabric became more faded—the only indication that time had passed.

Too bad I couldn't use any of those scratchy quilts.

"You both need to unpack before you run off!" Mom's voice carried from the lower level of the cabin to the open loft above.

"Done!" Ruby announced as she slammed a drawer on her side of the dresser closed with a hip check.

I looked down at the bags still hanging from my arms—the nylon straps making indents in my skin from their weight. Mom had packed me about twice as much as my sister.

Sucks to be me.

"See you, sis." Ruby brushed by me, a breeze of cool air hitting my face in the stifling hot loft.

"Where are you going?"

She paused, her legs straddling two different stairs. "Out."

A typical Ruby answer. "With your vacation friends?"

"Yeah…" She glanced down, peeking through the railing to where our mom unpacked below. "With them."

My sister jogged down the rest of the steps, and I heard the screen door squeak as it opened.

"Where are you going to be, Ruby?" Mom called out.

"I don't know yet." There was a pause. I braced myself for my sister's retort. "Maybe if I had a cell phone…I could let you know."

It was the current battle between Ruby and our parents. There were no cell phones in our family until you had your driver's license. For Ruby, it meant not having a phone or access to Facebook for the next three years. For my parents, it meant not always knowing where she was or who she was with. In my mind, it was a miserable compromise for both sides.

The screen door slammed against the doorframe, announcing her escape.

Mom let out a sigh.

I doubted I'd see Ruby until dark.

I took the shirts my mom had packed me out of the generic black duffel bag and put them in a drawer of the pine dresser

Ruby and I shared. She had already claimed the three drawers on the right side of the dresser, so I could only use the left ones.

We had to share the room, but at least we didn't have to share a bed. There were two beds in the loft, each with rustic log headboards that were far enough apart that I wouldn't be bothered by Ruby's snores while I slept.

A nightstand that matched the dresser bridged the gap between the two beds, and a single lamp with a bear-themed shade sat on top, which Ruby would make me keep on until late hours of the night so she could read the *Cosmopolitan* magazines she snuck up to the cabin with her. Ruby was only thirteen, but Mom said she acted like she was eighteen—already thinking she was an adult.

I sorted the shirts Mom had packed for me, shoving the ones I knew I couldn't wear to the back of the drawer. I counted how many that left me for the week.

Two. Two shirts that I could wear comfortably.

That wasn't enough to rotate for a week without Mom noticing. I'd have to wear something with a tag that'd annoy me all day. But maybe if I wore my swimsuit more often, I could get away with rotating the two safe shirts.

My heart sank as I pulled out the shorts she'd packed for me.

The same problem.

Mom loved to pack me denim shorts, even though she knew they felt rough against my skin. She thought they were more age appropriate than the soft, stretchy bike shorts I liked to wear. She called my favorite shorts *tumble shorts* to subtly remind me that little kids preferred to wear that style of bottoms.

My teeth felt funny just thinking about the denim shorts rubbing against my thighs. If I wore those, I'd be bothered by them all day.

I pushed the three pairs of denim shorts to the back of my drawer. There was one pair of the soft bike shorts I liked. Those would be the only bottoms I'd wear this week. And my swim-suit. I'd have to live in my swimsuit.

At least she hadn't noticed the three pairs of socks I'd snuck into the bag. They were my favorite. Seamless, no hard bunches of thread and fabric that would irritate the top of my toes with every step. I couldn't stand that. Even standing still, I could feel it—I couldn't focus on anything else when I had a toe seam.

My hands reached the bottom of my duffel, where I'd thought I'd find my tennis shoes, but it was empty.

"Mom!" I yelled from the loft. "Where are my tennis shoes?"

"What? Are you still here, Mia?"

I walked over to the wood railing that matched the pine of the dresser and nightstand. I leaned over the edge, glancing at my mother in the kitchen below. She was unpacking the two giant coolers that sat on the linoleum floor full of breakfasts, lunches, and dinners for the week. Two bottles of margarita mix sat on the counters next to the blender. My parents called it "vacation juice."

"My tennis shoes—did you pack them?"

"They're in your bag with your clothes." Mom continued to unpack the coolers, her head in the fridge with only her arms reaching out from behind the refrigerator door to grab perish-ables from the cooler next to her. "Have you looked there?"

I went back to my duffel bag, frantically searching every pocket and compartment one more time. "They're not in there!"

Mom mumbled something about wondering where Dad was, followed by something heavy landing on the kitchen counter that made a *thud*. "Then we must've forgotten them."

I closed my eyes, trying to control my increasing heartrate. "Can we go to the store to get a pair?"

Mom scoffed, and a cabinet door slammed shut. "Mia, do you hear yourself? We've just spent four hours in the car driving up here. No one is getting back in the car to drive forty minutes into town to buy you a pair of tennis shoes." Another cabinet door slammed. "Not when you have a perfectly good pair of sandals."

"But I like wearing tennis shoes." The kind that covered my feet completely. No dirt or sand ever met the skin of my feet when I had socks and tennis shoes on.

She stopped unpacking and tilted her head back to see me up in the loft. "Don't be ridiculous. Just wear your sandals and stop complaining."

Sandals were the worst. I always had to be on the lookout for loose gravel or the inevitable stray grain of sand that'd end up between the bottom of my foot and my sandal when I wore them.

Mom never listened to me.

I sighed, resting my forehead on the ledge of the railing, my nose pressed against the lacquered finish. It still smelled like polyurethane. From up here, I could almost see the entire lower level. Like the loft, the rest of the cabin was quaint and homey—but I didn't mind it. The cabin was just a place to sleep. The real vacation was outside these walls.

This summer vacation was a break for all of us, mostly from each other. Mom and Dad were both teachers, surrounded by students for nine months straight. They didn't seem to mind that Ruby and I went our separate ways while they sat by the pool or resort bar sipping margaritas. It was the only time of year I saw them drink. It was also the only time of the year they loosened their grasp on Ruby and me.

Usually they held tight—sometimes so tight I felt like my head would pop off my body. If it wasn't good grades at school, it was our manners at the dinner table. If it wasn't the extracurricular activities they signed us up for to "keep us busy," it was the incorrect way we'd made our beds in the morning. There was always something to comment on.

Enough that for this one week in the summer, it felt like someone pushed the release button on our family's pressure cooker.

Freedom. Blissful freedom.

I unzipped my second duffel bag. It was full of the things my mom knew I needed even though, when asked, would claim it was unnecessary. She always packed them for me or knew I'd end up in her bed late at night, insisting I sleep next to her with her arm draped over my stomach.

I liked to sleep feeling crushed.

There was no other way to explain it. I needed weight on top of me, holding me down, to sleep. Something about the pressure on me felt calming. No one understood it, but it felt good to me. Even in this stifling loft, I'd be hot, I'd sweat, but I'd endure the heat because I needed that weight on me to sleep.

The sheets came first.

I made quick work of stripping my twin bed, shoving the resort's sheets and quilt into their new home—under the bed and out of the way. I pulled out the fitted sheet from my twin bed at home. These were soft, not rough. The fabric didn't get caught on my toenails or the calloused skin of my heels. I stretched it over the mattress and smoothed the wrinkles out of the top.

One by one, I pulled out the four heavy blankets my mom had rolled up to fit into the duffel bag. The first was my favorite. It was pink minky fabric with thick batting. I laid it on the bed. The second was a heavy one from my grandfather's days in the navy. The third was a substantial knitted blanket that I'd found a couple of years ago in the back of our linen closet at home. The final blanket was a hand-tied fleece that I'd made at a sleepover. It had sweet butterflies on one side and solid royal-blue fleece on the other. After the sleepover, I'd brought it home and stuffed it full of the bean bags from my family's cornhole set. No one ever played it, and they never noticed the bags were gone.

It was a whole "Princess and the Pea" situation, only instead of being the princess sleeping on top of all the blankets, I was the pea.

By now it was late afternoon, and the loft was hot. I felt a bead of sweat drip down my back, following the curve of my spine. I took the box fan from the closet and propped it up in the open window, turning the fan to suck in the cooler outside air and blow it into the loft. Hopefully by the time I came back home, the room would be comfortable for sleeping, although how cool I would be under the blankets was debatable.

But that would be later—much later, when the sun had set and the outside air was chilly enough to require a sweatshirt. Right now I'd do anything, including leaving some of my things unpacked, if I could feel the cool breeze brush across my clammy skin.

Looking out the loft window, I could see the tree branches moving back and forth ever so slightly. I couldn't see the lodge, but I knew it was there, and I knew *he'd* be there, waiting for me.

I was twenty-two stairs and a few hundred feet away from starting the best week of my summer, but first I needed to get out of the cabin—preferably before Mom decided we needed to continue the whole tennis-shoe conversation.

I heard heavy steps on the deck as I snuck down the stairs, going one at a time so the treads wouldn't squeak. I was halfway to freedom—far enough that I could see the kitchen between the square spindles of the railing.

"Ah, what can I help you with, Darcy?" My dad opened the side door that led into the kitchen from the deck.

I tested the next tread for squeaks with my toes before putting my full weight on the wood.

"What have you been doing out there? I already have both the coolers unpacked." My mom's normally straight blonde hair was turning wavy in the heat of the cabin.

The brass handle of the cabin's front screen door was within reach. It took everything in me not to skip down the rest of the stairs, fling the door open, and run outside. I just needed to make it down a few more stairs.

"I'll get started on the margaritas," I heard my dad say.

I exhaled as my fingers wrapped around the cool metal handle of the screen door. The wooden stairs hadn't betrayed me.

I'd made it.

I held my breath as I pushed open the door, praying I was going slow enough that the hinges wouldn't whine.

"Don't tell me you're going out like that."

I jumped, letting go of the door. It slammed closed behind me, the hinges tattling on my almost successful escape.

Mom set the cooler she was carrying by the side handles right in front of my toes, her hands settling on her hips as she looked me up and down.

I followed her line of sight to my feet. I had on one of my tag-less blue T-shirts, soft black bike shorts, and my jelly sandals.

"You can't wear socks with sandals, Mia."

Ugh, she'd noticed. But I couldn't wear just the sandals outside of the cabin. All the paths and roads were gravel. Dust and rocks were just itching to jump on my skin. Socks were necessary.

"And your hair," Mom continued, frowning at me. "Can't you just wear it down for once? It looks so nice down. You have such pretty hair."

I ran my fingers through my ponytail on the back of my head. This was hardly the first time I'd heard this, a compliment that really wasn't a compliment. My hair might've been nice—it was blonde and long, but wearing my hair down meant little pieces blowing in my face, tickling my nose, and brushing along my neck. Having it tied back was much more comfortable.

"If you would just let me brush it—" She reached out toward me.

"Mom!" I yelled, twisting away from her hand.

"Fine, fine. It's your vacation. Look however you want."

I turned to leave, my head feeling like it might pop off of my neck at any moment. The screen door swung open, and cool air met my skin. It felt fresh, unlike the city air I was used to.

Outside was quiet except for the bird chatter and the occasional breeze that rustled the leaves of the trees. Peaceful. And mine for the week.

Chapter Two

Bower

"Mia's coming this week, right?" Dean asked me.

We were in the muck, up to our knees. Our feet sank down into the mud beneath the water, where it squished between our toes. We stood there waiting—we wouldn't be able to feel the bites. Leeches had something in their spit that numbed your skin right before they sank their teeth into you. But they were there. Dean had raised his leg out of the water a minute ago, and he'd already had three attached to his calf. Excellent bait for fishing.

"Yeah, she'll be here today," I said. "It's check-in day."

"Guess I won't be seeing much of you this week, then," Dean said.

My best friend lived just off the resort with his mom. She didn't like us hanging out. Something about me being a bad influence on him. Dean didn't care, though. He was always around since his mom worked constantly and didn't have anyone to watch him. Dean didn't need watching, though. Neither did I. We were twelve this summer, about to be thirteen—too old for babysitters.

My grandparents were too busy running the resort to keep

tabs on me. They owned this place, and I lived in the house attached to the lodge with them—where I'd lived since I could remember. When I'd been a baby, my mom's parents had taken me in after realizing my mom and dad were more interested in drugs than caring for me. Betty and Gill had become so much like parents that when my actual parents had died, it hadn't changed much for me. My grandma and grandpa had tried their best for my life to continue at Agate Harbors as usual.

Now I tried not to spend a ton of time around the resort. The lodge was always full of guests who wanted to chat and remark on how tall I had become, never bothering to talk about anything that actually interested me, like where the best fishing on the lake was.

Most days Dean and I were in a boat somewhere on the lake or climbing over shoddy ropes that had Private Property signs attached to them to get to the good fishing spots.

Except for one week every summer.

I flicked my wrist at the water level, sending lake water toward Dean's face. "It's not like that, dumbass," I said.

He loved to bait me.

"Oh, I know it isn't. You haven't even got pube hair yet."

I sent another wave of water Dean's way. "Just 'cause I like hanging out with her doesn't mean I *like* like her."

Mia was a girl I'd met at the resort a few years ago. Her family always came up the week of the Fourth of July. She didn't have anyone else to hang out with while her sister sunbathed and flirted with all the local boys. I didn't hang with her out of pity, though. Mia was fun. She was always up for whatever I wanted to do. I liked showing her stuff she didn't get to do in the city where she lived.

"Yeah, girls are weird. All the hair brushing and not wanting to break a nail…"

He snorted, but I knew Dean was lying. I saw the way he stared at the girls at the resort lying out on the beach in their bikinis, tanning in the sun. He was a half a year older than me, and maybe when I was that old I'd look at girls different too. But this summer all I wanted to do was fish, explore, and have fun.

"Do you think we got enough?" Dean asked.

I nodded, and we both waded toward the shore. We had ridden our bikes to the swampy part of the lake, where it was shady and the water was murky. A hotspot for leeches. I hoped we'd gotten enough. I was planning on fishing with Mia later today, and leeches were the perfect bait for bass.

The water lowered the closer we got to shore. Black blobs emerged from the water attached to our legs. I didn't have much hair on my legs yet either. Less hair made them less painful to remove. Dean's legs had recently sprouted dark hair that matched the hair on his head. He'd have some funny patches of leg hair missing when we finished plucking them off.

I studied my legs once our feet hit dry sand. Eight fat black leeches had attached themselves to my calves, and two were suctioned onto the top of my foot. Dean had gotten more than me —a few had attached themselves to the back of his knee.

Now the race was on. Before the leeches burrowed further into our skin, we had to remove them. The best way was with a flat rock. Dean and I scurried around the beach, looking for the perfect rock. It had to be flat and big enough to hold in your hand, plus have at least one thin, sharp edge.

Dean found two next to each other and tossed me one. We walked over to where our bikes were lying on the sand and pulled out the small containers we'd brought for collecting bait from our backpacks.

We bent down along the shore, filling them with lake water. The gray rock Dean had tossed me was perfect for leech removal. I slid its tapered edge up close to where the leech had attached itself to my skin and pushed down. The leech lost suction, its tiny teeth releasing my skin. With a flick of the rock, the leech fell off my skin and into the container I held below it. It splashed into the water, rolling and extending its body in its new environment. It likely was mad after being detached from its dinner.

We used to use lighters to get the leeches to let go—heat from a flame repelled them too—but Grandma had confiscated all my lighters last month after Dean and I had celebrated the Fourth of July early. I would have to wait until the end of the summer and scope out the lost-and-found box for some new ones.

One by one, I removed each leech from my legs. Trails of blood dripped down from the wounds their tiny teeth had made. Their saliva made it harder for the body to stop bleeding—it'd be a few minutes before the bleeding stopped—but it was worth it for a good afternoon of fishing.

Dean and I finished at the same time and snapped the lids on our leech containers. They wiggled in the water, trying to find their next meal.

"Guess I'll be seeing you." Dean dropped his leeches into his backpack and picked up his bike. He knew he was always welcome to join Mia and me, but he hardly ever did. "Hey, are you and Mia doing the crayfishing contest again this week?"

"Yeah, we are," I said. "She'll kick your ass again."

The resort hosted a crayfish-catching contest each week for the resort goers. I only joined the week Mia was here. It was only fun when she was here to catch them with me.

Mia was super competitive, even though she refused to touch them. She'd developed a particular way of catching the crayfish so she never had to touch them. She was good at it too—she'd gotten first place in the contest last year, besting out almost all the boys her age who'd had no problem getting crayfish slime on them.

Dean snickered as he threw his leg over the bike and mounted the seat. He pedaled away, his legs spinning quickly because of the faulty gear system on the old bike.

My bike had its own problems. The gears worked fine, but the brakes were starting to go out. I had to pull the hand brake just right to get the pads to squeeze the wheel tight enough to slow it.

Our bikes were old and our backpacks older. My grandpa had let us have a couple of bikes that had been sitting in the resort storage shed for several years, still waiting for the guests who had left them there to pick them up. The backpacks were finds from the lost and found after the summer season was over.

That was the best time of the year, when all the summer families had gone and Grandma gave me free rein over the lost-and-found box. At that point in the summer, everything that had been lost would never be found. Except by me.

The sun was straight up in the sky. Mia would be here soon if she wasn't already.

I pedaled down the gravel road to my grandparents' cabin. It wasn't a typical cabin. Instead it was attached to the lodge where the resort guests came to check in. The lodge had an enormous stone fireplace with chairs for guests to relax in and a small coffee station that was busy in the mornings. Two years ago, Grandpa had added a gift shop to the lodge and ordered T-shirts that said *Agate Harbors*.

Agates were like little nuggets of gold up here. People came from all over to search the shoreline for the colorful stones. The blue ones were the hardest to find—and my favorite—but guests loved bringing any agate they found up to the lodge to show off.

They were just pieces of striped quartz. I didn't see what was so special about them. Agates were plentiful—if you knew where to look.

"Bower! What happened to you?" Grandma stood at her clothesline, hanging guest towels with clothespins. We had a whole laundry facility, but she insisted on letting the towels air dry outside. Something about the outdoor smell.

I slowed my bike in front of the lodge. It took a couple of

false stops before my bike finally braked. My legs were still bleeding, drops of blood falling onto the gravel where I stood next to my bike.

"Dean and I were out leeching," I explained as I laid down my bike. It didn't have a kickstand.

"Come here and let me hose you off. We can't let guests see you like this. They'll think you got attacked by something in the woods!"

I followed my grandma over to the side of the lodge where there was a spigot and a green hose. I let her spray my legs, feeling the cold water wash away the blood. When she was satisfied, she sent me inside to change and put on antibacterial ointment. She knew Band-Aids wouldn't stay on my legs for long— they'd just end up floating in the lake.

It was only noon, and my clothes were done for. There was mud and blood all over my shirt and shorts. Fortunately I got a lot of my clothes from the lost and found too. The cabin cleaning crews always found a stray shirt or pair of shorts tucked in the back of a drawer, forgotten. They all ended up inside my dresser.

In my room, I pulled on a pair of orange shorts that matched the orange shirt I was wearing. They were the same shade and everything. I knew that'd annoy Grandma, but I didn't care. Maybe I enjoyed getting the reaction from her. She'd look at me disapprovingly and say, *That rebellious streak of yours is gonna get you into a heap of trouble someday.*

I swung open the screen door, ready to take the heat. But when I stepped outside, any thoughts of riling up my grandmother flew right out of my head.

There she was, in an embrace with Grandma.

Mia was here.

Chapter Three

Mia

It was like I was a moth and the lodge was a flame—I was drawn to it. I knew *he* would be there. *They* would be there. I was just as excited to see Bower's grandparents as I was to see him. They were a comfort like I had never known. They didn't get impatient or frustrated with me, didn't look at me funny when I wore socks with my sandals. Bower and his grandparents just liked having me around, in whatever state I was in.

A breeze blew the towels on the line upward, revealing my presence.

"Mia!" Bower's grandma, Betty, was hanging blue-and-white striped towels on the clothesline when I turned the bend to the lodge. She dropped the towel she was hanging and rushed over to me, wrapping me in a loving, squishy hug.

I didn't enjoy hugging. The last time I'd hugged my parents might've been a few months ago. Their hugs weren't brief, nor were they restrained. Maybe it was because I didn't hug them often, but when their arms were around me, they always squeezed me tight, holding me against their warm bodies for longer than I thought necessary. I'd tried tapping on their shoulders, pulling away—anything to let them know their body squished against mine was no longer appreciated. They never seemed to understand that if I accepted a hug, I wanted it to be brief with minimal body contact, and when I pulled away, it was time for them to do the same.

Betty's hugs were different. I always let her give me a welcome and goodbye hug this week during the summer. Hers were warm and doughy. Her gray hair was always pulled back into a low bun, so it never flew out and tickled my face. And the clothes she wore were soft. She never held me for long and picked up on my cues when I'd had enough.

"I'm so happy to see you," Betty whispered into my ear as I breathed in her scent. She always smelled like fabric softener. She let me go, still holding on to my arms as she took me in. "You've grown since last summer. Almost a young lady."

I grinned, then saw movement behind her. Something orange was coming through the lodge door. Betty turned to follow my gaze.

Bower. Dressed obnoxiously in all orange.

"You look ridiculous," I said. "It's not even deer-hunting season."

Bower smiled, crossing his arms in front of him. He was always so fun to tease. He had grown a lot over the past year. Definitely taller. Maybe a little broader in the shoulders. His blond hair was longer, a little shaggy. He was still Bower, though, with that twinkle in his blue eyes.

"This outfit gets a lot of *bang* for a buck." His eyebrows moved as he spoke.

My hand covered my mouth as I held in a laugh.

"Bower Lee Hanson!" Betty scolded. "Where did you learn to talk like that?"

"School," he answered. "Maybe I shouldn't go back in the fall."

She groaned and rolled her eyes, turning back to me. "Keep

an eye on him this week, Mia. This is the one week his grandpa and I get a break from his shenanigans."

"You know I will," I said.

I'd been told rumors every year about Bower and all the trouble he got into at the resort. Mostly from my sister. She'd heard stories from the kids she hung out with. I'd seen Bower tease his grandparents, maybe push their buttons, but I never saw him do anything that wild—nothing a boy up north with a lake at his fingertips wouldn't do.

It wouldn't surprise me if the stories Ruby brought home were just that—stories. It was a small world on the lake. It seemed that everyone knew a little bit about everyone, and rumors were bound to fly.

"Is that Mia?" Bower's grandpa, Gill, emerged from the lodge, brushing his hands off on his plaid short-sleeved button-down. He smiled as he walked around Bower to approach me. He placed his hand on my shoulder for just a moment, his blue eyes twinkling as his warm voice welcomed me back to Agate Harbors.

And just like that, I felt like I was home. I was comfortable here with Betty, Gill, and Bower. They never pushed past my boundaries; instead they respected the way I wanted to be touched—or in this case, not touched. Betty and Gill always treated me like one of their own this week of the summer. I greedily allowed them to coddle me, while also pretending I had supportive parents who didn't care about my many quirks.

Bower grabbed my wrist. He led me away from his grandparents and walked me toward the beach and the docks.

"Come back this afternoon for Popsicles! I've got orange, your favorite!" Betty called out.

I waved goodbye to her as Bower pulled me along, clearly with some kind of plan in mind.

"I hate when she uses my middle name like that," he complained once we were out of earshot of his grandparents.

I laughed. It was easy to laugh with Bower. It always had been. He was one of those friends where even if we didn't see each other for a year, we always picked back up right where we'd left off. There were never any awkward moments.

"What are we doing today?" I asked.

"I thought we could fish. I found this new spot a couple months ago and got bait this morning." He motioned down to his legs that had little red welts on them.

I scrunched my nose. *Boys.*

The resort's beach was a wide expanse of shoreline. Lounge chairs lined the water with folded blue umbrellas stuck in the sand between them. From the gravel stairs that led to the beach, a wooden boardwalk floated on the sand. We stepped right from the gravel onto the boardwalk—it was long and transitioned into a dock that suspended people over the water. The dock had places for boats to be tied and a small marina hut at the end.

We walked until we met the edge of the lake.

Bower jumped off the wood planks and into the sand. He turned to me, expecting me to jump as well.

I stood there looking at the sand. It was crunchy. The pieces were small and abrasive. The sand would inevitably penetrate the socks and sandals I was wearing. My teeth hurt just thinking about the grains rubbing against my skin.

"My canoe is over there on the beach." Bower gestured toward the silver canoe that was partially pulled onto the shore. Two paddles stuck upright from the sand like stakes in the ground. "I've already got two rods and my tackle box in the hull."

Tiny bead of perspiration dotted my upper lip. Yes, I could do it. I could step onto the sand, get the tiny pieces stuck between my sandals and socks, let the grains push through the fibers of my socks and touch my feet. I could sit on the canoe for a couple of hours while the sand rubbed my skin.

I shuffled back. No, I couldn't. I tried to take deep breaths but could only expand my lungs so far before I took another breath. And another.

"Mia, what's wrong?" He walked over to the boardwalk, flicking sand from the backs of his sandals. I backed up further.

This was so embarrassing. I couldn't walk on the sand. Who couldn't walk on sand? Everyone did it. They didn't even think about it.

Bower looked at me, waiting for an answer. He knew I was different—had things that bothered me. He'd never judged me before.

"The sand," I said. "I can't walk on it. I don't know how to explain it…"

How did I explain I couldn't think of anything else except the sand rubbing against my skin? How I couldn't walk on sand because it made my teeth hurt? Then I'd have to explain that even though my teeth weren't connected to my feet, my body was somehow wired differently. It never made sense to anyone I'd tried to explain it to.

"You walked on the beach last year." He was confused, like everyone else who interacted with me.

My stomach dropped. "It's gotten worse."

"It" was the unspoken thing that caused me infinite amounts of stress and trouble. Something no one understood. Even I didn't understand it, and it was happening inside my body.

Bower turned his back to me.

I sucked in a breath. He was done with me, giving up like everyone else in my life.

Then he crouched down and looked over his shoulder. "Hop on."

It took a moment for his words to register in my brain. I stood there with my mouth open.

"Come on, Mia." Bower snapped me out of my trance, and I jumped onto his back, wrapping my legs around his waist and my arms around his neck.

He put his forearms under my knees and stood up. I squeaked in surprise as he jostled me around, adjusting my weight on his back.

We set off toward the beached canoe. Bower made sure not to kick up sand with his sandals as he walked—he even turned around and let me slide off his back directly into the canoe.

Zero sand contact.

Just like that, we were ready to go out on the lake. No problem at all.

He brushed the grains off the handle of the oar he pulled from the sand before giving it to me. I made my way to the front of the canoe, sitting in the forwardmost seat, and laid the oar across my lap.

Bower was an experienced canoer. He threw his oar into the bottom of the boat, letting it fall on top of his fishing rods, tackle box, and coils of rope. With a single thrust, he pushed us into the water and jumped into the back of the canoe without getting wet. The canoe wobbled back and forth, but it soon found its balance as Bower started paddling, steering us away from the beach. I stuck my oar in the water to help. The front passenger of the canoe was there for paddling, and the back passenger was the rutter, the one who steered the boat. I had the simple job— paddling a couple of strokes on each side of the canoe at my leisure.

The lake was tranquil for it being the afternoon. We kept to the edge of the lake, gliding past other resorts and houses big enough to be resorts themselves. We hardly ever spoke while we paddled. I liked it that way. Nature was meant to be enjoyed quietly.

Between resorts, a side channel hidden by old, waterlogged trees and brush became visible. Bower put his oar into the water on the left side of the canoe, dragging the water and turning us right. I kept my paddle close to the canoe, not wanting it to get stuck when we entered the small space. Bower and I ducked under the arbor of trees that bent over the channel's entrance.

As I sat back up, I felt transported to a magical fairyland. Knotted tree roots lined the channel, their brown bark covered with fuzzy green moss. Trees bent over the water, making a tunnel for us to glide through. Frogs croaked and crickets chirped. I looked back at Bower, who held his oar behind the canoe, steering us through. He smiled at me, and I smiled back. He knew how magical this was. I felt special that he chose to share it with me.

The channel opened to an area of clear, shallow water. It was small but could fit our canoe. I could see the sandy bottom of the lake and the seaweed waving back and forth under the water. We were still under a canopy of trees, completely hidden from the outside world. At the top of the canopy, I could make out a circle of blue sky, the light from the hole in the canopy casting a spotlight on the water.

"This is the best spot for bass." Bower slid his oar underneath his seat and pulled a container filled with water out of his pocket. Black blobs squirmed inside. "And this is their favorite food." He held up the container. Leeches. They gave me the creeps.

"I'm not touching those," I said.

Bower laughed. "I figured you wouldn't." He pulled a fishing rod from the bottom of the canoe and released the line. Detaching the hook from the metal eye, he held the sharp hook between his fingers on one hand while he opened the container of leeches he held between his legs with the other. He plucked one out of the container and pierced it onto the hook. I reached out to grab the rod from his outstretched arm.

"Remember how?"

"Of course I do." I snatched the rod from him, rolling my eyes.

He laughed again. "It's been a while."

It had been a year since I'd fished, but I remembered. It was one of those things that had been engrained in my mind ever since Bower had taught me. Everything about this week every summer was imbedded in my brain. They were the best memories of my summer—maybe of my entire year.

I cast the line out and reeled it in until it was taut, then watched the bobber float in the water and waited. The whirling of Bower's cast and the plop of his bobber hitting the water quickly followed.

We glanced at each other and grinned. This was great. It was quiet and peaceful. Easy. Everything was easy with Bower. He got me.

"How's your summer been?" I kept my voice low and quiet. Just like me, the fish also liked the quiet.

"The usual. Fishing, lighting things on fire, keeping my grandma sharp."

I smiled and shook my head. "Why do you give her such a hard time? She's so nice."

"That's what kids are supposed to do, right? Give their parents grief?"

I couldn't imagine purposefully giving my parents trouble. I did that enough without even trying. "Maybe if it's your parents, but those are your grandparents. They're sweet."

"Well, since my parents are dead, I don't have a choice who I cause trouble for."

My stomach dropped. "Bower, I didn't mean—"

He waved me off. "I know."

Last year, Bower had told me about his parents. They'd both died from overdoses in the city. He didn't remember much about them. He'd been young when his grandparents had taken him in.

I glared out at the water, furious with myself. We'd barely been together, and already I'd said something so stupid. How could I ruin things so quickly?

"Seriously," Bower said, looking over at me. "I was just kidding. It's fine."

He gave me a big, goofy grin, and I couldn't help the smile that crept up in response. Like I said, easy.

My bobber went under the water before I felt the tug on my rod. I gasped, and my heart started pumping fast. I gave my line a little yank before I started reeling it in. The end of my rod bent toward the water. Whatever was at the end of my line was heavy.

Bower set his rod down on the bottom of the canoe as he grabbed a silver net with green plastic netting. When the fish was by the edge of the canoe, he bent down and scooped it up. The fish flopped back and forth as its scaly body hit the air.

"Nice one!" Bower exclaimed.

I smiled, beaming with pride. The bass was huge—it'd eaten its fair share of leeches. Bower made quick work of unhooking the fish and holding it up for me, his thumb in the bass's mouth.

I leaned in close to take a look, admiring its yellow-green scales. My chest puffed up with pride. Then I rocked back in my seat, giving Bower a nod. "Thanks," I said.

He lowered it into the water and let it go before grabbing my hook and re-baiting it with a fresh leech.

Bower knew without asking that I didn't want to touch the leech or the fish. But he knew I still wanted to be there, still wanted to participate. It just had to be in a different way. And he got that.

Chapter Four

Bower

It was already Wednesday—halfway through her week here. This part of the summer always went by too fast. Dean was fun to fish and get into trouble with, but this week with Mia was different. I didn't have to match Dean's wisecracks or make sure I was keeping up with the shenanigans I was known for. By this time of the summer, my grandparents had gotten used to bracing themselves the moment I walked through the door—ready to hear about whatever trouble I'd gotten into that day.

There was no pressure with Mia to act a certain way or say certain things. Everything with her was easy, comfortable, and I liked it that way.

Today was the crayfish-catching contest—a popular weekly event with the guests. The crayfish were plentiful around Agate Harbors. They always stuck around even though they were caught and thrown into a bucket every week by guests. Maybe it was because their brains were tiny. They resembled miniature lobsters, although they were dark brown instead of the typical lobster red. The four-inch-long crayfish that lived around the resort almost looked black as they skittered along the sandy bottom of the lake.

Everyone came with their own methods of catching them. Some had fishing lines, some had nets, and some brave guests used their hands. There was skill in catching crayfish. First, you had to find them. They often hid under rocks or logs. Second, you had to be patient. They were skittish creatures that scurried away from any disturbance to the water. If someone thought they could just dip their hand into the water and grab them from the bottom, they were in for a rude awakening. Some of the bigger crayfish had big pincers that hurt when they snapped your skin.

Mia always did well in the contest. She was smart enough to know where to find them and patient enough to catch them.

Mia smiled when she saw me standing in the grass outside the front door of her family's cabin. She wore the same shirt and shorts as yesterday. But who cared? Everyone here was on vacation—no one wanted to bother with laundry.

"Where are you going, Mia?" Her mother's voice followed her out of the cabin. "Oh. Hi, Bower."

She'd never really liked me, and I knew it. My grandmother told me to be polite to the guests, but there was something about the way Mia's mom talked to her that always bugged me.

I couldn't stop myself from giving her a two-fingered salute, hoping it would make Mia laugh.

Instead, my friend stared at me with wide eyes as we all stood there silently.

I cleared my throat, then finally said, "Hi, Mrs. Miller."

Mia's mom just pursed her lips before looking back at her daughter.

"I'm going to the crayfish-catching contest with Bower," Mia said. "It's down at the marina."

"You'll touch a slimy crayfish, but you won't wear sunscreen?" Mia's mother clucked her tongue. "You're looking a little pink."

She opened her mouth to explain to her mother, but I interrupted. "She has an entire system," I explained. "She never touches them. Good thing too—some of them have big pincers."

Mrs. Miller narrowed her eyes in my direction.

Mia tried to hold back a smile, biting her lower lip with her teeth.

"Fine, go on, then." Her mom started to retreat into the cabin. "If you see Ruby, let her know she needs to come back to the cabin for a bit. At least long enough to change her clothes."

"Sure, Mom!" Mia said quickly, then took off to the marina.

I snorted. The chances of us running into Ruby while we were busy with the resort activities were extremely low. She was probably out on someone's boat frying herself in the sun.

But before I could say anything like that to Mia, I turned to find her already several cabins away. I jogged to catch up.

We held the contest on the dock in the small marina of the resort, where the water level was shallow. In some places, only a paddleboat or canoe could float without scraping the hull. It was perfect for crayfish catching. Every participant got a five-gallon bucket, and we had an hour to catch as many as we could.

The marina was full of five families and a few single participants standing around, waiting for the contest to start. It seemed busy, but I didn't know how many guests usually participated, since this was the only week I took part in it.

Grandpa counted down and whistled, signaling the start of the contest.

As usual, Mia borrowed one of my fishing rods and baited the hook with a kernel of corn. She'd brought a baggie of it from her cabin, probably from last night's dinner with her family. When she found her target, she dipped the line into the water slowly, so as not to startle the crayfish. With the corn positioned right in front of where the crayfish were hiding, she waited until it got curious and ventured out to investigate the kernel. Only after it grabbed the corn with its pincers did Mia lift the line and shake it over the bucket until the dangling cray-fish let go.

She was clever. Mia always went off on her own, away from the competition to quieter areas along the dock. While some kids were trying to grab them with their hands, either getting pinched or having them skitter away, Mia was catching one after another, each landing with a thud on the bottom of her bucket. I liked to watch her. The smile that would make her eyes crinkle every time a crayfish pinched onto the line. I almost enjoyed watching her more than catching the crayfish myself, and I always made sure not to catch as many as she did.

Maybe it was unfair, but I also tried to figure out who else was catching a lot of crayfish and find some way to sabotage them—without Mia knowing, of course. Sometimes I would "accidentally" kick a rock into the water near where guests were hunting, causing the crayfish to scatter.

Last year, when I had my lighter, I burned a guest's fishing line when he was counting his crayfish so he had to re-thread the whole rod. He'd cursed out my grandpa, claiming interference, but it was worth it to see Mia's face when she'd realized she'd won. I'd do a lot to see that face.

Time was winding down in the contest. My grandpa gave the five-minute warning. The number of crayfish in my bucket was small. I'd been too busy keeping tabs on Mia and the other guests to catch many of my own. I could tell from the way the sun illuminated the inside of Mia's bucket that she had a large pile of crayfish—she'd win again this year.

Everyone else was either too impatient or too forceful. It was always like that. Even outside of the crayfish contest. People were impatient, not wanting to take the time to understand or learn. Or they were forceful—but not in a good way. They'd use brute strength or harsh words to get what they wanted. The two things were intertwined, people's impatience leading them to use cruel words or their bodies to scare others to get what they wanted.

Mia seemed to be at the brunt of both qualities with her parents. They didn't understand her because they were too impatient to take the time to listen, then they used cruel words to speak to her because they didn't take the time to understand her and became frustrated. I thought back to the cabin earlier, when her mom had commented on her looking pink because she wasn't wearing sunscreen. There was a reason Mia couldn't rub the lotion into her skin. They didn't take the time to listen and find out why. It was a vicious cycle that she was dealing with.

"Time!" Grandpa called, and everyone stopped their hunting.

One by one, everyone lined up with their buckets of crayfish. Grandpa would count each crayfish aloud before throwing them back into the lake, then he'd write the participant's name and number of crayfish caught on his clipboard. It was all very official.

When it was Mia's turn, Grandpa winked at her before he started counting. Just looking at her bucket, he knew she had the win in the bag.

"Fifty-two!" he called out as he counted the last crayfish and tossed it into the lake. It made a splash as it hit the water and slowly floated down to the sandy bottom, skittering away to find a new hiding spot.

It wasn't even close. Mia had won by fifteen crayfish.

My grandpa presented her with an *Agate Harbors* tie-dye T-shirt that she pulled on over her clothes. It was huge, probably an adult extra-large. It hung past her knees, but she didn't care that it fit more like a dress than a shirt. Her smile stretched across her entire face. It would be there for the rest of the day, and that made me smile too.

Chapter Five

Mia

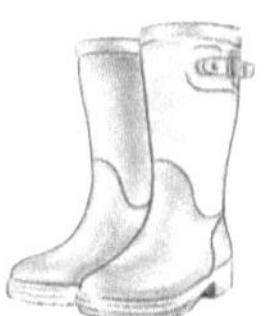

I wore the Agate Harbors T-shirt like a badge of honor for the rest of the week. The shirt didn't even have a tag on the collar—it was one of those nice shirts that had the label printed onto the fabric. My mom didn't say anything, even though I wore that shirt day after day. She and Dad were too busy enjoying their own vacation. Which was fine. I was enjoying mine too.

It was Friday—the end of the magical vacation I looked forward to every year. It was hard knowing it was coming to an end and that I would have to wait a whole year for it to come again. The freedom I had for this one week was like jumping into the deep, cold part of the lake. It had my entire body tingling. I felt alive. I didn't want the week to end.

It was almost time to go back to the constant ridicule I was used to. I'd almost forgotten what it was like to be under a microscope, to have my hair forcibly brushed and to wear clothes I wasn't comfortable in. A week up here did that to you, let you escape from reality.

I wasn't the only one escaping. Mom and Dad had met their quota for the number of margaritas a person could drink in a single week, and I hadn't seen Ruby much at all. I already knew that tomorrow she'd sit next to me on the long car ride back to the Twin Cities with dark bags under her eyes and a smile on her face.

But it was still Friday for a little bit longer, and Friday meant fireworks. It was an Agate Harbors weekly tradition. I bet Bower was really missing his lighters this summer. He loved a fireworks show, whether it was the one his grandparents set off every week or his smaller, maybe-less-than-legal display. Bower was supposed to meet me at the beach at sunset—well, at the boardwalk on the beach. There was no way I was going to walk on the sand with my socks and sandals.

The sun looked like a scoop of ice cream, melting into the horizon. With every moment that passed, the orange color melted into pinks and reds, so different from the dark lake beneath it. It'd soon be dark enough for the fireworks to start.

The view from here on the boardwalk was fine, but I knew Bower would want to watch the fireworks from the rocks we'd sat on last year, back when I'd been able to walk on the sand to get there. They were the perfect viewing spot. But they were across the beach and up some rocks that he wouldn't be able to piggyback me over.

"Hey," Bower said behind me.

I turned, a smile automatically on my lips. "Hi."

"Ready to go?"

When I nodded, Bower started walking across the sand. I stood there watching him, sand flicking up every time he took a step in his flip-flops. I was jealous. What it must be like to walk across the sand, not caring about the grains rubbing against your skin, making your teeth hurt. I could only stand there like an idiot. At least I felt like an idiot.

Bower stopped and turned around once he realized I wasn't following him. "Shit, I forgot."

I was a little taken aback. He'd never sworn in front of me before.

"Give me a minute. I'll be back, Mia." Bower held his palms out in front of him, willing me to stay where I was.

A minute later, he came back out of breath like he'd been running, a pair of yellow rain boots in his hands. They were tall —adult-sized.

He held them out to me, and I took them in my hands. "So you don't have to worry about the sand."

My stomach did little somersaults inside my body. I didn't know what to say to him. No one had come up with a solution like this for me before. It was like my quirks weren't even a problem for him.

"They're from the resort's lost and found," he said. "Don't worry about ruining them."

I gladly kicked off my sandals and pulled on the rain boots. They were hot for a summer night and way too big, but there was no way I'd ever complain. I could walk on the sand like everyone else now. How had I not thought of this before?

I left my sandals on the boardwalk for later and stepped into the sand. I sunk down a bit, the sand spilling over the tops of my feet, but it didn't touch my skin. The rubber blocked all the sand, letting it tumble off with each step.

I followed Bower across the beach, enjoying the view of the lake now that I didn't need to worry about the sand. The sun had fully set, but there was still an orange glow around the horizon. Bower's grandpa had his motorboat tied to the small island out in the lake away from the beach. I could see his silhouette unpacking boxes of fireworks. Young kids ran around with sparklers in their hands, their mothers following behind them, warning them to be careful.

We got to the end of the beach where the sand turned into rocks, which turned into boulders, and Bower and I carefully climbed up. He put his hands on the rocks to balance himself. I was slower since I didn't want to touch the rocks and the sand that would inevitably be on them. It turned into a balancing act, my arms outstretched to counter my body.

Bower stopped at a flat rock among the boulders. The rock was level and large enough for us to sit. There were even a couple rocks behind that we could use as back rests as we watched the fireworks. If I remembered right, this was the exact spot we'd watched the show last year—the fireworks would explode right in front of us.

I closed my eyes and took a deep breath. I needed to commit this moment to memory. The waves slapped against the rocks before withdrawing back into the lake. The birds were singing their good-night songs. I opened my eyes, taking another look around. There were rock cairns built all around the sitting area—stacks of flat stones balanced on top of each other. Some were tall with ten or more rocks, while others were built with just a few.

"Look what washed up," Bower said. There was a pile of rocks near his feet, and he bent down to pick one up. He brought it over to me, holding it out in his hand. "An agate."

I'd seen them in gift shops around here but never found one in person before. They were so popular with tourists and rock enthusiasts that you had to go far off the beaten path to find one in the wild. This one was yellow, with dark bands around it.

Bower took a minute to wipe it off with his shirt before he gave it to me. I took it in my hand and spun it around in my fingers. It was gorgeous. "There's a whole bunch of them." I motioned to the pile at his feet.

"Yeah, I started collecting them this spring after the snow melted," Bower said. "Maybe I'll sell them to guests or something."

I walked over to one cairn and crouched down to admire the configuration. Every rock had to be picked specifically to balance the rock on top of it. "Did you build these too?" I asked.

"Yeah. I can't usually find that many agates around here, so while I'm looking I like to build the cairns with the other rocks."

I couldn't stop the grin from growing on my face. The time it must have taken to build and balance the cairns. I was sure my mom wouldn't believe he'd built them. Maybe not even his own grandma.

No one saw this side of Bower except for me.

"I want to build one," I said.

Bower's face lit up. "Sure! Let's find a good base to start with."

We searched around the boulders, looking for smaller rocks between them. Bower pulled a flat rock about the size of a dinner plate from between two boulders near the water. He set it down on one boulder near our firework-viewing spot. "Now we need to find rocks to balance on top of each other."

I pointed to one near my feet. It was smaller than a dinner plate but still flat.

"Nice." Bower picked it up and used his hands to brush off any sand that was on the surface.

He handed it to me. I walked over to the first rock and placed the rock in my hand on top of it.

We climbed around the boulders, finding smaller and smaller rocks to stack. I pointed, and Bower retrieved the rocks. He always brushed them off before handing them to me to stack.

It got harder to see as the sun fully set, but slowly my eyes adjusted as the sunlight dissipated and the moon took over, casting its soft light onto the earth.

In the end, we had a beautiful cairn about eight rocks high with a mix of brown and black stones. Bower bent down to his pile of agates and studied them until he found one he liked. He picked up a red one with lots of banding and took his time brushing any debris off the smooth surface. When he handed it to me, it fit snuggly in the palm of my hand. "For the top," he said, motioning to my cairn.

I carefully placed the agate on top of the stack and stepped back a few paces to admire our creation. It looked steady, like it'd be here next year. Hopefully the wind or a wave wouldn't knock it over and mess up what we'd built together.

It took me a minute to notice that Bower had gone quiet.

I looked over to where he stood next to me. My face heated as soon as I realized he was staring at me. I glanced just past him, pretending I was looking out onto the lake. The waves were calm, and in the dark, the water seemed to stretch on forever. I breathed through my nose, but the cool breeze blowing off the lake did nothing to cool my reddened cheeks.

I couldn't stare out at the lake forever—I was acting weird enough as it was. The lake was pretty and all, but I'd never just stood and stared at it for this long…

This was starting to feel awkward when it shouldn't. This was Bower—I knew him. I could look at him. I'd looked at him a million times this week.

After another moment, my ears buzzed with the much too quiet silence between us.

I glanced back over to see if he was still staring.

He was.

This time I didn't look away; instead I watched his eyes as they darted around my face.

"Mia, I think—"

Pop! Pop!

Bower and I turned around to the lake just in time to see a red-and-yellow firework explode in the air over the water. Bower grabbed my wrist and guided me back over to the flat rock with the backrests. We sat there watching the fireworks. I pulled my legs in, wrapping my arms around my shins, staring at the sky.

It was funny how a place could feel like home even when it wasn't. It hadn't happened quickly, but over the course of the last several summers, Agate Harbors had begun to feel like home to me. I felt safe here. I could be myself without having to worry about hiding the awkward parts of me.

The grand finale of the fireworks show was loud and bright. We could hear his grandpa hoot and holler from the island when it was over, and everyone on the beach cheered before packing up their gear to head in for the night.

The moon's glow cast just enough light that Bower and I didn't need a flashlight to climb back to the beach. I took one last look at my cairn and the little oasis Bower had built. He was busy sifting through his agates, pocketing a few to bring back. I plucked the red agate from the top of my cairn and tucked it into the side pocket of my shorts.

I sighed, my shoulders slumping. It was time to go back.

Bower offered his hand to me, and I took it, using him as leverage as I balanced over the rocks. By the time we reached the beach, it was already deserted.

I thumbed the agate in my pocket, making sure it was still there. Making sure I had a piece of Agate Harbors to take with me when I left.

Nine Years Ago

Chapter Six

Mia

"This is it! This is the last summer I'm coming up here with you guys!" Ruby snapped from the back row of the van. She'd decided she needed the entire back row to herself this year for the drive up to Agate Harbors. I sat in one of the captain's chairs in the middle of the car.

"Ruby…" our dad cautioned from the driver's seat after glancing at her in the rearview mirror.

"I'm eighteen now. This is the last year you're making me come up here."

It was the summer before Ruby left for college, and she was never home, always babysitting or off doing *super important things* with her friends. My parents had thought making her come with us this last summer would force one last chance at family bonding, but they didn't realize this week wouldn't be any different. She'd disappear with the girls from the resort who she always hung out with.

Mom sighed, cradling her forehead between her thumb and index finger in the passenger seat.

"I think that's enough, Ruby…" Dad said. "You've already put us through plenty today."

Ruby had climbed into the van without the sweatshirt she was always wearing recently. I'd thought it odd that she'd been wearing sweatshirts in June but had brushed it off as just Ruby being Ruby. She always did her own thing.

I'd come to expect that, but this time, she'd really put our parents over the edge. It turned out that under her sweatshirts, she'd been hiding new tattoo sleeves and some ink on her chest, which she'd chosen to reveal to us all today.

It had taken several threats from our parents to cut off her cell phone data to get her up here this year—now I wondered if they regretted threatening to cut off her data when they should've been threatening to cut off all the time she'd spent babysitting, saving up for what had to have been a very expensive tattoo.

Fighting against my curiosity, I tried not to stare at it, or at least what I could see of it beneath the V-neck shirt she wore, as I pulled up my socks that had fallen toward my ankles. I hated that feeling. My quirks hadn't gotten any better over the past year. If I was being honest with myself, they'd probably gotten worse.

"Mia…" Mom said from the passenger seat.

My face scrunched up at the sound of my name. How typical. With Ruby already slinging attitude, I became the easy target to harp on.

"Make sure you check in with us at least once a day. We need to know you're okay."

Our car passed the welcome sign for the small town where Agate Harbors was located, reading *Population 207*. The only people who lived in the small town of Northpoint year-round were the resort owners and employees.

"If I had a cell phone, I could just text you." I'd just turned sixteen and had already completed all the behind-the-wheel hours required. I was ready to get my license.

It was my turn for a pointed glance in the rearview mirror

from Dad. "You'll get a cell phone after you get your driver's license."

"I'm ready right now," I argued. "I'd pass. I'm a good driver."

"I know you're a good driver, Mia." Mom turned around in her seat to look at me. "But your father and I agree you need some time to mature before you get your license."

My dad grunted in agreement.

I groaned. This wasn't the first time we'd had this conversation, but it didn't get any easier to hear.

"You can't even dress properly." Mom looked down toward my feet. "You wear rain boots every single day."

"I've already explained to both of you why I wear them—I don't have a choice." My voice was flat, almost monotone. We'd literally had this conversation every morning during the school year before I'd left for the bus in my rain boots.

I had Bower to thank for the rain-boot idea—they were lifesavers. The boots kept all the dirt away from my skin from the knees down. The yellow ones Bower had given me had stayed at the resort, but I'd bought a black pair back home that matched everything I wore. They worked great in the winter and on rainy days—no one looked at me funny when I was wearing them. But in the spring and summer, everyone gave me strange looks when I wore them. Especially at school, when all the girls were wearing cute sandals and I showed up in my cumbersome rain boots, but I had to wear them. I couldn't think about anything else if I wasn't.

I'd tried other types of boots, but they weren't the same. They squeezed my feet unevenly or had laces that pressed against my feet too tight. Nothing compared to the smooth insides of rain boots. The rubber remained in a permanent shape, and there were no laces to mess with. Every time I slid my foot inside them, I knew what I was getting. The boots would be comfortable, and my feet would stay protected. They'd become a safety net of sorts.

"Don't pretend like you don't have a choice," Mom said, turning back around. "You have at least three pairs of sandals in your closet at home."

I put my head in my hands, bending over and stretching the seat belt. They didn't get it.

"Look, I packed a pair for you. A nice pair. Birkenstocks." I sat up and watched Mom pull out a pair of brown leather Birkenstock sandals from her bag. "The ones we got you for your birthday last year. All the girls are wearing them."

They were my version of a nightmare. The leather rubbing against my skin, the sand and dirt that would inevitably get under my feet and between my toes…

She handed them back to me. "Put them on."

"No, thanks." I pushed them back toward her.

Dad cleared his throat. "Listen to your mother."

The van's walls suddenly felt closer, the tall trees we were driving by moving faster. The seat belt cut into my lap and my shoulder, holding me in place. "But I—"

"Put them on, Mia! You're not going to walk around the resort all week in rain boots. It's supposed to be ninety degrees and humid. You'll look ridiculous."

"I can't, Mom—"

"Do what your mother says!" Dad yelled from the driver's seat. Our car swerved a little as he yelled. I hunched over in my seat, trying to make myself small. "It's time to grow up, Mia," he spouted, his forehead red and splotchy in the rearview mirror. "You can't wear rain boots for the rest of your life." He ran his hand through his hair before he let out a breath and gripped the wheel.

I took the sandals from Mom and pulled off my boots. My nose felt tickly, and a tear trailed down my cheek. They didn't get it. They never let me fully explain. But even if I did have the chance to and they listened, would they understand? Probably not.

A hand slid onto my shoulder from behind, and I looked back to see Ruby looking at me with sympathy. I lifted my shoulder and bent my neck to the side, giving her hand a squeeze between my shoulder and ear. We didn't always get along, but she knew how Mom and Dad could be. She'd been rebelling against them her whole life.

Next year, when Ruby was gone, it would just be me at home. I wasn't looking forward to the undivided attention.

I finished pulling off my boots and slid my feet into my sandals. I still had my socks on. It was at least a small barrier.

Mom's hand reached back toward me again, this time empty. "Boots please."

I put them into her hand with the dirty soles resting against her palm. That was about as rebellious as I got.

An arched sign over the gravel drive read *Agate Harbors*. I let a sense of relief wash over me. We were here.

The resort looked the same as it always did. Brown cabins scattered among tall oaks and evergreen trees. Small bonfire pits sprinkled among the cabins with wood stacked next to them, ready for an evening fire.

My dad stopped at the lodge to check in and grab the keys before we parked at our cabin. Ruby and I jumped out and grabbed our bags from the trunk. I took a minute to breathe in the fresh air. It always felt different up here.

I walked cautiously up the gravel walkway to the cabin, careful to not let any stray pieces of gravel flip into my sandals. We climbed up the deck and entered through the back door. Ruby and I hightailed it up the stairs and into the loft, throwing our duffels onto our beds. I had an extra bag of blankets with me as usual.

"Let's get out of here before she makes us help unpack," Ruby whispered.

I nodded in agreement. The four-hour car ride had been enough time with our parents for today. We snuck out the front of the cabin just as Mom and Dad made it through the back door with bags of groceries in their hands.

Ruby waved at me before she trotted off to find her friends. I knew exactly where I was heading. It would take me longer in sandals, but I'd get there just the same.

"Mia!" Betty's voice rang out the minute she saw me walking up the gravel road toward the lodge. She gingerly got up from the flower bed she was weeding to greet me.

"It's always such a treat to see you," Betty said as she held me. "Come inside and have a Popsicle with me. Bower will be back soon. He's off on the boat with Dean."

I followed her into their cabin, and Betty pulled out a chair from the round table in the middle of the kitchen before she opened the freezer and started digging around. I sat there, surrounded by photos of Betty and Gill in front of different parts of Agate Harbors throughout the years and photos of Bower as a little boy.

"So, how are your parents and your sister?" Betty asked as she handed me a packaged Popsicle. I ripped open the wrapper, pleased to discover it was orange. The best flavor.

"They're fine," I answered quickly before shoving the Popsicle into my mouth. I didn't really want to talk about them. Especially after what had happened earlier in the car. I looked down at my new Birkenstocks, which had probably already given me a blister.

The creak of the screen door had both of us turning to see Bower stumble through the door into the cabin. The door slapped against the outside wall before slamming closed behind him. Dirt covered his legs up to his knees. His hands and wrists were equally as filthy.

He scanned the room as if he was searching for something—until his eyes landed on me.

"*Mia*." His voice was several octaves lower than it had been last year. He looked different too. He was taller and had filled out with muscle. A slight shadow of brown facial hair covered his chin and cheeks.

My heart began to beat faster, and my palms started to sweat. Nerves danced along my limbs. I'd never felt like this around him.

"Oh, Bower! Don't track dirt into this house. Go wash off!" Betty shooed him out of the cabin, and I heard the hose turn on outside.

I stood up with the Popsicle in my hand and peered out the screen door of the cabin, watching Bower grumble as he hosed himself off.

"I think Bower has some fun plans for you this week," Betty called out from the kitchen. "You're going to the crayfish contest again, right?"

I nodded, unable to stop myself from staring through the screen again at Bower. He was bent over, letting the hose water run over the top of his head. He flipped his head back up, smoothing the wet hair over the top of his head with his hand.

"Good. You can't let anyone take that winning streak away from you!"

Bower finished up and walked back toward the cabin to turn off the hose. I scurried back to the table, sitting in a chair with my back to the door.

His voice met my ears. "So, don't be mad, Grandma…"

I froze, the Popsicle halfway out of my mouth.

Bower stopped in the doorway, his eyes widening as he saw me sitting in his kitchen. He paused at the Popsicle I had my lips wrapped around before his gaze went lower, stopping at my feet —at my sandals. His eyes narrowed, and his mouth sunk into a frown.

Betty's sigh brought Bower's eyes away from my shoes.

"Dean and I had some trouble with the boat today." He

walked past me toward his grandma, still dripping from the hose he'd sprayed off with.

I slowly slouched down in my chair.

"What happened now, Bower? Don't tell me the sheriff's involved again." Betty stopped what she'd been busying herself with in the kitchen to turn to him.

"No, no, nothing like that. We just kind of…sank it."

"You did *what*? How's that even possible?" She put up a hand. "Wait. Don't tell me it was your grandpa's motorboat."

Bower combed his fingers through his wet hair, looking at the ground before he looked back up at Betty. "So, Dean had this rifle—"

"What in the hell were you boys doing with a rifle?"

My body hunched even further, the wooden Popsicle stick clenched between my fingers.

"It's Dean's mom's new boyfriend's hunting rifle," Bower explained. "And well, it went off in the boat and the bullet put a hole in the hull. We tried to drive it back, but it filled up with water right before we got it back to the dock." He ran his hand through his wet hair again. "It's underwater just outside of the marina."

That explained the mud and dirt he'd showed up in. He and Dean had probably swum from the boat into the marina, then walked through the muck to get to shore. Was I getting a glimpse of the Bower everyone gossiped about but I'd never seen?

"How does a rifle 'go off' in a boat?" Betty's face was red, her eyes shooting lasers toward her grandson. "Answer me that, Bower." Even I could feel the heat coming off her.

He looked down at the floor. "We thought we could shoot fish from the boat."

"You're something special, Bower." She shook her head and began feverishly wiping the counter clean with a rag. "You're lucky Mia's here and I want her to have an enjoyable week."

They both glanced at me, and I tried to sink even deeper in my chair. If I got any lower, I'd be on the floor.

"If she wasn't here, you'd be attached to my hip for the rest of the summer," Betty continued. "You know what? After this week, you will be. You're going to be my personal assistant for the rest of the summer. Screaming children at Kids Camp? You're dealing with them. Five-a.m. doughnut pickup on Sunday morning? You're on it."

Bower groaned, looking down at the floor.

"You've shown me you need supervision, Bower, so that's what you're going to get." She opened a few cabinets in the kitchen just to slam them closed. "Mia, get him out of here before Gill gets here."

I pulled myself up out of the chair and threw my Popsicle stick away before hurrying toward the doorway. Bypassing Bower, I opened the screen door and exited the cabin. The door didn't slap closed behind me, so I knew he was following. Even as I walked further away from the cabin, I could hear pots slamming and the odd curse word coming from Betty.

I turned around once we were a decent distance away from his cabin.

Bower still had his eyes on the ground, every so many steps launching a rock off the trail with the toe of his shoe. "The boat was old," he grumbled. "It was an accident. No one got hurt. It isn't that big of a deal."

I held back my opinions on shooting a rifle on a boat. It seemed unnecessarily dangerous—but I didn't want to sound like his grandmother.

He'd always been happy when I showed up each year. This grumpy Bower wasn't who I was used to seeing.

I didn't like it.

We only had a week together, and I didn't want to waste a minute of it.

I cleared my throat. "I guess you're lucky I'm here, huh?" My breath caught in my chest as I waited for a response.

It took a second, but he looked up and smiled at me. There was the Bower I knew.

I couldn't help but smile back. Over the course of the last year, he'd grown into someone my friends back home would call "cute." I'd grown too, a little taller and in other ways... I wondered if he thought his friends would think I was cute too.

"I want to forget about earlier. Let's go fishing." Bower nodded toward the beach.

"With what boat?" I asked.

He rolled his eyes at me. "One that isn't at the bottom of the marina."

I held back a laugh, turning before I saw his reaction to walk toward the beach, where I knew he kept a canoe packed and ready to go.

"Hold on a sec," Bower called out.

I turned around, watching him jog back up to the lodge. He was headed back into fire—Betty was still in there.

I curled my toes in my sandals, waiting.

A minute later, he emerged with yellow rain boots.

He remembered.

Grabbing the boots from his hands, I kicked one of my Birkenstocks into a nearby bush, pulling the rubber over my socked foot. They were still several sizes too big. Balancing on my now booted foot, I kicked off my other Birkenstock. Bower's hand latched onto my elbow, instantly balancing me. My socked foot slid easily into the boot, and I stood on two feet, unafraid of what lay beneath my soles.

Chapter Seven

Bower

I'd seen the caravan of new guests arriving from where we'd been fishing on the lake, right before Dean had shot a hole in the bottom of the boat. It was amazing how fast that thing had sunk. Luckily we hadn't been too far offshore, or I would've gotten some serious swimming in. I'd jumped off the boat, leaving Dean to try to pull it ashore. Knowing him, he'd probably already given up and sacrificed the boat to the lake.

Mia was finally here. I'd waited all summer for this week— all year. I didn't have any way to contact her. She still didn't have a cell phone, and my teachers had called my handwriting "unreadable." Not that I'd sit down and write a letter anyway.

Just another thing on a long list of my missteps. There was always something I was doing wrong or just not right enough. I was the troublemaker at school, and home wasn't any better. I figured my grandparents held their breath every evening when I walked through the door, bracing themselves for what I'd look like or what I'd fess up to. At least I wasn't a liar—the one thing I wasn't. But it wasn't like I had much of a choice in this small town. The truth would inevitably get back to them, and then I'd be in even more trouble than if I'd just told them the truth about something to begin with.

When Mia was here, my grandparents were happier, definitely less stressed. They smiled when I walked through the door because they knew Mia kept me busy and out of trouble. Instead of lectures each night, I would sit down at the kitchen table with them and we'd talk, even joke around.

It was nice having Mia here, even if our only connection with each other was this week. After I'd hosed off, I'd hardly recognized the girl sitting at my kitchen table. She'd grown in the past year—in a good way. Her blonde hair was longer, her lips were redder, and her breasts were... I'd had to pull my gaze away quickly.

It wasn't like that with her. We were close—just friends.

Suddenly the plans I had for us this week seemed immature. I was going to take a girl like *that* fishing?

She deserved more than that.

But she liked that stuff too, right? That was why she always came to find me every year. She wanted to do those things.

We'd start with fishing. After that, I'd figure something out. Do something that would impress her.

———

Mia was quieter than she'd been last year. Maybe it'd been the interaction between me and my grandma that'd scared her. I'd watched her sink lower and lower in her seat as she'd watched me and my grandma go back and forth. She never saw that side of me. When she was here, I was always on my best behavior—I never wanted to get her in trouble or mess up the short time she had here.

But maybe it was the rifle that'd scared her. Yeah, it was probably that.

We paddled out onto the lake, Mia at the front and me

steering in the back. She wore her hair tied up in a ponytail like she always did, but this time the tip of her ponytail brushed below her shoulder blades—accentuating the way her waist dipped in before her hips flared out. She was in those bike shorts she always had on, and I had to pull my eyes away from the way the canoe's seat pushed the top of her ass up.

Mia was the same girl I'd always known, just in a much more attractive package. Looking back, she really hadn't changed all that much. Or maybe I was just now noticing how attractive she was. Dean always gave me shit for being a late bloomer. Maybe I was. Guys had probably been drooling over Mia for years.

I dragged the paddle in the water, slowing us down once we got to a spot I knew was good for bass. She already had the tackle box open by the time I laid my paddle on the bottom of the canoe.

"Would you like any help?"

Mia had a knife out and was cutting the fishing line. She shook her head. "It needed a new hook."

I watched as she dangled the line with the bent hook between her fingers, dropping it into the bottom of the tackle box.

At first, it'd surprised me that Mia enjoyed fishing, especially since so much of it was slimy, wet, and sometimes sticky. But there was a lot to enjoy about fishing that didn't involve getting dirty.

She held out her newly tied hook, sporting the same knot in the line that I'd taught her to tie last year. I couldn't help but smile. I took the hook, my fingers brushing against hers before she let go. My eyes bounced from the hook I was baiting back to where she sat, holding the rod in her hands. There was a smile on her lips—there she was, the Mia I knew. Now we could forget what had happened earlier, and we could be just regular Bower and Mia again.

Both of our lines were in the water, and our bobbers were

barely moving on the still lake. With a flick of my wrist, I tapped the tip of Mia's rod with mine.

"Hey!" she yelled, taking her rod and hitting mine in retaliation.

I gave her my best serious face. "We aren't going to catch any fish with you acting like that."

"You're a terrible actor, Bower," Mia said through a smile.

I scoffed, "Me? An actor?"

She rolled her eyes.

"I swear, even my theater teacher would tell you I'm a terrible actor."

The canoe rocked a bit as Mia resituated herself. "Speaking of school…"

I frowned. Apparently fun time was over.

"What are your plans after you graduate?" Her sister, Ruby, had graduated in the spring. I'd follow suit the next year.

"I don't have a plan yet." It was the truth; I hadn't really thought about it. My grades were mediocre at best. School wasn't a priority for me.

Mia gasped.

I opened my mouth to explain my situation further but then realized that it wasn't my dislike of school that had Mia in shock, it was that her bobber was being aggressively pulled beneath the water.

I didn't have to say anything. I just sat at the ready, holding on to the net I kept in the bottom of the canoe and watching her expertly reel in the fish. It had to be big based on the way her rod bowed down toward the surface of the water.

"Hold steady," I called out as soon as I saw the scales of the fish glistening near the side of the boat. I dipped the net into the water, scooping the fish and lifting its flipping body out of the lake.

I pushed the net toward Mia. "Nice catch!"

She smiled, admiring the fish from a distance. "I'm not touching it."

I grinned because I already knew that. I knew her. "I'd never ask you to."

I set the net and the fish down in the bottom of the canoe and grabbed its jaw with one hand and its belly with the other, then lifted it up to show Mia. It was a big one.

Too bad neither of us had a phone to take a picture—to remember this moment forever.

This was the week that went by the fastest each summer. Mia and I did everything together, including every activity the resort offered. We competed in the crayfishing contest and bingo by the pool. There was a medallion hunt that we'd never been very good at, but she never complained and always seemed to enjoy looking for it even if we didn't win.

Today the activity was tie-dying. My grandma stood in front of the group, demonstrating how to twist the white shirts into perfect spirals. Mia sat next to me, her fingers easily manipulating the shirt into a spiral identical to my grandma's. I struggled to get the shirt to fold correctly, my spiral looking more like the bottom of the lake, a mess of uneven elevations.

A rubber band hit my cheek. I looked over to find a young kid snickering with his buddies. Mia bit her lip as she watched. If she weren't here, I might've said something to the little shit, but that would've just gotten me into trouble.

I glanced around the tie-dying group—we were the oldest "kids" here. We both sat waiting for the next set of directions while everyone around us was still completing the first set. Were we too old for this? I looked over at Mia, who was patiently waiting, surrounded by kids who were having more fun braiding rubber bands together than tying T-shirts.

Was she bored? Maybe she'd outgrown the resort activities.

My friend's parents had left for some cruise in Europe—leaving the house and their son unsupervised. A rookie mistake. If Mia had outgrown these activities, I wanted to show her what a real good time on the lake was.

"Hey, there's a party on the lake later tonight," I whispered to her. "Do you want to come?"

Mia glanced over at me. "A…party?"

"Only if you want to," I was quick to assure her. "It'll be pretty chill."

She nodded, thinking it over, then smiled. "Sure, that sounds fun."

Grandma picked up a bottle of dye and demonstrated how to make colored triangles on the rubber-banded spiral so our shirts looked like a rainbow pie.

"Pick you up at nine?"

Mia picked up a bottle of red and began squirting it onto the shirt. "It's a date."

Chapter Eight

Mia

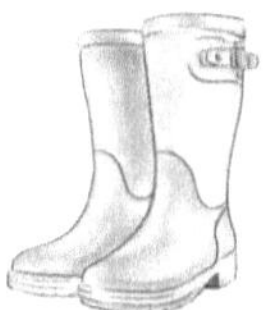

I loved being immersed in Bower's world. Even the things he did every day, like fishing, were exciting for me. And now a party? I couldn't hide the fact that I was nervous. I hadn't been to any besides the birthday parties my friends' parents threw for them at a bowling alley or movie theater.

The high school parties were more of a Ruby thing. I often heard her come in late at night, past the curfew my parents set for her, smelling like alcohol.

Now it was my turn. Maybe I'd get a little crazy, do something out of my comfort zone…

First, I had to find something to wear to this lake party. I stood in my room, looking over my options. Not much. I'd packed for myself and had brought only the clothes I felt comfortable in—shirts without tags and soft bike shorts that didn't rub against my skin. I didn't have fancy shoes. No one else at the party was going to be wearing yellow rain boots, but I didn't have a choice. My sandals were lost in the brush, and I never wanted to see them again.

I settled on an emerald-green racer-back tank top and black

bike shorts. Hopefully the yellow boots didn't clash too bad. If anything, I could claim I was a Green Bay Packers fan, right?

I looked in the bathroom mirror and pulled my hair back into a low ponytail. My hair was full of flyaways, but Ruby had a bunch of products lined up along the sink. I scooped out a pea-sized amount of pomade onto my fingers. I held my breath as I smoothed it through my hair. Immediately, I washed my hands, ridding my fingers of the sticky serum.

I took one look at all of Ruby's makeup before I glanced at myself again in the mirror. Natural would have to do. If I wore anything on my face, it would annoy me all night, when I was supposed to be enjoying my time with Bower.

I poked my head out of the bathroom to check the clock on the nightstand between the two beds. Bower would be here soon. Mom and Dad were at the resort bar, so I didn't need to worry about sneaking out. They'd probably think I was already in bed when they got home late, but I should leave some kind of note—just in case Ruby somehow made it home before I did.

The nightstand had a drawer with an Agate Harbors–branded notepad and pen inside. After scribbling a quick message to Ruby, I slipped it under her pillow.

I skipped down the stairs onto the main level of the cabin and pulled on my rain boots. I pushed the screen door open and hopped down the stairs onto the grass.

Bower was standing there, waiting.

I gasped, stumbling back a couple steps.

He gave me a closed lip smile. "Sorry—I didn't mean to scare you."

"It's fine. Are you ready?" My words came out quickly. What was I supposed to do with my hands? They fidgeted at my sides. I hadn't brought a purse—but who needed a purse when you didn't even have a cell phone?

"Yeah, I've got the boat all ready." Bower motioned with his arm for me to follow him.

I smiled. It was hard not to smile around him.

I followed him down the gravel path to the marina, carefully making my way down the stairs. A boat that *hadn't* sunk to the bottom of the lake waited for us. I ignored Bower's offer of a hand into the boat and climbed in myself. I untied the rope at the bow of the boat as he untied the one at the stern, jumping in once the boat was free from the dock.

We worked in perfect unison. We didn't even need words.

Bower started the motor and flipped it into reverse, backing out of the marina. A few moments later he pointed down into the water on the starboard side of the boat, just when we got outside the marina.

I leaned over the side to see the outline of Gill's motorboat resting at the bottom of the lake. My hand flew over my mouth as I tried to hide a laugh. Bower hadn't been kidding about sinking it—at least he hadn't lied to Betty.

He pulled on the throttle, the tip of the boat rising into the air. Carefully, I balanced behind the windshield of the boat, flipping the middle portion closed behind me. The front of the boat was my favorite, feeling the breeze on my face, but I had just pomaded my hair—I didn't want to risk any flyaways after I'd endured that sticky stuff to flatten them.

I sat in the passenger chair next to Bower, watching him drive. His arms had gotten muscular and veiny over the last year. Every time he gripped the wheel, I could see the muscles and veins beneath his skin move.

Why did I like that?

I felt the beat of the music before I heard it. Bower slowed the boat as we approached the party. Boats lined the beach next to an enormous house that must have cost millions. There were people everywhere with red Solo cups, sitting on the dock, the beach, and still on boats.

Bower guided the boat onto the beach in an open spot between two pontoons. I braced myself as he hit the sand and killed the motor. I watched as he jumped into action, grabbing the coiled rope from the seat at the bow of the boat and tying it to a nearby tree. He pulled until the rope was taut.

He was suddenly in front of me, offering me a hand off the boat. I had to blink several times to remoisten my eyes from the way I'd just been staring. Waving my hand, I declined his and instead jumped off the bow and into the shallow water of the beach. The water splashed up onto my boots, but their height protected my skin.

Bower seemed to know everyone at the party. We stopped often for a high five or a handshake-hug-type thing that was popular between boys. He never failed to introduce me to everyone who stopped him.

We got to the bonfire in the center of the party, where coolers repurposed as seats surrounded the fire. Bower leaned over, opening one, and pulled out two beers. He offered me one, and I took it in my hand, unsure of what to do. Bower cracked his open, the hiss of the carbonation leaving his can meeting my ears. He took a swig, his neck pulsing as he swallowed. I looked down at my can, unopened.

I'd never drank before. It wasn't like I was opposed—I'd just never had the opportunity. I pulled the tab of the beer and cracked it open. Slowly, I put the can to my lips and took a sip. I couldn't stop the face that followed.

It was disgusting. It tasted like dirty water. I struggled to swallow and grimaced as I felt the warm liquid going down my throat.

Bower chuckled, taking the beer from my hands. "It's fine if you don't like it," he said.

I let him have it. Beer was gross. He finished his can, crushing it against his leg before he started on mine.

"Mia? Is that you?"

I'd recognized that voice anywhere. Any sister would. *Ruby.*

"What are you doing here?" She seemed surprised and

maybe a touched impressed to find me attending the same party she was. Ruby had a red Solo cup in her hand. She took a sip of her drink while her eyes bounced between Bower and me.

Another guy came up behind Bower and bear-hugged him around his shoulders. I recognized the shaggy brown haircut.

"Hey, Mia," Dean said.

"Hey, Dean."

"Betty put you in charge of Bower for the week?" he asked.

"Pretty much." I shoved Bower playfully in the chest. "No sinking boats on my watch."

"You sunk a boat?" Ruby asked.

Dean looked up, surprised to see her. He backed up a bit and crossed his arms over his chest. He pursed his lips, not willing to divulge any more information.

"It figures. You're a fuckup," Ruby said.

I heard a growl come from Dean's chest.

My eyes bounced between the two of them.

Dean opened his mouth, ready to argue.

A girl I recognized from the resort came over and grabbed Ruby's arm, pulling her away. Her eyes were glassy, and her speech slurred. "*Come on*, Rubes, I know where we can find some cigarettes."

My sister steadied her friend as she glared at Dean. "Okay, Annie, let's go." Ruby almost fell to her knees as she struggled to hold up Annie. "Find me before you leave," she whispered to me. "I might need a ride back to the resort."

The corners of my lips lifted. She wanted a ride back with me—her annoying little sister she always ditched during the family trip. Maybe she would finally see me as her equal. Or at least someone worthy of her time.

"Sure," I said.

Ruby's friend pulled her away into the crowd.

Bower crushed my beer he'd just finished against his leg. He reached down for another one from the cooler.

It was his third beer, but this was a party. Everyone was drinking.

He looked at me with his cheeks flushed red and a goofy grin plastered on his face. I couldn't help but smile back.

"So, your sister…" Dean looked at me, his eyebrows raised.

I shook my head. "She'd eat you alive."

She would. I'd seen her around our high school with many boys but never with a boyfriend. Ruby was the girl that all the boys chased but no one ever caught. She was cunning and witty —everyone loved her.

"I'd like to see her try." He wiggled his eyebrows.

I pushed his shoulder. "Gross, Dean. Keep it in your pants."

The music was getting louder, and so were the voices. It sounded like everyone was yelling, their hearing dampened by the alcohol they were ingesting. The bonfire was unattended and glowing brightly in the center of everything. Everyone gravitated toward it like it was the heart of the party.

Weirdly, no one had touched the s'mores supplies that leaned forgotten against a cooler near the fire. I supposed everyone put the consumption of alcohol over that of sugary carbs.

I'd never been against sugar or carbs. They were delicious.

"Can I?" I asked Bower, like it was his party or something. I just felt weird, like I needed permission before I opened a brand-new package of marshmallows.

Bower put his hands up like he didn't care. I took it as an open invitation to dive in. I was somewhat of an expert at s'mores. It was one of the few talents I possessed. The marshmallow had to be perfectly goldened the whole way around. Puffy but not burned. A burned marshmallow was a tragedy. The chocolate and graham cracker had to be premade, ready to envelope the hot marshmallow on both sides. It was the only way the chocolate melted to a perfect soft consistency that wasn't too runny.

I laid out the crackers and chocolate atop one of the free

coolers near the fire and set off to roast the most perfect marsh-mallows. It wasn't hard. The fire had been burning for a few hours at this point in the night, and the flames had created pockets of embers that were perfect for marshmallow roasting. Warm but away from direct flames that would burn it.

One at a time, I cooked the marshmallows, squeezing them between the crackers and chocolate as I pulled them off the long metal fork I'd cooked them on.

I gave my first creation to Dean, my second to Bower, and saved the last for myself. Then I squeezed myself next to Bower on a cooler, biting into my s'more, making sure to keep my fingertips on the graham cracker and away from the marshmallow.

It was perfect.

"These are fucking delicious, Mia," Dean mumbled with a full mouth.

Bower nodded, looking at me with a twinkle in his eye before he took another bite.

This entire night was perfect.

I was in my favorite place with my favorite person. The sky was clearer up here. There was no light pollution like in the Cities. Every star shone brighter, and the night seemed darker. I exhaled, letting my breath join the night air.

I sat back and enjoyed my dessert, but I enjoyed watching Bower eat his even more. He did so much for me during my week up here; it felt good to do something for him too, even if it was as small as making a s'more.

Bower took his last bite and crushed his beer can.

"Going slow tonight?" Dean asked.

"What do you mean?" He tossed his crushed can into a garbage bag next to one of the coolers.

"That's only your third beer. Usually you're five deep by now."

Bower rubbed his palms on his pants, glancing over at me.

I kept my lips closed, squeezing the s'more between my fingers. I hadn't drank before, let alone been drunk. How many beers was a lot? Did he normally drink a lot? Bower seemed fine to me.

"Fuck off, Dean."

Dean smiled as he raised both of his hands above his shoulders, stood up, and walked away from the fire. I watched as he jogged down to the beach, greeting a pontoon full of people that'd just showed up.

Bower turned to face me. "This is my favorite week of the summer."

I finished my s'more, leaving my sticky fingers extended away from my body. The only failure of the perfect dessert. "Yeah, I bet it's nice to have your grandma off your back."

Bower gave his head a quick shake. "It's—"

"Incoming!"

He looked up, and his forearm hit me across my chest, pushing me back. I instinctively shriveled up as a full beer came flying toward us, flipping end over end. Bower caught it in the palm of his hand right before it would've hit me square in the face.

Someone from across the party cheered at his catch. Bower raised the beer in thanks and set it on the ground next to his chair unopened.

I sat there stunned for a moment, not even able to get out the words *thank you.*

"Yeah...because of my grandma," Bower said quickly, filling the silence.

I unfolded myself from my chair, keeping my sticky fingers in front of me so they wouldn't touch my clothes or hair. My teeth were starting to hurt.

"Do you want to—" Bower motioned to the lake after glancing at my fingers covered with sticky marshmallow fluff.

"Yeah, sure," I said, standing up.

He followed me down to the lake. I waded a little bit into the water, the yellow rain boots once again protecting my feet. I bent down and rinsed my fingers off.

The lake was warm. I made ripples in the water with my fingertips, sending the reflection of the stars above bouncing along the waves.

Bower stood by my side, his sandaled feet welcoming the lake water brushing against his skin. Another reminder that I was different. I was wearing tall yellow rain boots to a party where most girls wore sandals or just went barefoot. No one had said anything, probably because Bower had been glued to my side all night.

I finished cleaning my hands and brought them to my tank top to pat them dry. The lake water wasn't the cleanest and I could feel a film already forming on my fingers, but it was the best I could do right now.

Bower grabbed my arm, his fingers circling the entirety of my wrist. The veins in his forearm pulsed under his skin as he pulled my hand close. With his other hand he lifted his own shirt by the hem, bringing the fabric up. I watched as he guided my wrist, tucking my hand beneath his shirt, covering it—drying each finger individually with his free hand.

"You shouldn't put lake water on your clothes—the fabric is going to dry funny, and it'll rub against your skin…"

I kept my hand limp as I held my breath. He was holding my hand beneath his shirt. If I flexed my fingers, I'd be touching his bare skin.

I looked up at Bower, the left side of his face illuminated by fire and the lights of the party, the right side lit by the moonlight's reflection on the lake. The ripples of the waves made moving patterns on his skin.

He paused.

My hand twitched, the pads of my fingers finding his warm

skin. I felt goose bumps pop up beneath my touch, his stomach drawing in as his breath caught.

Slowly, beneath his shirt, he guided my hand from his sternum down his abdomen. My senses were amplified when it came to Bower. I could feel all the ridges of his stomach as he held my hand against his body, leaving a trail of heat in its wake. My finger hit the waistband of his shorts, my knuckles instinctively buckling and my fingertips dipping beneath the elastic.

He let go of my wrist, my hand dropping before I pulled it back.

I watched my hand float between us. That had felt natural, easy, like it hadn't been the first time. I blinked, the break in my stare breaking the spell between us.

Quickly, I pulled my hand to my chest, holding it in my other hand, willing it not to shake. I looked up at Bower. His eyes were wide as they bore into mine.

We had never touched like that before—I had never touched anyone like that before. There was something illicit about it that made my heart beat faster in my chest. Nothing about the touch had felt wrong or dirty like health class had made it seem. It'd felt natural, right, like my hand was meant to be there, touching his chest—feeling his warmth against me.

It already felt different between us. Not a bad different, just different. For once, I didn't know what to say to Bower. What could I even say? At the end of the week, I would leave and not see him again for an entire year. A lot could happen in a year.

It took a moment for the both of us to realize that the music had stopped playing. Girls in bikinis and jean shorts ran past us toward the dock and into the water, jumping onto boats. Guys followed behind them, yelling about cops and telling everyone to leave. I froze, looking to Bower for direction. This was my first serious party, complete with underage drinking and other debauchery. I hadn't had more than one sip of beer. Was it still in my bloodstream? Would a cop know I had had one sip? It was just a sip, and it had been gross. I shouldn't have even tried it. Sweat pooled under my arms.

"Hey! I need that ride home now." Ruby's face was flush, but there was a twinkle in her eye. This wasn't her first busted-party rodeo.

"Sure." Bower leapt into action, wrapping his arm around my waist, guiding me toward my sister.

Dean trotted up behind Ruby.

"Take the keys, man." Bower tossed the boat keys to him, which he caught by the red spongy flotation keychain attached to them. "Get the boat started, and I'll push us off."

"Hey! Freeze!" The voices were close. Lights from flashlights circled the beach, blinding me if I looked away from the water. Police lights flashed from the front of the mansion, casting a red-and-blue glow around the house.

We ran down the beach, Ruby glancing behind her to make sure I was following, the water splashing around our feet. Dean led the way, hurling himself onto the boat Bower and I had taken to the party. Ruby lifted herself up and over the bow, rolling onto the boat. Yep, she'd done this before.

"Stop right there!" A flashlight shone brightly in my eyes. They were so close.

The boat's engine roared to life. "Come on!" Dean yelled from on board.

Bower swept me off my feet, his arms cradling my body, holding me along my shoulder blades and under my knees. He tossed me up into the boat. It wasn't a graceful throw, but it got me inside the boat. I landed on the seats in the bow.

"We've got to go right now!" Dean yelled.

"Go!" Bower yelled.

Dean threw the boat into reverse and hit the gas. I sat up, ready to help Bower into the boat. Branches snapped, and the rope he'd anchored the boat with pulled a tree from the shore.

Bower stood knee deep in the water, watching our boat back

away, bent over from having just pushed it out into the lake. Cops splashed into the water to apprehend him. He kept his eyes on me as they wrestled his hands behind his back.

"No!" I shouted. He wasn't fighting them. They didn't need to be so rough.

Dean backed the boat up ninety degrees before he flipped the boat into forward and hit the gas. I ran along the length of the boat to the back, kneeling on the seats, watching Bower being pulled out of the water that was littered with floating beer cans. The officers had him in cuffs, the red-and-blue lights still flashing.

Chapter Nine

Mia

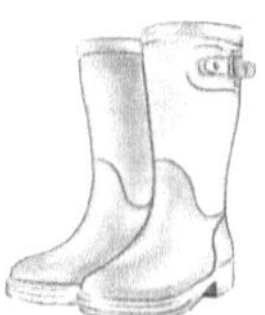

"Dammit!" Dean yelled over the roar of the boat engine. We were flying over the water. I sat crunched into a ball at the back of the boat, watching the beach become smaller and smaller.

"What's the big deal?" Ruby asked. "He'll get a slap on the wrist or a minor. His grandparents will pick him up tonight. We'll see him in the morning."

"It's not like that for Bower," Dean said.

Ruby came up behind him and pulled the throttle back, slowing the boat. "I think we lost them."

Beats of anxiety rushed through my veins. I'd lost Bower. I'd left him at the beach. He should have jumped or at least tried to get into the boat.

"Bower isn't going to get a slap on the wrist. His grandparents aren't going to pick him up. They're already on their last straw with him," Dean said.

"What do you mean?" Ruby asked.

"They've picked him up from the police station too many times this year."

It was barely July. How many times had he been in trouble

with the police within six months? He'd mentioned none of that to me.

"The last time his grandparents picked him up, they swore it was their last time," Dean continued. "They'll leave him in there. And the police will keep him. I think they're sick of his antics."

"I didn't know Bower was such a badass," Ruby said.

"More like a dumbass." Dean turned to me. "He saved you, you know. The cops would've gotten you if he hadn't thrown you into the boat."

Those beats of anxiety were replaced with waves of guilt. Bower had saved me in place of himself. I didn't have any priors. I would've gotten into trouble with my parents, but I hadn't been drinking. Not really. He could have jumped into the boat and left me there instead.

"Hey, Dean?" Ruby said. He looked her way. "Shut up." She came over and sat next to me. My sister didn't say anything or reach out to touch me, but I felt her there.

Dean docked the boat, and Ruby helped me out. I was still numb, the image of Bower getting smaller and smaller still fresh in my mind.

"Get back to your cabin," Dean called out as he pulled the ropes attached to the boat's cleats closer to the dock. "I don't need anyone else getting into trouble tonight."

"Are you headed home?" Ruby asked.

"Yeah, straight there after I finish tying up the boat—I'm sure the cops will be patrolling the bays, looking for stragglers."

She waved at Dean before grabbing my hand and pulling me with her along the dock. My hand shook in hers. "He'll be okay, Mia. He's still a minor. They can't charge him with anything serious."

"Still, just seeing him on the beach all alone…" I swallowed the giant lump in my throat. "I've never seen him like this before."

Bower had done a lot of things tonight that I'd never seen him do before. He'd been drinking, he'd gotten taken away by the police—and apparently it wasn't the first, or even second, time it'd happened. I only saw Bower for a week each summer, and I'd thought from that time we spent together that I knew him—that I really knew him.

"Maybe he isn't who I thought he was…"

"You know Bower," Ruby said. "You spend enough time with each other every year we're here. Just because you saw an unfamiliar part of him tonight doesn't mean every other part of him is different too. He's the same person; you'll still have the same connection tomorrow and the day after that."

She pulled me off the dock and onto the gravel path. "You both keep coming together year after year. I don't think one night's going to change that."

I looked at my feet as I walked. My sister's words couldn't wipe the guilt away. Bower was in a cold, sterile police station, while I was back at the resort, his home. He should've been here with me, holding my hand instead of Ruby. After the way he'd held my wrist, I could only imagine what his hand in mine would feel like. There had been a moment between us on the beach—there was no denying it.

Loud music came from the lodge. Ruby stopped and listened. It was karaoke. A woman was singing "That Don't Impress Me Much" by Shania Twain. She was butchering it.

Ruby turned to me and smiled. "I know what will cheer you up." She pulled me through the threshold of the lodge and into the warm bar area.

The room was packed with bodies, making it muggy. The bar was a U shape, with two bartenders inside the arch, rushing to fill everyone's drink orders. Neon beer signs hung from the walls, lighting the room.

Ruby took a minute to scan the bar, pulling me with her once she decided on her destination. We weaved through tables, knocking knees with the drinkers and slipping between occupied chairs that were pulled out too far from the tables.

The song finished, and the crowd clapped. The next drunken resort guest got called to the stage.

Mom made her way back to our table, pausing for a minute before looking between Ruby and me, where we sat sharing a single chair next to our dad. "What are you two doing here?"

My sister smirked. "We heard your beautiful singing voice and had to come watch."

"Ruby…" Mom warned her, giving her *that* look. Then she glanced down at my feet. "Where are your sandals?"

In a bush, never to be seen again, I wanted to say.

"Bower found these boots for me," I said instead.

"You and that boy." Mom sat down and grabbed hold of my wrist. Her hands were smooth, but it made me think of Bower back at the lake, what his bare skin had felt like. "You spend a lot of time with him, Mia."

"Yeah, he's my friend."

"Boys aren't friends at your age." Mom's eyes were glassy, like Ruby's friend Annie's were at the lake party. "It'll never work out. Young love never does."

She let go of my wrist, and I let my hand fall into my lap.

"*Shut up,*" I whispered beneath my breath. She didn't get to tell me about young love. She was married, drunk, and had no idea what had happened tonight.

Ruby's eyes went wide.

Mom's eyes narrowed. "What did you say?"

"You're right, Mia." My sister slid off her half of the chair. "We should *get up* and go back to the cabin. It's late."

Mom gave us both a look like she didn't believe us but couldn't prove otherwise.

I stood up, curling my toes in my boots while I pushed the chair back under the table. I led the way out of the bar, weaving between tables.

"Wear your sandals next time!" I heard my mom's voice cut through the noise of the bar. "You look ridiculous in those boots."

My shoulders sunk, folding into my chest. Ruby put her hand between my shoulder blades, giving me the smallest push to keep moving.

The cool outside air sucked us out of the warm lodge. I took a deep breath, enjoying the fresh air. The stars were out, glowing against the dark night sky. I quickly looked down. I shouldn't be enjoying them when Bower's only view was fluorescent ceiling lights.

Mom was wrong—I didn't have feelings for Bower. We weren't in love. We were friends. But there was something about him that was different this year. Not just his appearance, but how he acted around me. He was intentional with his words and actions, making sure I was safe, introducing me to all his friends. He'd made me feel special during those few seconds on the beach, the way he'd dried my hand for me.

But at the end of the week, we'd pack up and go home, and I wouldn't see him again for a year. Nothing could be permanent between us.

"She's drunk." Ruby grabbed my hand and squeezed it. "She didn't mean it."

We stood outside the lodge, the music from inside mixing with the crickets and frogs on the outside.

"She's right." I sighed. "Bower and I would never work. We're going home at the end of the week."

Ruby gave me a funny look, her head cocked to the side. "You thought I was talking about you and Bower?" She laughed, shaking her head. "I meant your boots."

I looked down at my yellow rain boots. The outside rubber was speckled with drops of liquid, but my feet inside were perfectly clean and dry.

"Your boots are awesome."

I smiled.

Ruby linked her arm with mine and pulled me to the trail that led to our cabin. "We'll see your *friend* Bower when he gets back tomorrow."

Tomorrow.

I'd see him tomorrow and thank him for putting me on that boat—for sacrificing himself so I wouldn't get into trouble. I'd apologize for leaving him on the beach, doing nothing as we'd pulled away.

I had to make things better between us before I left Agate Harbors.

Eight Years Ago

Chapter Ten

Mia

As soon as the car parked outside our cabin, I opened the door, letting my yellow rain boots hit the wet gravel. It had rained a lot this summer, and the ground was continuously damp.

"Mia, get back here! You need to help us unload the car!" I ignored my mom and took off toward the lodge. Toward Bower.

I still had the boots he'd given me. I'd never gotten a chance to give them back.

Bower had never come back to the resort last year.

The morning after his arrest, I'd gone up to the lodge to see him, but his grandmother had shooed me away.

He's not coming back this week, Mia, Betty had told me. I could tell she'd been disappointed in me. I was supposed to be Bower's shield that week, keeping him protected from his bad decisions. I had failed.

You're going to let him sit in there? I'd asked. The thought of Bower sitting in a jail cell or even a juvenile detention center had made me angry. He hadn't deserved to be there.

Mia, Betty had begun. She'd sounded tired, worn out. Probably from being up all night dealing with Bower. *This isn't a onetime occurrence. Bower's been having trouble for a while now. I know you don't see that side of him, but Gill and I do every day you're not here. We can't help him anymore. We don't know what to do.*

For the rest of our vacation, Dean had kept his distance and I'd tailed Ruby in my yellow rain boots. They'd never left my feet except when I'd slept.

Bower didn't have a cell phone, so I'd called the resort phone every month for the last year hoping it would be him who picked up the phone. It never was. It'd always been Betty or Gill who answered, letting me know that Bower wasn't available and skirting around any of my questions about when he *would* be available. After winter, they'd stopped answering my calls entirely and I'd been too embarrassed to leave a voicemail.

Now I was back at Agate Harbors and finally had the chance to track him down and find out what had happened last year.

The lodge looked the same as it always did. Nothing really changed up here. I liked that about it. Stability.

I looked through the screen door of Bower's cabin. Through the haze of the metal screen, the cabin looked empty. I knocked on the wooden panel of the door. "Hello?" I called.

They were usually around the lodge and their cabin. I heard shuffling from the side of the cabin that housed the bedrooms. Inside, I saw the door to Betty and Gill's bedroom slowly open, Gill's gray head of hair popping out.

"It's me, Mia."

"Oh, hi, Mia." He made his way out of the bedroom and walked over to the screen door. I moved out of the way as he pushed it open.

"Where is Bower?" Greetings and small talk would have to wait.

"Bower isn't here, Mia," Gill said.

"Will he be back this afternoon?"

He ran his hand through the thinning hair on the top of his

head. I sometimes forgot that they were Bower's grandparents. They had raised two generations of children.

"He isn't coming back, Mia."

I froze, my body numbed. *What?*

"He's joined the Marines."

I took a step back, tripping down the steps that led to the cabin.

"I'm sorry, Mia. I know you two were close," Gill said. "Betty and I just couldn't do it anymore. We gave him a choice: enlist or get out."

I steadied my feet but couldn't stop my knees from weakening. "But I called…so many times last fall."

The outer ridges of Gill's eyes turned red and pooled with tears. "We just couldn't watch him turn into his parents."

My jaw dropped. Bower wasn't like that. He'd had a few beers at the party last year, but he wasn't an addict.

Gill continued to explain, seeing the look of shock on my face. "You were with him one week out of the year. We were with him the other fifty-one. He wasn't doing well. We caught him so many times with alcohol and drugs, we just—"

"Yeah. I got it," I cut him off. I had heard enough. I didn't want to believe it.

Bower had never shown me that side of himself. I had shown him every facet of myself. Even the ugly parts. The parts that my parents were embarrassed of. The parts that *I* was embarrassed of. He didn't feel comfortable enough around me to let me all the way in. Apparently I had read the entire relationship wrong.

I'd thought we were closer than that.

I'd thought Betty, Gill, and I were closer. "You couldn't have told me on the phone that he was going to enlist? That he wasn't just unavailable—he was gone?"

"We didn't know how to tell you." Gill rubbed his face with his hand. "We didn't want to upset you."

I bit my tongue. It was more upsetting to find out this way. It was more upsetting to have been ignored for the last year, especially when I saw Betty and Gill as my second family.

I stepped out of the yellow rain boots I had held on to for the past year. They'd sat in the back of my closet, an everyday reminder of summer and the freedom it brought me. Even on tough days, when my sensitivities overwhelmed me and my parents were jumping down my throat, they reminded me that better times and acceptance were there for me at the resort. The socks I was wearing instantly absorbed the moisture on the gravel. I could feel the grains of sand penetrate the woven fibers of my socks.

"Here." I held out the boots. "Bower let me borrow them last year."

"Keep them, Mia," Gill said.

"I don't want them." I put them on the wood porch and walked away.

He didn't call out or beg me to stop. Our relationship was over. Like the one between Bower and me.

I'd thought I meant something to Bower.

That night on the beach last year, the way he'd looked at me before it had all fallen apart… I knew that'd meant something to him. He couldn't have left me a note before he left? Snuck my home phone number from the resort's records?

The Marines were serious business. How long was he going to serve for? When would I see him again? *Would* I ever see him again?

The tiny particles of sand from the gravel road worked their way through my socks and rubbed against my skin. It made my teeth hurt. I could feel the grains between my toes, scratching with every step. I practiced holding my breath, trying to forget about the uncomfortable feeling overwhelming me. It didn't work. In the end, I just let my teeth hurt.

It felt like an appropriate punishment for me. Letting myself open up to someone who was essentially closed off. Letting myself feel comfortable, feel loved and wanted by adults who weren't even my family. Ultimately they were just acquaintances, people I saw once a year for seven days. There were three hundred fifty-eight days that I wasn't a part of their lives. A lot could happen in three hundred and fifty-eight days—birthdays, holidays, happy and sad times.

I wasn't a part of their family. Just a girl who was a guest at the resort they owned.

Present Day

Chapter Eleven

Mia

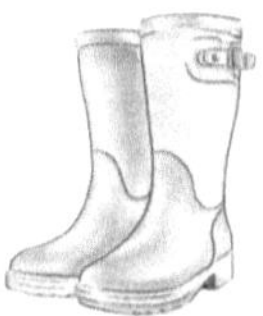

Archer Owns had gotten us a party bus. Not just any party bus, but one of the nice kinds. It had lights, a sound system, a stripper pole, an entire bathroom in the back, and air-conditioning to offset the sticky late-June humidity.

I just want you to have a good time, he'd said before he'd kissed me goodbye, pushing back the jet-black hair he kept long on the top of his head.

Archer was staying behind with his buddies for his bachelor party weekend. We'd all waved goodbye as the bus had pulled away. His large stature got smaller the farther we got, his driveway that led to his four-car garage and five-bedroom house also shrinking. It was the house that I'd move into after we were married at the end of the summer.

He could afford it. That was what he always said when I commented on his lifestyle. He had enough money for every-thing, it seemed, and I wasn't used to that. Our family had taken a single summer vacation each year when my parents had time off because they were teachers. I'd grown up in a three-bedroom, two-bathroom house that had a toilet whose handle needed jiggling and a roof that needed replacing. After a year of dating him, I still wasn't used to it—the money and the frivolous spending.

"This is so nice!" Mindi, one of Archer's friend's wives, crooned from the seat next to me. "I was so happy when Jake told me Archer was getting the bus for us. Four hours in the back seat of Laura's BMW? No, thank you."

Ruby rolled her eyes next to me. She mouthed *BMW* before sticking out her tongue. I tried to hide my smile, but Laura wasn't exactly wrong—squished together in a back seat during Friday-night cabin traffic would've been a nightmare.

"Oh my god, it would have been so uncomfortable. Ruby, you and me crammed in the back seat?" Rachel said.

"Mia would've had the front seat," said Laura.

"Of course she would've," they all agreed, mimicking each other like parrots.

All three of the girls on the trip besides Ruby were my friends. Well, they were our friends—mine and Archer's. They were the wives of his best friends and, therefore, my friends. Ruby didn't approve. All three of the girls looked the same— blonde (although Mindi had some help in that department), tall, and lean. For some reason, she didn't point out that I looked the same. Except that Mindi, Laura, and Rachel were thin from counting calories and their daily Pilates classes and I was lean from being so busy with my first-grade class that I forgot to eat. Ruby called them the Towhead Triplets. I'd had to look up the word *towhead* when she'd first said it. I often had to do that when I was around her now that she was an adjunct English professor.

If we were name calling, I supposed I was a towhead too. My hair was blonde—much blonder than when I'd been a kid. Archer insisted on setting up hair appointments for me every six weeks to *help me feel my best.* It was his way of suggesting I go blonder and wear my hair down more often.

He'd assumed at first it was because I hadn't liked the color or cut. But that, of course, wasn't it. Going blonder was fine, but I preferred to wear my hair back, away from my face. Those flyaways still irritated me. When I'd tried to explain that to him after my first hair appointment, he'd brushed it off, blaming my inability to speak critically of the stylist—as if I simply hadn't liked the haircut—and found me a new stylist, insisting that this one was better. Once again, that wasn't the problem.

Archer had recently given up on me wearing my hair down. He'd instead bought me a pair of diamond stud earrings that shone from my earlobes, *even with my hair pulled back.*

"Can we see the ring again?" Rachel reached out her hand, flashing her manicured nails.

"Sure." I slid the ring easily off my finger, since it was still two sizes too big. We hadn't gotten it sized yet.

He'd only proposed a month ago after a year of dating. Everything was being fast-tracked—we were getting married in two months, right before school started up. I was so busy during the school year and didn't get much PTO, so because Archer didn't want to wait until next summer, his checkbook was helping expedite everything.

They passed the ring around, each trying it on, admiring the weight of the giant diamond Archer Owns had given me.

"I'm going to make Jake propose to me again, just so he'll buy me a bigger ring," Mindi said. The Towhead Triplets all laughed.

Ruby held the ring in her palm for a moment before passing it back to me without trying it on. As far as I knew, my sister didn't have a boyfriend. She kept her personal life private. I slid the ring back onto my finger. My hand felt a lot heavier with it on.

My parents were thrilled. When I'd introduced them to Archer Owns, they'd positively lost their minds, bending over backward to welcome him into the family. Although they never let him stay past ten o'clock on school nights, as humiliating as that was. They claimed it was because we all had school in the morning—my parents and me. I taught first grade now at a STEM school, a job which my parents had helped me get after I'd graduated from college. I'd moved back in with them right after I'd graduated to help save money. I had four years of student loans to pay off.

I'd met Archer shortly after starting my job. He'd been touring the school since he was a donor, being the owner of a tech start-up that had made it big. Archer had been looking to give back, fund some STEM programs for kids who hoped to follow in his footsteps.

When he'd stuck his head into my classroom mid-song, I'd been at the board teaching a science lesson, my students reciting ROYGBIV in a cute song perfect for first graders. He'd flashed his thousand-watt smile at me, and I'd dropped the dry erase marker I'd been holding. I'd made a fool of myself stumbling around the front of my classroom trying to pick it up.

At the end of the school day, he'd been waiting in the parking lot for me, leaned up against his Maserati. I'd looked at my twenty-year-old sedan, one of the bumpers being held on by duct tape, and thought that this guy must've had his life together, must've been comfortable and secure—just what my parents had been wanting for me my entire life.

It was what I wanted too, I reminded myself, downing my second glass of champagne.

"Where's this place you're taking us again?" Laura asked.

I had planned the trip. Archer had insisted on me having a bachelorette party, and I didn't want to end up in a spa or Las Vegas. I wanted to be somewhere I had the best memories growing up, somewhere that felt familiar and warm.

"It was my favorite place to go as a kid," I explained. "We went every summer—it's magical."

"We each have our own rooms, right?" Mindi asked.

"Of course." I nodded.

The girls all breathed a collective sigh of relief.

"I reserved a five-bedroom cabin for the weekend."

"Mom and Dad are going to flip when they hear we went up to Agate Harbors without them," Ruby said. Against everything she'd said at eighteen, now at twenty-seven, Ruby still went up north each year for our summer weeklong family vacation. It was what our parents called an "important tradition," and at twenty-five, I still hadn't broken it.

I purposefully hadn't told my parents where I was having my bachelorette weekend. It was important that I kept the plans vague around them. I'd even reserved the cabin using the address to the school I worked at. That way no flyers or mailings came to my parents' house. They'd been a little too excited about my relationship with Archer. I wouldn't have put it past them to show up to "support" me. Agate Harbors was their favorite place too. Luckily, we'd all be together again in two weeks, for our family vacation to celebrate the Fourth of July.

"Are you sure this is where you wanted to go for your bachelorette party?" Ruby asked. "Archer would've flown us all to the Bahamas if you asked."

I laughed; he totally would have. "Yeah, I'm sure. My best memories are of Agate Harbors. Might as well add to them." I helped myself to a third glass of champagne. The cheap stuff the party bus had provided was finally starting to taste good.

"We had some good times, didn't we?" my sister asked. She sat back in her seat, smiling. Ruby and I had gotten a lot closer as we'd gotten older, our mutual wariness of our parents fueling our relationship. Mom hadn't gotten any less critical, and Dad still hadn't found his ability to cross her.

My ring cast a reflection of light onto the roof of the bus. I wiggled my fingers, watching the orb bounce around. This was my bachelorette weekend—I was on my way to celebrate my upcoming marriage at my favorite place. I was the happiest I'd ever been.

I blinked at my reflection in the window. My bleached blonde hair made my brown eyes pop, but the window didn't reflect the twinkle that'd been there when I'd been younger.

I should be the happiest I'd ever been.

Turning away from the window, I settled in my seat to watch the scenery change from strip malls and chain restaurants to towering pines and shimmering lakes.

Funny how every time I drove up here, I thought of him.

It was hard not to. So many of my summer memories had him in them.

I shook my head.

It was time to make new summer memories. Good ones that didn't end with me broken-hearted.

Chapter Twelve

Mia

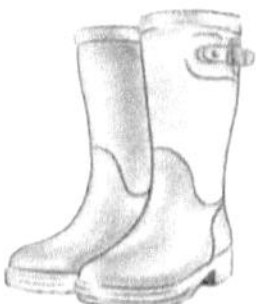

"There has to be a dead body in this bag." Ruby lifted one of my duffel bags. The party bus driver had unloaded our luggage to the sidewalk in front of our cabin. Apparently after we'd picked up the keys at the front desk from a resort employee I didn't recognize, that was as far as his "job description" said he had to take them.

Mindi and Rachel made scoffing sounds at him and whispered to me that I shouldn't give him a tip. I snuck a standard twenty percent into his hands when they weren't looking.

"Just my weighted blanket," I said, grabbing my other duffel that held my clothes and shoes for the weekend.

"What's that weigh?" Ruby asked.

"About twenty pounds."

"Okay, a watermelon, then."

"Don't tell me that someone else brought watermelon shooters!" Mindi whined.

My sister laughed. "Nope, Mia just brought an entire watermelon in her duffel."

Mindi looked confused. "Okay, well, I have stuff for watermelon shooters. I'll get started on those."

Ruby dropped the duffel onto the porch of the cabin with a thud. I'd bought the heaviest weighted blanket I could find. The salesperson had recommended a blanket around twelve pounds for my body weight, but nothing that had been recommended for me had ever worked, so I'd jumped right to the "big guns." It was like a big hug that lasted all night long, and it reduced my anxiety tenfold and relaxed my nervous system. It was a lifesaver. The blanket was the only reason I got a decent night's sleep.

"I'm not carrying this up the stairs." My sister breathed heavily, resting her hands on her thighs.

"Do I have to pull the bachelorette card?" I asked. "You *are* the maid of honor."

"Ugh." Ruby grabbed the duffel and brought it into the cabin. I followed her in, while the others each claimed their own rooms.

She found the sunlit primary bedroom and hoisted the bag onto the bed. "There, princess." I laughed, throwing the bag I was carrying next to the one with the weighted blanket. "Should I help you unpack too?"

"Isn't that on the list of duties for the maid of honor?" I quipped.

It was somewhat of an inside joke between us. When Archer and I had gotten engaged, Mindi had sent me a checklist of maid-of-honor "duties" from a bridal website. She'd sent it under the guise of not wanting me to miss out on the "full experience." Ruby had claimed it was her way of vying to be the maid of honor.

"Fine, I'll help you," she said. "Only so I won't get demoted."

We both laughed. I would never demote Ruby. She was my ride-or-die.

I unzipped my duffel and started pulling out the outfits I'd packed for the weekend. It was a mix of clothes I was comfortable in and clothes Archer had bought me for the trip.

"This is cute!" Ruby held up a sequined halter top. An Archer purchase.

"You can have it."

"What, really?" She held it up against her body.

"Take it." There was no way I was going to wear it. The sequins rubbing against my skin would drive me crazy.

Archer meant well. He wanted me to have whatever cute, trendy women were wearing. Even after all these years, I still couldn't force myself to put things on my body that made me feel uncomfortable. Made my teeth hurt. Made me think of nothing else except the way they rubbed against my skin.

In college, as part of my elementary education degree, I'd taken several special education classes. One of the classes had been a general overview of the wide array of support and accommodations our students might need in the classroom.

It was in that class that I'd realized that I'd been accommodating myself my entire life without knowing what I was doing. The socks and closed-toe shoes, the tagless shirts and non-denim shorts. How I always had my hair tied back away from my face. I was accommodating for the way my brain negatively received the information through the receptors on my skin. I wasn't a freak. I just needed support. Accommodations. Understanding. The one thing I hadn't gotten from my parents growing up.

So I did something else that my parents had never done for me: made an appointment with a specialist. It had been a freeing moment for me—being officially diagnosed with sensory processing disorder, or SPD. The way I'd been feeling my entire life finally had a name. The way I'd always felt wasn't some flaw or inconvenience to others...and most importantly, it wasn't my fault. I'd worked with the specialist to locate an occupational therapist who helped me find adjustments to my daily life that made my life more manageable, and we'd been slowly working over the years on building my tolerance to the textures that'd previously caused me so much anxiety.

At my teaching job, I'd become close with the special education teacher in the building. Ms. Weber was patient and kind to everyone in her classroom, no matter how "troublesome" some of her students were labeled. She was a wealth of knowledge regarding SPD, having taught for the last twenty years. She was the one that had turned me on to weighted blankets. Her experience gave me a lot more confidence, knowing I wasn't alone with my SPD.

I was still picky about my clothes, and that was okay. I no longer viewed wearing shirts without tags and staying away from textures that bothered me as problems—they were accommodations.

"I'm wearing this tonight," Ruby said, watching the shirt's sequins reflect rainbow orbs around the room.

I moved to continue unpacking, and the sunlight from the window hit my ring, its rainbow orbs joining the sequin shirt's dancing against the wall.

My sister looked down at my ring. "Are you sure you want to do this?"

It wasn't the first time she had asked me. The first time she'd uttered those words had been when I'd showed her my ring. It had put a damper on the moment, but that was Ruby. She was critical but realistic.

"I'm engaged to the man of our parents' dreams. What's not to be sure about?" It was meant to be a joke, a jest. But there was some truth behind it.

I threw another top Archer had picked at Ruby. This one had fringe.

"That. That's what you shouldn't be sure about. Yeah, Mom and Dad love him, but what's more important is that *you* love him."

"I do," I said.

"Is that what you want to say to him at the altar?" She draped the two shirts across her arm.

I pursed my lips and became very busy hanging T-shirts in my closet.

A scream echoed through the cabin. Ruby and I glanced at each other, then dashed out of the primary bedroom and down the hall.

Laura stood outside of her room, a look of disgust on her face. "There's…there's a spider on my pillow."

Ruby snorted behind me.

I walked into her room and saw the culprit. A daddy longlegs sat perched on top of the white pillow on the queen-sized bed in her room. I jogged over to the bathroom, grabbing one of the paper cups stacked on the counter.

Carefully, I picked up the spider, using the cup, and walked over to the window. Laura watched from the doorway in horror.

With a practiced hand, I unclipped the screen from the window frame and reached outside, giving the cup a gentle shake. Eventually the spider wandered off the lip of the cup and onto one of the wooden logs of the cabin's exterior.

After resecuring the screen and the window, I smiled at my friend. "There," I said. "Crisis adverted."

"You should've squished it," Laura whined. "It'll come back tonight and crawl into my ear. I'll wake up with spider babies pouring out of my head."

"Don't be stupid—spiders aren't going to seek out your ear to crawl into," Ruby said from behind her.

Laura glanced at Ruby, a sour look on her face as her cheeks went rosy. "I think Mindi said something about watermelon shooters?" She walked past us and toward the kitchen, where it sounded like our other two friends were.

"Stop it, Ruby."

"Stop what, Mia?" She knew exactly what I wanted her to stop doing.

"Don't be mean to my friends."

"Your friends?" Her eyebrows rose high on her forehead.

I crossed my arms in front of my chest.

"If those are your friends, and this"—Ruby held up the sequined shirt I'd given her—"is the kind of shirt your fiancé thinks you like, then I'm not sure you'll be happy a year from now."

"*Ruby!*"

She stood up and wrapped her arms around me. "Okay, okay, I'll stop." I half-heartedly tried to push her away with my crossed arms. "I just want what's best for you—a life that's going to make you happy."

"I know." I relaxed into her hug. She never had the best delivery, but I knew her intentions were good.

"Did I hear something about watermelon shooters?" Ruby whispered into my ear.

I laughed. "If you haven't heard about the watermelon shooters by now, we need to get your hearing checked."

We linked arms and turned to head to the kitchen. Watermelon shooters seemed great right about now.

———

"You didn't say this place was so…rustic," Rachel was saying. As promised, Mindi had made us all watermelon shooters.

I looked around the kitchen of the cabin. It opened to the living room and a small eating space. The cabin was clean, just not updated. It had a classic homey style, with embroidered pillows and linoleum floors. All the appliances were white rather than stainless steel, but they were clean and worked fine.

"It's been owned by the same family for four generations." It wasn't what I would consider rustic. But maybe to Rachel, who lived with her husband in a trendy downtown condo, it was.

"You would think one of those generations would invest in a new showerhead," Laura said.

"Or get rid of the doilies under the lamps," Mindi said.

I hadn't noticed any of those things. They were just part of the charm of the cabin.

"Is the restaurant nice? How many stars does the chef have?" Rachel asked.

Ruby snorted next to me.

I willed my eyes not to roll. We had reservations at the resort's restaurant for tonight. It wasn't a Michelin-star restaurant. The kitchen consisted of a flat top and a couple fryer baskets.

Before I said anything I'd regret, I picked up another shot. The liquid fell down my throat before I even tasted it on my tongue.

They might've been high maintenance and a sometimes a bit ridiculous, but Rachel, Mindi, and Laura had always been kind to me—they'd welcomed me into Archer's friend group without hesitation. Their significant others were Archer's best friends. They'd be around for the rest of Archer's and my life.

I just needed to keep Ruby's snorts and my eye rolls under control for the rest of the weekend.

Chapter Thirteen

Bower

"That's the last one." I lifted a case of hard seltzers onto the bar.

The truck had just dropped off a pallet of them. It had taken me several trips to bring them all inside. It was what everyone was drinking these days. Not that I would know. I was almost nine years sober. Fortunately being around the bar didn't tempt me. I'd realized at a young age that alcohol didn't make me feel better—instead it made everything worse.

"Thanks, Bower," Dean said. "I'm going to need a hand behind the bar tonight. We have a bachelorette party coming in."

He'd been promoted to bar manager a few years ago by my grandpa while I'd been away. He was still a good friend after all these years. Keeping in touch when I was overseas, letting me know when I was needed back home.

This was my first summer back at the resort since I'd been seventeen. Most things were still the same—weekly rentals coming in on Saturdays, weekend rentals on Fridays. Bachelorette parties hitting up the bar on a Friday night was nothing new.

"Sure thing." I tapped my hand on the bar before turning around to head back to check on the kitchen.

I stuck my head through the swinging doors. "All good?" I asked Tim, our cook, who was elbow deep in onions, chopping them up for burgers tonight.

He gave me a nod as he scooped the onions and threw them onto a hot skillet. The onion juices snapped and popped against the sizzling surface, and I flinched. Sometimes it was little things that affected me, reminded me of the sounds I'd heard during my time in the Marines.

I backed out of the kitchen before another noise could trigger a full flashback. I didn't have time for that—I had a resort to run.

"I'll be back before dinner!" I yelled in Dean's direction before I stepped outside. I'd help him out with dinner service, disappear for my Friday-night shower while the fireworks popped off, and then work behind the bar until we closed up.

Nothing had changed. That had to be the biggest shock when I'd gotten back last month. It was like stepping into a time machine, returning to the summer when I'd been seventeen, right before I'd left.

I'd been an idiot as a kid, made my grandparents' lives a living hell. Still, they'd welcomed me back nine years later with open arms. Grandpa said I felt different. Sure, I'd put on some muscle during my time in the Marines and could finally grow a decent beard, but I knew he meant something else.

All the mischief had been beaten out of me in the time I'd spent in the National Guard Youth Challenge Program to finish out high school. As soon as I'd turned eighteen, there had been no question that I was going to enlist in the Marines. The structure the program provided had changed my character. I'd still been young and a little dumb, but at least after my time at the academy, I'd had a purpose—I'd found out I was good at making quick decisions and leading my comrades.

By the time I'd found my footing in the Marines, all that

young, dumb energy had been replaced with grit and a strong work ethic. I wasn't some drunken teenager anymore headed down the wrong path—I had a drive, I was a leader. It had felt good to know that others looked to me for direction, trusted me to lead them. I'd never wanted to screw that up. I'd never wanted to revert back to that kid who'd caused trouble and hadn't cared who it'd caused trouble for. That had meant leaving Agate Harbors and my past behind—the best I could.

All that had changed when Dean had reached out last year.

Somehow, a year ago, he had gotten ahold of my commanding officer's contact info. Dean's urgency had been enough that the commanding officer had ignored my wishes for no phone calls and insisted I talk with Dean. My friend had been calm but direct: Things were changing at Agate Harbors, and it was time to come home.

It'd taken me six months to finish my tour and get back to the resort.

I'd hardly talked to anyone back home for the last nine years. It wasn't for my family's lack of trying—it was my choice. I'd been angry enough at my grandparents in the beginning that I hadn't responded to my grandma's letters, and eventually she'd stopped sending them. Dean had sent me letters every couple of months. I'd responded sporadically, asking about the resort and sometimes about her…mostly about her.

I didn't do email, and everyone in my platoon knew that I wouldn't take phone calls. The letters were one thing—I could receive an envelope and choose whether to open it. Emails had a subject line that I could shy away from, but I couldn't escape what someone said on the phone. I hadn't wanted to feel those emotions—not when I'd needed to focus on my career in the Marines. Maybe it had been selfish, but a large part of me had wanted to put a bit of distance between myself and all those Agate Harbors memories. There'd been a lot of good memories, but also so many I wished I could forget.

That hadn't stopped Mia from popping into my mind now and then, but all I'd had to do was picture that look of disappointment across her face and I'd remember why I'd left—that I'd needed to change, to become a better person.

I'd made a fool of myself on that beach all those years ago. I'd known I was on thin ice with my grandparents, but I hadn't taken their threats seriously. They'd already been claiming that they were going to stop bailing me out, going to send me to a military school, but I'd always seen their words as hollow threats.

It'd come as a shock to me when I'd woken up the next morning still in the cell, the image of Mia's face slowly getting smaller and smaller as the boat drove away lingering in my mind. I'd been embarrassed. I'd disappointed her. And worse—I'd put her at risk of getting into trouble. There'd been no chance for explaining myself or apologizing, because that was the last time I'd seen her.

Now I was back where it had all started, where my messy slate was waiting for me. Now I had to prove to everyone who remembered me that I was different, changed—a responsible adult who didn't shoot holes in bottoms of boats and didn't have run-ins with the cops every weekend.

For the most part, everyone had forgiven me for my teenage shenanigans, welcoming me with open arms, ready to give me another chance. I'd taken over a lot of the day-to-day management of the resort from my grandpa. He had been willing and grateful for someone to step in and help out, and I was happy to put my leadership skills I'd gained from the Marines to work.

There was one person I hadn't seen yet—who I might not see now that she had grown up. Her family's standing reservation wasn't until the week of the Fourth of July, and for all I knew she might not even come up with her parents anymore.

I spied a flash of white hair along the docks of the marina, pulling my thoughts away from Mia.

Damnit. Who was supposed to be watching her? It took me a minute to get down to the marina, as the lodge was on higher ground. I booked it down the set of steps built into the hillside, ignoring the handrail.

"Grandma!" I yelled, but my voice didn't carry far enough. She was climbing into one of the resorts motorboats. The boat key in her hand glittered in the sunlight. "Stop!"

My feet hit the wooden boards of the dock, and I ran, leaping over the water between the docks to get to her faster. After my fourth jump, I slowed. "Grandma, don't get in the boat." My heartbeat wildly in my chest even though I wasn't out of breath. "Give me the keys."

"I don't need some boy telling me what to do!" Her eyes were wide, her voice angry. "This is my resort. I'll go where I please."

My eyes closed as I let out an exhale. Calm, I needed to be calm. I still wasn't used to the Grandma I'd come home to. She wasn't the same one I'd said goodbye to nine years ago.

"Can I have the keys, please?" I kept my voice level. "Let me drive you."

She eyed me, scowling. "Do you work here? One of the boys Gill hired for the summer?"

I looked down at my feet. It never got easier, however many times she didn't recognize me. "Yeah, Gill hired me."

"Fine, drive me somewhere away from that awful girl. She's been up my ass all morning." The swearing was something new too. The Grandma I knew never swore.

She held out the keys, and I snatched them from her hand before she changed her mind. There was no way she should be driving a boat. I'd have to get Caleb, who I'd hired to work in maintenance, to install a lockbox with a combination code on the keys in the marina. She couldn't have access anymore. We'd done the same thing with the car keys at the house. They sat in a lockbox in the garage. The code was my birthdate, which she didn't remember.

"Betty!" The dock shook as someone stepped onto the boards. "Oh my god. I'm so sorry, Bower. I went to the bathroom, and she was gone." Chloe, Caleb's wife, carefully walked along the dock toward us. "I can only waddle so quickly!"

Chloe was eight months pregnant with their first. Caleb had left the Marines a year before I had to marry her. I'd served five years with him and my buddy Gus, and I considered them my brothers.

We'd eaten together, played cards together, slept in the same bunkhouse. We'd been part of a larger group of marines there to assist Syrian forces in their efforts against ISIS. Sometimes that meant helping patrol parts of the cities we were stationed around. It wasn't often that we'd been under fire, but it had happened. We'd always had to be watching, scanning, aware, but sometimes we hadn't seen the militants until it was too late.

When I'd gotten back this summer, I'd hired Caleb on as the head of maintenance for the resort. He'd needed a new job, and I knew he was a hard worker. Plus, the resort needed some serious upkeep. My grandpa and I couldn't do everything. They stayed in one of the two-bedroom cabins in the resort next to Dean's one-bedroom place, across the gravel road from my small studio cabin. I wished I could've hired Gus as well—but that hadn't worked out.

"It's fine, Chloe," I said, watching her to make sure she hadn't overexerted herself coming down here.

Chloe usually ended up watching Grandma during the day, as it had gotten to be too much for my grandpa to be her sole caretaker twenty-four seven. Grandpa spent his time puttering around the resort, trying to tackle various projects. There was always something that needed fixing, but I knew the real reason was he had a hard time when Grandma didn't recognize him, which was often.

I didn't blame him. Losing your partner like that? Slowly, then all at once. Watching them become a shell of a person. It would be hard for anyone. Grandma had been slipping away for the last seven years.

"That's the girl! That horrible girl who's been up my ass all day!" Grandma pointed a finger at Chloe.

"Watch your language, Betty. Babies can hear inside the womb," Chloe scolded. Grandma glanced down at Chloe's swollen belly and quickly closed her lips. Chloe had a sharp tongue and wasn't easily offended. She'd been a godsend to my grandpa and me. But there was only a month left until Chloe had her baby, and I needed to figure out care for Grandma by the end of the summer. Another task for me to do.

I ran my hand through my hair. It was longer now that I was out of the service. There hadn't been any time to get a haircut.

Chloe reached out, and Grandma tentatively placed her hand inside Chloe's. "There we go." Chloe helped her out of the boat. "Let's get back to the cabin, and I'll make you some tea. Wouldn't that be nice?"

"Tea, yes. That sounds nice." Grandma held Chloe's hand as she led her off the dock and to the stairs up to my grandparents' cabin.

I should talk to Caleb about installing some sort of barrier or fence at the top. Just to deter her from coming down to the boats. I trailed behind them a bit, not wanting to spook my grandmother further. She didn't know me. She had only recognized me twice since I'd gotten back, fleeting moments before a glaze had once again covered her eyes.

I put the key back on the empty hook next to the other resort boat keys. Like most things at Agate Harbors, the boats were old and in need of repair or replacement. I added it to my ever-growing mental to-do list to look into getting a few new boats once we had the funds.

First things first: Getting ready for this weekend's events.

There was a bachelorette group coming in tonight. The reservation had been put under the name of an elementary school in the Twin Cities—first time I'd seen that. Maybe we'd be getting a bunch of teachers up here, looking to let loose. We needed to attract more parties like that to the resort. It guaranteed a large cabin rental and big spending at the resort bar. Agate Harbors needed money, and maybe hosting more of those big parties would bring it in.

Maybe this city-girl bachelorette had city-girl friends who were also engaged and looking for a place to have their own last-fling parties. I'd have to introduce myself to the group—I needed to make sure Agate Harbors looked good so I could keep business rolling in.

Chapter Fourteen

Mia

After two watermelon shooters a piece, we were off to dinner. I could smell burgers and other bar food well before we got to the restaurant attached to the lodge. It smelled glorious. Even if my friends weren't impressed, I was going to enjoy some fried food.

I walked arm in arm with Ruby, the other three girls walking together behind us. It was like I was back in my classroom, leading the line down the hallway. They screamed as a chipmunk ran across the path in front of them, then laughed at each other's reactions. Ruby rolled her eyes. I glanced back, hoping the other girls couldn't read my sister's body language. I didn't need anything getting back to Archer.

I'd worn heeled booties and a soft spandex dress with a camisole and bike shorts underneath, with my hair pulled back into a low French twist and the diamond studs Archer had given me sitting in my earlobes. He was right—they did make me look more mature, like a woman instead of a girl. I'd let my freckles fly free this weekend. Usually I covered them up with powder, the way Archer preferred, but the minerals irritated my skin. The freckles across my nose and cheeks made me look younger—not how I wanted to be seen, but I was on vacation. It'd be fine.

The musty smell and neon lights of the restaurant welcomed us in. I stepped into the bar area, immediately noticing that my feet didn't stick to the floor like they had previously. It didn't smell like spilled liquor either.

A five-top table near the bar had a laminated *Reserved* sign with *Bachelorette Party* written on it with a dry-erase marker. The sign matched the scratchy bachelorette sash the girls had made me wear. They'd also insisted on a rhinestone-incrusted tiara with fluffy feathers lining the bottom band that sat on top of my hair. I'd been trying to ignore the stiff plastic combs that dug into my scalp, keeping the tiara on top of my head the whole walk over.

We took our seats while Rachel flitted around the table, giving everyone feather boas and tiny crowns that they could clip into their hair. She also threw a plastic penis straw into each of our water glasses. Public fellatio—fantastic.

I looked over the menu that had been stuck between the plastic mustard and ketchup bottles at the table. To be honest I was more excited about eating some of the resort's fantastic apps than I was about any silly bachelorette-party antics.

"What can I get you ladies to drink?" A server came from around the bar to take our order.

"Do you have any specials?" Laura asked.

"We've got tap beer, bottled beer, and liquor," the man answered.

Laura looked disappointed. I was sure she wanted something with floating herbs that smoked because of the dry ice added to it.

"Dean?" Ruby asked suddenly.

My eyes shot to our server. It *was* Dean. His mop of curly brown hair was cut short and styled. He looked good. Older, more filled out.

"Ah, shit. Ruby?" His neck went red. He placed his hands on the table and leaned in. "I haven't talked to you since…"

"The summer it all went to shit," Ruby finished his sentence. Ever since that summer, Dean had made himself scarce during our family's week up here.

He looked a little taken aback as he glanced around the table, finally landing on me. "Mia? Is that you?" A huge smile came across his face. He glanced down at my sash and back up at my crown. "You're the bachelorette?"

"Guilty," I said, giving a shy smile.

"You know who'd love to see you…" Dean looked over his shoulder at the bar.

I followed his gaze and felt my heart stop inside my chest.

Every muscle in my body squeezed.

Static filled my ears.

Bower.

He couldn't see me from where he stood behind the bar, pouring a beer into a pint glass. His arms were bigger than I remembered. Bower pulled the tap handle, the veins in his arms bulging out from his skin as he smiled at the patron at the bar, obviously shooting shit with him. He looked good. His hair was shorter than when we'd been young. He wore a baseball hat on his head—backward—and had tattoos on his arms now. A lot of them.

It had been nine years since I'd seen him being taken away by the cops on that beach. I remembered it all, probably remembered it too well. How I'd sat in the back of the boat watching as he was taken farther and farther away from me. How I'd looked for him the next year only to find him gone, without so much as a goodbye.

I looked away as quickly as I had looked at him. "I'll take a margarita, please," I said.

Dean paused for a moment, looking at me before writing my order on a pad of paper.

After Dean got everyone's drink orders and went back to the bar, I felt a hand on my thigh. I looked over at Ruby. She gave me a sad smile before letting go. She knew.

"Oh my god, everything they have here is fried," Mindi said.

"Have they ever heard of a vegetable?" Rachel asked.

"They have fried pickles," Ruby suggested.

"I'm going to be so bloated," Laura said.

"Booking an extra Pilates class now," Mindi said, pulling her phone from her purse.

"I'm going to order for the table!" Ruby shouted.

The girls stopped squabbling for a moment. My sister headed over to the bar, where Dean was taking a long time to punch our complicated drink order into the POS system.

When he'd been taking our drink orders, Rachel had asked if the bar had blow-job shots. I'd cringed while Dean had laughed, telling her they didn't have them on the menu but they could improvise something. Rachel had giggled, brushing her hand down his arm, and ordered a round for the table.

I tried to listen to the conversation happening at the table, but I was too busy trying to keep tabs on Ruby and Dean. She leaned in close to talk to him. Occasionally they both glanced back at the table, making eye contact with me before I could turn away and pretend that I wasn't watching them.

Ruby returned to the table and plopped back into her seat. "I got fried vegetables for the table."

A few minutes later, Dean brought over our drinks. I took a sip of the margarita right before making the biggest mistake of my life.

I glanced over at the bar. *He* was looking at our table. At me. His eyes met mine, and I stiffened, salt from the margarita still on my lips. His face froze, his stare endless.

I broke eye contact, turning back to the table and adjusting the crown on my head. The bottom of the crown had little white feathers that kept falling on my face. I brushed one off my nose, letting it fall to the ground.

I hadn't seen Bower since the night I'd left him at the beach. I hadn't talked to his grandparents since they'd shooed me away, carefully avoiding them whenever we'd come here since. What was he doing here? He was supposed to be gone, out of my life. He hadn't been a part of it for nine years.

I shifted in my seat, making sure I was sitting up straight. Why was I letting him affect me like this?

Needing a distraction, I took the blow-job shot, licking the whipped cream from my top lip.

"You're supposed to take the shot without the whipped cream touching your lips!" Mindi screeched. "Like a blow job, swallow it all…"

I set down the shot glass, confused. The girls looked at me funny before they started laughing.

"Don't tell me you've never given a blow job before," Mindi said.

My face turned red. I could feel the capillaries on my skin expanding, warming my cheeks.

"Oh my god. She hasn't."

"Archer proposed to you without ever getting a blow job?" Laura asked. I had her full attention and the complete attention of the table.

"Shut up!" I whispered, much louder than I'd intended.

"Oh my god. Are you a virgin?" Rachel slammed down her drink, waiting for my answer.

Was my hair turning red? It felt like it should be from all the heat radiating off my face.

"She is!" Rachel yelled.

I pushed back from the table, my chair falling over behind me and clattering against the floor. The entire bar looked over at our table. I smoothed my dress before I bent down to pick up the chair.

Ruby met me on the floor, our hands grazing each other's as we reached for the chair. "Take a minute," she whispered.

I nodded and stood up. My eyes felt wet, and I tried to breathe normally but couldn't. I walked toward the bathrooms, trying to act poised and normal, but it was hard on heels.

The bathrooms were next to the bar, down a short hallway. I kept my eyes on my boots, making sure I didn't trip and make an even bigger fool of myself. This hallway had horrible lighting, and the fluorescent bulbs in the ceiling flickered.

"Let's not pretend like we don't know each other."

In an instant, I stumbled, catching my back against the wall. I sucked in a breath, my eyes shut tight.

His voice was several octaves lower than I'd remembered.

I lifted my head and opened my eyes.

Bower.

He was standing right in front of me. His eyes were the same as I had remembered them, although there was a depth I hadn't seen before. His skin was tan, his hair bleached from the sun. I closed my eyes as I inhaled. He smelled the same. Like cedar. Like outside. Like home.

With one hand, he lifted the crown from atop my head. The combs that'd been pushing into my scalp released, and I let out an involuntary sigh. With a flick of his wrist, he threw it to the ground. I turned and watched the crown bounce a couple of times before hitting the wall.

What was he doing? I looked back up at him, our eyes locking. His had that twinkle I remembered, the one that dared me to look away.

Stop.

I made my eyes close, breaking the spell.

I put my hands on his chest—his chest now filled out with muscle—and pushed.

He made it easy, backing up far enough that I was able to turn and walk across the hallway to the women's bathroom. I set the lock as soon as it closed, leaning my back against the door. I breathed like I had run a 5K, my lungs begging for air.

At the single sink, I turned on the cold faucet and splashed cold water onto my face. The mirror had one of those horrible fluorescent lights, just like the hallway. I looked like a wreck—red face, red eyes, freckles everywhere.

I pulled a couple of paper towels from the dispenser and dried my face, willing it to pale. The fucking sash was rubbing on my neck again. I pulled it out in front of me, hearing the cheap fabric tear. It dangled in my hand, reading *Bachelorette!* in pink glitter letters. I pushed it into the trash can, pulling brown paper towels from the dispenser to cover it up. Fuck feeling uncomfortable. I'd had enough of it tonight already.

I looked down, smoothing my dress. It had ridden up my thighs, exposing my bike shorts underneath. Why was I such a mess? It was just a boy—a man I knew from nine years ago. Why was I letting him get to me like this? Why was I letting my friends get to me? So what if I was a virgin, at pretty much everything. Archer was a gentleman. He didn't push me to go further than I was comfortable with.

This was my bachelorette party. I was supposed to be having the best time.

I smoothed my hair against the side of my head before unlocking the door. As I slipped out into the hallway, my eyes met a pair of tan work boots crossed over each other. I followed up the legs they were attached to. Blue jeans, faded and worn. Black Henley T-shirt. Tattooed arms crossed. Bower's blue eyes.

I stopped, the door to the bathroom swinging closed behind me, pushing me out into the hallway.

"Those girls out there," Bower said. "They're your friends?" He uncrossed his arms and legs to take a step closer to me. I felt small next to him. My view from the bar hadn't done him any justice. He had packed on a lot of muscle in the last nine years.

"Yeah." They were my friends. Probably. Kind of. Although

they were more friends by proxy. The start of this weekend was already a reminder that I'd only spent a handful of dinners and attended the occasional get-togethers at their houses—we weren't close.

They were obnoxious. I knew they were. Bower had probably already heard offhand criticism from their big mouths about the resort.

But I wasn't close with anyone from the school I worked at, and I hadn't exchanged more than a couple of texts with any of my friends who lived nearby since I'd started dating Archer. My close friends from college were halfway across the country. Even though I hadn't seen them in a long time, not since I'd met Archer, I wasn't going to ask them to fly out for a single weekend. They'd promised they would come for the wedding. That was enough.

Rachel, Laura, and Mindi weren't my first choice of bachelorette guests, but they were the partners of Archer's good friends, the women I'd be seeing regularly once Archer and I were married.

"If those are your friends, then maybe I don't know you as well as I thought I did." Bower reached out his hand toward my face.

Without meaning to, I flinched.

He paused, his arm extended in the air between us. His eyes were the same blue I remembered. He'd always had those kind eyes. Bower's thumb contacted my lower lip, sweeping along the outer edge, before he pulled away to swipe at the whipped cream he'd just removed from my face with his tongue.

I brought my left hand to my lip, tingling after his touch. Bower's eyes widened when he saw what perched on my finger. It felt heavier than ever.

"Wait, *you're* the bachelorette?" He backed up several steps, his back hitting the wall in the narrow hallway.

I motioned to the crown that he'd thrown onto the floor. "What did you think that was?"

"I didn't think—all of you are wearing feathers and shit."

Forcing myself to look into his eyes, I confirmed, "I'm the bachelorette."

Bower's nostrils flared before he tore his eyes from mine and headed back toward the bar. Leaving me to watch him walk away.

Chapter Fifteen

Bower

Mia was here, back at Agate Harbors. At her bachelorette party. When Dean had mentioned a bachelorette party coming in tonight, I never would've guessed it was Mia's.

Though there was no mistaking that it was her, she looked… different. Her hair was a little blonder, her body curvier. The tight dress she was wearing left little to the imagination. I'd be lying to myself if I said I wasn't attracted to her.

The ring on her hand was more like a rock. She must've found someone rich, but did he take care of her like she deserved? Did anyone in her life nowadays?

Earlier, I could tell from the bar that the crown on her head and the sash on her body had been irritating her. She'd been constantly fidgeting in her seat, adjusting the monstrosity on her head. I'd ripped it off the first second I could, and the relief in her eyes had been instant.

She was with a group of girls who looked like they walked out of Barbie boxes and into the bar. They were too fancy for this place. They looked like they belonged in a swanky downtown bar or a VIP table in Las Vegas. Not here. They acted like they didn't want to be here either. I'd heard them complaining about the food and asking for drinks we didn't have. Was this the company she kept now? Being engaged to a rich man had changed her.

When I'd enlisted, I'd known I needed to make myself into the man Mia deserved. I'd thought I had, thought I'd turned into someone Mia could respect, be proud of. But that was all for shit now. She was engaged. I was too late. I'd thought I'd maybe see her in two weeks, when her family came up for their annual vacation, but it was better this way. This way I didn't have to keep my hopes up for any longer. Finding out she was engaged should've been a relief, a reminder of where things stood.

I was no prize. Those years in the Marines had changed me. She didn't need to deal with my shit. Especially when she had a man that could afford to buy her the life she deserved. I could barely afford to keep the resort up and running. Dean, Caleb, and I had done our best to clean up the place and were slowly updating it, but it was expensive. The resort was low on funds coming out of the winter months, the slow season.

Mia didn't need those burdens and everything else that I brought to the table. She deserved to be happy. She was happy, wasn't she? Shrieks of drunken laughter filled the bar, which I knew was coming from their table. I tried not to look over at her.

It'd been nine years since I'd seen her. A lot had changed. If those women sitting at her table were the company she kept, I wasn't sure I'd have anything in common with her anymore. Maybe I'd been keeping her memory alive for so long in my head, adding to the fantasy of Mia, that I'd turned her into a made-up, fictionally perfect woman that didn't exist.

Drinks needed pouring, and food started coming out of the kitchen. I made sure Dean was the one who delivered everything to their table. I didn't want to make her feel uncomfortable.

Without warning, I heard a series of loud pops and jumped back. Only to see the pop gun Dean was filling a glass with had misfired. "Shit, man, I'm sorry." He patted me on the back. "I'll go replace the syrup."

I straightened my fingers, stretching them before curling them back into my palm, returning the heel of my hand to the edge of the bar top. I looked down the bar hoping no one had seen me jump. No such luck. Ruby was sitting on a barstool in the back of the bar, leaning against the wall, and clearly had seen my entire reaction to the pop gun.

The older, wilder of the two sisters. Ruby looked the same as she had nine years ago—she still had that mischievous glimmer in her eyes.

I walked over to where she was sitting, glancing quickly at Mia's table. Had they sent her over here? It didn't seem like it. Mia and the three blondes were sitting at the table, not paying any attention to her.

"Bower, how are ya?" Ruby asked.

"Ruby." I nodded back at her.

"So, our girl's getting married," she said. She lifted the lid to the garnish tray and snuck out a cherry. "He's not the one." She popped it into her mouth like she owned the place. "I know it, and I think she knows it deep down."

I froze in place.

"The only time I've seen her truly happy was all those summers ago…with you."

Ruby reached for another cherry, and I slammed the lid shut before she could get a second one.

I looked back at the table. Mia was hunched over, twirling her drink with her straw. She didn't look happy. It looked like she was bored—maybe daydreaming about something else…

"What are you going to do about it?" Ruby asked.

I shook my head, prying my eyes away from the table. Mia was engaged. At her bachelorette party. *Fuck.*

"What's there to do?" I snapped. "She's engaged."

I grabbed the cleaning rag from the soap bucket and slapped

it onto the counter. What was Ruby suggesting? I wasn't about to break up a relationship because I'd had a childhood crush on the girl. Especially since she seemed so different than the girl I used to know.

But what if she wasn't? What if she was the same Mia I'd fallen in love with all those years ago? Mia wasn't married yet. If there was a chance…

"What do you…" I paused, shaking my head again. Nope, I couldn't go there. "Forget it."

"I think she needs a little reminding of who she used to be." Ruby leaned in, opening the garnish tray again, this time taking an olive. "Remind her, Bower."

Chapter Sixteen

Mia

I refused to take another blow-job shot. The girls had dropped the sex talk after I'd returned to the table sans crown and sash. They didn't ask what had happened to them, and I didn't give any explanations.

My fingers traced my lip as I sat at the table listening to the ramblings of the girls. I could still feel his finger on it, the way he had studied my face when I exited the bathroom. I noticed what I was doing and put my hands in my lap. I was fantasizing about Bower. The blue-eyed boy who had turned into a man over the last nine years.

The man I, somehow, had disappointed tonight.

Why did his words affect me? *Maybe I don't know you as well as I thought I did.* Of course he didn't know me like he had all those years ago. I was nine years older and a hell of a lot more mature. I was engaged. I had lived another life without him being a part of it for a week every year.

Was he the same Bower I used to know? Probably not, judging by his enlarged frame. He had lived another life as well. We were both different people. We finished growing, apart from each other.

So why did I still feel we were connected? He had been such an important part of my life for so many years. My safe place when I was floundering with my SPD. He'd never judged me. So why was he judging me now?

"Let's go watch the fireworks." Ruby came from the bar and pulled me up out of my seat.

"Fireworks?" The girls squealed and jumped out of their chairs. They were already feeling the effect of the drinks and shots during dinner.

We left the bar out the back doors. The sun had set about an hour ago, and the stars twinkled in the night sky. I stared up at them from where we were standing on the large deck outside the bar, looking over the lake. The reflection of the stars glittered in the water.

It was a short walk to the beach. Laura, Rachel, and Mindi ran ahead of Ruby and me, arms linked, blonde hair flowing behind them. I heard their shoes thump into the sand as they kicked them off and their shrieks and splashes as they waded into the water. My toes curled in my boots. I still couldn't bring myself to go in the lake. All the sediment and algae floating around touching my skin.

Small steps still get you to where you want to go. It was one of my therapist's go-to sayings. I was doing so well making accommodations and exposing myself to things that'd previously made me uncomfortable—now I even wore sandals sometimes. Eventually I'd get to the point where I'd be able to put my feet in the lake. Small steps.

There weren't any lights out here, just the stars and the moon that was almost full. The first pop of the fireworks met my ears before color burst across the sky. I didn't know who was setting them off this year on the little island out in the lake.

I looked over to the end of the beach where it got rocky. Where Bower and I had climbed to find the perfect firework viewing spot all those years ago. My breath got caught in my throat, and I stopped walking for a second, the sand slipping under my boot.

Tiny cairns stood on the rocks. Around fifty of them. All varying heights.

I still had the agate from that summer, the top of the cairn I had built, kept safe in my purse. It was always a reminder of that firework show with Bower. When I had felt like I was home.

But my home wasn't here. It hadn't been in many years.

Forget it, I told myself. *Forget him.* I looked back up at the sky, watching the fireworks.

———

The bar became crowded as soon as the firework show ended and everyone hustled back inside for a refill. Dean was hustling to get the drink orders of the resort guests and the needy members of my bachelorette party. They kept asking for drinks he didn't have or didn't know how to make. He wasn't a mixologist. He was a can cracker and beer pourer.

The air left the room when Bower walked into the bar. His hair was wet beneath his backward cap, a few stray drops of water running down his neck. Where had he been?

Dean was struggling. Luckily he didn't harbor hard feelings toward me. Even after he had been so angry nine years ago when Bower got arrested. He made sure to keep my drink full. Ruby sat next to me, an empty glass in front of her. I could only assume he was purposefully ignoring the empty glass. She resorted to stealing sips from my drink.

We took over the back of the bar, along the end of the U-shape against the wall. It was by the jukebox that Rachel kept feeding money to play her favorite songs. The entire bar was currently listening to "Call Me Maybe."

The clink of a shot glass hitting the bar in front of me caught my attention.

"Congratulations, Mia," Bower said from behind the bar. He pushed the glass closer to me.

I reached out to grab it, our fingers briefly touching in the exchange. Ruby smirked before she stood up and joined the rest of the bachelorette party by the dance floor.

"Thanks, Bower." I tucked my left hand in my lap between my legs.

"I'm sorry about earlier." Bower took his hat off before he ran his hand through his wet hair. He put his hat back on and put both of his palms on top of the counter. He made a cage with his body, boxing me in with his arms even though he was on the other side of the bar. His black Henley covered his arms and chest like a second skin. He had my full attention. "You surprised me by being here…like this."

I looked down at my lap, at the hand that wore the ring Archer had given me. I hadn't expected to see Bower here either. He had been gone so long; I didn't think he was ever coming back.

"The resort looks good," I said, changing the subject. "It's cleaner."

"Yeah, it's been a lot of work. Dean's been—" Bower paused. He breathed sharply out of his nose, glancing down the bar before he looked right at me with his blue eyes. "I'm gonna cut the shit, Mia."

I squeezed the shot glass in my hand. The liquid inside the glass quivered.

He looked right at me. "There was never a day after that night on the beach that I didn't think about you. I thought about you every fucking day." Bower brought his face closer to mine, and the noise of the bar became dull in the background. His voice became the only thing I could hear. "And now that you're here, in front of me again, all grown up, I don't think I'm ever going to forget you. All those summers we had together."

I shook my head and closed my eyes for a second. My

thoughts raced through my head a mile a minute. I couldn't catch them. What happened to *It's good to see you*? It was like he couldn't manage small talk. But then, neither could I.

"You never even said goodbye."

"Fuck, Mia, I couldn't. I'd already put you at risk on the beach that day. I saw the way you looked at me from the boat after the party got busted, and I just couldn't." Bower backed away from the bar, his hands linked against the back of his neck.

The way I'd looked at him? I tried to think back to how I might've reacted in that moment on the boat, but all I could remember was feeling terrified for him.

Not that it mattered now. It had been nine years without a word, and today was the day he decided to pour his heart out.

I picked up the shot glass with my left hand, intentional, and tipped the glass back, letting the liquid burn my throat on the way down. As I slammed the shot glass back onto the bar top, Bower zeroed in on the ring on my finger.

"It's a little too late." Tears welled in my eyes, but I willed them away. I looked around, anywhere but back at him. I couldn't look at his face. Or let him see mine.

I saw Ruby on the other side of the bar. She had escaped the other girls. I slid off the barstool and didn't look back at Bower, though I felt his eyes on me as I walked around the U, dodging drunken resort guests.

"Hey, how did that go?" Ruby asked when I sat next to her. Bower remained on the other side of the bar. Hopefully he would stay over there.

Dean stopped by where we were sitting, two open beers in his hand. "Why does Bower look like he just swallowed a brick?"

"Probably because he confessed his love for me and I shut him down," I said cooly, trying not to flinch as I did so.

"You what?" Ruby swiveled in her seat, facing me. Dean

looked back at his patrons before handing the beers, intended for them, to us.

"Dean! We're waiting over here!" a resort guest yelled from several seats down.

"You can wait, Johnny. You've had five beers already!" He bent over, resting his elbows on the bar. "What did he say?"

"That he never stopped thinking about me. How he can't forget me." I picked up the beer Dean had placed in front of me and took a drink.

"And you told him to take a hike?" Ruby asked. "What were you thinking?"

"I'm thinking that I'm engaged. That I'm at my bachelorette party."

Bower looked over his shoulder at me as he pulled a tap handle, filling a beer. I made sure to look away.

"Would you have said yes to Archer if you knew Bower was still an option?" Ruby asked.

I looked at her before sighing, my shoulders slumping. I didn't want to answer that.

"He hasn't been around for years; you didn't know he was a possibility until tonight."

"Nine years without communication. He thinks we can pick up where we left off when I was sixteen." I looked down at my ring. That hand felt heavy again.

"I don't think he ever left Agate Harbors. Maybe physically, but mentally he's been here," Dean said. He bent down beneath the bar and grabbed a cold beer out of the refrigerator.

"Dean!" Johnny yelled from down the bar. "Beer!"

Dean held out the beer he had just taken out of the fridge, showing Johnny it was on the way. "Every letter he wrote was about the resort. Wanting updates," he said to me. "He asked about you every summer."

"So he wrote to you? Where were my letters?" I asked. I took another drink of my beer. My insides were starting to heat. It wouldn't have been that hard to drop something in the mail for me too. Something like, *Sorry I left you hanging* or *I'm in the military now traveling the world—maybe I'll be back someday.* Something, anything.

"He didn't like that you saw him like that, that night on the beach. He was embarrassed," Dean said.

For nine years? I'd forgotten about a lot of embarrassing things that had happened to me in nine years. I'd never forgotten about Bower, though. The way he'd made me feel. He'd been embarrassed? He had saved me that night from getting in trouble with the police. Who knew how *that* would have gone over with my parents. Maybe we would have never come back to Agate Harbors.

"What about social media? He couldn't have found me somehow and reached out?" Even a thumbs-up or a smiley face would have been something. Something to show me he still cared.

"You think that guy has social media? He wrote me letters for nine years, Mia. Letters. With a stamp. Not even an email," Dean said. He popped off the top of the beer bottle and left to deliver it to Johnny.

"A guy like that is rare," said Ruby. Her eyes were on Dean as he walked away. Was she talking about Dean or Bower?

"I can't do this." I finished the beer Dean had given me and looked at my sister. "It wasn't even real."

None of it. Was what I remembered between me and Bower what had actually happened? Sometimes when you were younger, you remembered things more magically than they really were. Like looking through a pair of heart-shaped, rose-colored glasses.

"Oh, it was real." Ruby laughed.

"Nine years was such a long time ago." I rested my forehead on top of my hands, my palms flat on the edge of the bar.

"You disappeared with him for a week each summer. You left

the resort every year happier than when you came. I was a teenager and I pretended I couldn't see it, but I could. Mom and Dad could see it too."

"Mom told me that night that young love never works," I said, talking to the floor. At least from here I couldn't see Bower.

"Maybe young love doesn't last..." Ruby put her hand on my shoulder. I turned my head to the side to look at her. "But you aren't young anymore. You've grown up. Maybe that love grew with you."

Tears welled in my eyes. Bower and I had both changed. Growth was unavoidable. But had our feelings grown with us? Or were they just a magical childhood memory we were trying to relive?

I scrubbed at my face, sighing. I'd been crying all too often for it being my bachelorette party.

"I can't hear how he asked Dean about me all these years," I said. "It brings back too many feelings." Feelings of safety, warmth, magic. Everything I felt as a girl at Agate Harbors with Bower.

"Those feelings you're having..." Ruby said, shaking her head. "I wouldn't be getting married if I felt them."

"Mia, can we talk?"

That voice. I'd heard it for the first time outside the bathroom today in all its baritone glory.

I lifted my head. Bower was standing there, in front of me, his arms tensing through his shirt. I quickly wiped my under eyes.

Ruby grabbed my forearms. "Talk to him. Just give him a minute."

I nodded, taking a deep breath.

"Cover me for a minute, Dean," Bower called out.

His friend gave a wave of his hand in acknowledgment. He was bent over the bar trying to understand the girls' latest drink order. Good luck to him.

Bower stepped out from behind the bar, then grabbed my wrist, like he had when we were kids, and pulled me outside the building. It was late, but they wouldn't close until the people stopped buying drinks. We walked far enough down the gravel drive that the music and voices from the bar turned into ambient sounds.

"What do you want, Bower?" I pulled my wrist out of his hand. I felt too comfortable with him holding it.

"Do you love him?" he asked.

"Love who?"

"If I have to tell you who, you must not love him."

I shook my head. I hadn't forgotten about Archer. It was just this place, the memories. All I could see was Bower.

"I'm engaged to him," I said.

"That wasn't my question."

"Don't do this to me, Bower."

"Do what?"

"Confuse me with…everything."

He knew what this place meant to me. Now that he was here, in my favorite place, looking like he did, I was second-guessing myself, the choices I made when he wasn't around.

Bower took a step closer to me. I could smell him. It was his body wash or something—no, it was the lake again. It flooded my senses.

"How about this? I'll make it less confusing for you," he said. "Don't do it. Don't go back to him. Give me a chance, a real one this time."

I didn't know what to say; I just stood there like a deer in the headlights. Bower grabbed my left hand, then dug into the pocket of his jeans. He dropped an object into my palm, bending my fingers around it before I could see what it was. It wasn't heavy, but it was solid.

He still had his hand wrapped around my wrist, used it to pull me close to him.

I stood like a statue, scared to move—to make the wrong move.

He bent down, his warm breath against my cheek sending goose bumps down my legs, and hovered there for a minute. I couldn't breathe. My brain still wasn't functioning.

His lips touched my cheek, lingering longer than a greeting or a goodbye kiss. This felt like a promise. "I never left you," he said with his mouth against my skin.

Bower let go of me all at once. The absence of his warmth left me feeling like I'd jumped into the lake before ice-out. He turned around, heading back to the bar. I didn't look away from his silhouette, and he never glanced back.

When he disappeared back into the bar, I took a breath of air. It burned my lungs like they'd been deprived of oxygen for minutes.

What had he left in my hand? I got brave enough to look. Finger by finger, I unfurled my hand, revealing what he had given me. An agate. Like the one at the bottom of my purse. A memory of happy times. A promise of more memories made together.

I let the tears fall and my knees hit the gravel, ignoring the abrasive grain on my skin.

I cried because I now would have to wash my knees off in the bathroom sink.

I cried because Bower had left me with an awful decision to make: Leave my fiancé to give him a chance, or marry Archer and live with the what-if of Bower.

I cried because Agate Harbors was always my favorite daydream and now it was turning into a nightmare.

"Mia? Is that you?" Ruby bent down next to me, wrapping her arm around my shoulder. "What did he say?"

I opened my hand to show her. That said it all. She knew I kept the agate from summers ago in my purse.

"Ah, fuck." My sister pulled me up to standing and bent

down to brush the gravel debris off my knees. "Let's get you to the bathroom and cleaned off."

"No." I suddenly wanted to feel the grit against my skin. It distracted me from the way my life was tumbling down around me.

"Okay. Drinks." Ruby grabbed my wrist as Bower had earlier.

Only this time, I wasn't pulled toward a man but to a bar. With alcohol. Lots of alcohol.

Chapter Seventeen

Mia

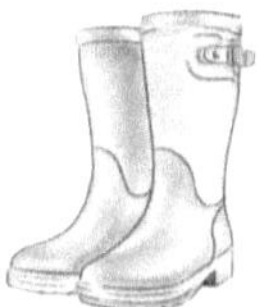

Something hard was pressing against my sternum. The sheets of the bed underneath me were rough, scratching at my skin. What was I wearing? I rolled over, immediately regretting that decision. It was so bright in here. What time was it?

I kept my eyes closed, slapping my hand along the edge of the bed, looking for my phone. I found it halfway down, near my hips, plugged into the charger.

I tapped twice on the screen to see the time. Eight thirty in the morning. Too early. My mouth tasted like sour milk. Water. I needed water.

I threw my legs over the side of the bed. My head pulsed. I breathed in sharply, willing the vomit in my throat to recede, when I felt it again—the hard lump in my chest.

Glancing down, I saw that I was still wearing my clothes from last night and fished out the culprit from my camisole. An agate, like the one from all those years ago with Bower. Memories from last night came flooding into my brain. One after another punching me until I was knocked over on the bed. I looked up at the ceiling fan, making lazy circles. What was my life?

"Yoo-hoo! How's the bachelorette feeling this morning?" Laura came into my room with way too much enthusiasm. Had she not been at the same bar I was at last night? "That was a bachelorette party for the ages! Archer is going to be so jelly."

She sat down on the side of my bed, bouncing the mattress. Whatever was left in my stomach sloshed around as I groaned. "That guy last night—he was something else. He carried you out of the bar like you were light as a feather."

What?

"And tucked you into bed. It was so sweet."

I blinked at her. *Who?*

Ruby rushed into my room, out of breath. "You're awake. Sorry—I tried to get here…first." She looked at Laura with a touch of disdain. "It smells horrible in here." Ruby went over to the window and forced it open.

"What the fuck happened?" I sat up on the bed. Laura was being vague, and I needed facts.

"You got super drunk," Ruby explained.

Yep. My head confirmed that loud and clear.

"And you passed out on top of the bar, and Bower carried you home." Ruby talked fast, cringing, waiting for my reaction.

I didn't give her one. My face froze in horror.

"A hot lumberjack carrying you home?" Laura said. "Ugh. What I wouldn't give. It's like a romance novel." Her comments were unwanted and unnecessary. The guilt and embarrassment ravaged my body all on their own.

"Laura, why don't you get the bachelorette some water?" Ruby suggested.

Laura skittered out of the room, glad to be of use.

"Bower refused to let anyone else help you," Ruby said once she had left. I let my head fall into my hands. It was more comfortable there. "He carried you back to the cabin and tucked you into bed."

No. How was I going to explain this to Archer? How was I going to justify this to myself? What had happened last night with Bower and me, the agate I held in my hand? I was going home with more baggage than I had brought with me.

"You're going to have to make a decision, Mia."

Ruby was right. I had to figure out what I wanted. I'd come on this trip with the mindset of marriage, as Archer's fiancée. But that was before Bower had reentered the chat. Could I get married in good faith knowing what Bower had proposed? Giving him a chance? That would mean breaking things off with Archer, canceling the wedding and disappointing my parents. They loved Archer and all the support he offered me. Mostly support of the financial nature.

After last night, watching the fireworks on the beach, seeing the cairns brought back so many happy memories. Memories that had nothing to do with money. Bower had been my safety net all those years. He'd never let me fall. Bower was a landing place, like a hammock I could comfortably rest on.

Right now Archer's net held me in place, promising safety so long as I pleased him—the way he wanted me to dress, how he wanted my hair to look, covering my freckles. I had tried to explain, tried to make him understand how it bothered me, but he never did, and I was afraid he never would. Just like his friends. Ruby was right. They were awful.

Bower had never tried to change me. Even as a little girl who couldn't walk on the sand. He'd seen through my issues and accepted me for who I was.

I had to decide what I was going to do. And quick. Mom, Dad, Ruby, and I would be back up at Agate Harbors in two weeks for our summer vacation. And there was no way I could bring Archer if Bower was here.

Two Weeks Later

Chapter Eighteen

Mia

"I still don't understand, Mia," Mom was saying from the front seat. Dad was driving, and Ruby and I were sharing the back seat. I was eleven years old all over again.

Mom insisted on us driving up together for our summer vacation, just like we always had when we were younger. *It's a tradition,* she'd say when Ruby or I brought up driving ourselves. If the tradition excuse didn't work, she'd pull out the *Your dad and I are both getting older, and we don't get to spend enough time with you.* That guilt trip always worked, no matter how much I dreaded spending four hours stuck in a car with my parents.

Ruby's promises of never coming on the annual family trip never held up. Mom used the same strategies she used on me to guilt her into coming—and for that I was thankful. I couldn't do a week with my parents without her. Particularly this week, since they'd found out just this morning that Archer wasn't coming with us as planned.

"We're taking a break," I explained.

That was what I'd said to Archer too. A break seemed less final than breaking up. Maybe after some time being on a break, it would be easier to end things permanently. Especially if for the first part of it we were four hours apart.

It wasn't the right thing to do. I should have completely ended it with him, but when I'd brought up taking some time apart, he had lost the unflappable attitude I was accustomed to. He at first blamed Laura, Rachel, and Mindi, claiming that they must've told me something about him that made me look at him differently, which made me wonder what they had seen of him in the past.

When he'd realized that wasn't the case, he'd quickly shifted blame to Ruby, knowing that she wasn't his biggest fan. I'd shut that down quickly. Finally, Archer got into self-deprecation, bringing up regrets about all the things he'd been doing to help me "better myself." He'd said it in such a way that I questioned if he was being genuine or just trying to say the things I wanted to hear.

Though he was partially right—his unacceptance of me and how I was had put a wedge between us. I couldn't bring myself to tell him the truth: that Bower made me feel things he never did and never could. We had a history together that couldn't be replicated, and I would be forever wondering what we could've had if I stayed with Archer.

So when tears had begun falling down Archer's cheeks, something I had never seen before, I'd folded. Just a little. I'd called it a break, told him we would talk when I got back. I already was not looking forward to that conversation.

Mom was still rambling on. "I just don't get it. You leave a man with all of *that*." By *that*, she meant money. Influence.

I didn't have a good excuse for her. To someone on the outside, it looked like a stupid decision. I couldn't tell her I still had feelings for Bower, feelings that I needed to explore. She had already made it quite clear what she thought about young love and how it would never work.

"We wanted better for you," she said. "More than what your father and I could give you girls growing up."

That took me back. I looked at Ruby next to me. Her lips pursed, shaking her head. I'd known they'd struggled raising a family on two teachers' salaries, but I'd never realized this was why she wanted me to have Archer's money.

"You brought us on this vacation for a week every year!" I said, unable to stop from raising my voice. The money talk and how I had given up a man whose only feature in my parents' eyes was the wealth he had was getting on my nerves.

"To Agate Harbors?" She almost let out a laugh. "Like I said, we wanted better for you!" Mom was speaking in raised tones now too. Dad put his hand on her leg.

Steam was coming out of my ears. Suddenly she was too good for the resort that Bower was working hard to fix up? The place where I'd made my happiest childhood memories? It was far from the dump she projected it to be. In my eyes, it was the most beautiful place on earth. Agate Harbors had that aura. It was someplace magical.

A piece of hair fell out of my ponytail and tickled my nose. I ripped the hair tie out of my head and got to work retying it. Mom glanced in the rearview mirror at me before looking away disapprovingly.

"We have twenty more minutes until we're there," Ruby whispered, resting a hand on my arm reassuringly.

I needed to last twenty more minutes without blowing up. I could do that. Then I would be in Agate Harbors.

This week was going to be an experiment of sorts. I'd avoided Bower for the rest of my bachelorette weekend. It was embarrassing enough being continually reminded by my "friends" that he had carried me home the night before—I couldn't risk embarrassing myself further by running into him. I had been hungover and didn't have the slightest idea of what I would've said to him.

We'd ordered pizza to our cabin—much to the girls' disappointment—and watched old rom-com DVDs until we'd fallen asleep on the couch, only crawling to bed once the title menu music had woken us up.

Sunday morning, everyone had been up early and ready to go home. Ruby had called a car service to drive us home, and I'd texted Archer to cancel the party bus that was scheduled to pick us up after lunch. We'd dropped the cabin keys into the lodge's mailbox before driving away.

The moment Agate Harbors had disappeared from the rearview mirror was the moment I'd decided to end things with Archer. It'd felt like I'd forgotten something—a part of me—back at the resort, and I knew I had to go back and see if what I'd felt between Bower and me was more than just a spark.

Had I made the right decision? In first-grade science, I taught my students the word *hypothesis*. This week I had one to test. *If I spend the week at Agate Harbors, I will leave knowing that I made the right decision.* There were a lot of variables to take into consideration. First, who Bower was as a person. I didn't know the man who had cornered me in the hallway of the bar two weeks ago. I'd like to think I did, but people changed a lot over nine years.

Second, Bower's feelings toward me. He'd asked me to give him a chance, but he'd never outright said exactly how he felt about me. That was more of an assumption on my part. Third, my feelings toward Bower. I had felt a spark between us. Was it just because we hadn't seen each other in nine years and he looked like a hot-ass lumberjack? I didn't think so. That spark still had to be there.

It was time to put my hypothesis to the test. If only it would prove true.

———

"Go find him, Mia."

I was standing on the deck, trying to get a glimpse of the lodge between the trees. If I could see him, figure out where he was, I could plan my approach. I wanted to see Bower—I really did—but the anxiety of what was riding on this week was beginning to get to me. The smell of the cabin, the magic of Agate Harbors had already infiltrated my body. I was a different person up here, and I didn't want anything to change that. Even Bower.

"What if I'm wrong? What if the spark isn't there anymore?" I bent over the deck, propping my elbows on the drink rail, my head in my hands. "What if I dumped my fiancé for no reason?"

Ruby laughed. She crossed her arms, leaning her back against the railing next to me. "You two practically started a fire at the bar two weeks ago. The spark is there." Ruby shook her head. "And as for dumping your fiancé, you had a shit ton of reasons to dump him. It's the best decision you've made all year."

I frowned at her, taking a step back from the railing. "You never liked Archer."

"Archer is fine. I didn't like who you were when you were with him," she said. "You were always trying to become something you weren't. It was like watching eleven-year-old Mia try to please our parents, except you were trying to please someone who was supposed to be your partner. Someone who is supposed to love you unconditionally. Archer gave you a lot of conditions."

"So, you never liked Archer," I pressed.

Ruby tilted her head. "Nope. I guess I never did."

"Fine, I'll go find Bower. Only because you're making me." I turned and walked toward the stairs.

I heard her chuckle behind me. "Mm-hmm. Keep telling yourself that."

The path to the lodge was etched into my brain. I could find it with my eyes closed. The familiar sights of Betty's clothesline and the porch we'd sit on with our Popsicles brought a smile to my face. It felt like coming home.

"Let's go back to the cabin," I heard Gill say. "You've had a long day, and it's time to relax."

"Don't tell me to relax! I don't know you!" Betty's voice rang clear from behind the towels hanging on the clothesline.

I picked up my pace, jogging, ripping towels off the clothesline to see what was going on.

I hadn't exchanged more than pleasantries with the Hansons since Bower's sudden departure, only a simple "Hello" during the week our family vacationed, and I hadn't seen them at all during my bachelorette party. But something sounded off in Betty's voice, and I was determined to find out what was the matter.

Behind the third towel I pulled down were Gill and Betty. I stood there looking at them, out of breath from the adrenaline spike coursing through my body.

"Mia? Is that you?" Betty's voice sounded like music to my ears.

Gill looked at his wife with trepidation.

"Yeah, it's me. What's going on here?"

Gill looked between me and Betty, his mouth open.

"You'll catch flies in that trap if you don't close it up," Betty said to him before walking toward me. "I'm so glad to see you!" She pulled me into her bosom, wrapping her warm arms around me. "Boy, you've gotten a whole lot taller since last year."

"Have I?" I asked. I hadn't grown taller since I'd been in high school. I looked between Gill and Betty when she released me. "Is there a prob—"

"No problem. No problem here." Gill was quick to interject. "We're happy to see you, Mia."

I didn't know what was going on. Maybe I'd heard wrong. I

could've sworn Betty had said *I don't know you*, but if she was saying that to Gill, that didn't make sense.

"I've got something for you, Mia. It's inside. Let me go see if I can find it." Betty turned around and shuffled toward the cabin.

Gill paused, like he wanted to say something to me, but he took a breath before turning around and following his wife.

I had so many questions, but it seemed this year would be the same as every other year. Only pleasantries with Betty and Gill now.

"What are you doing here?"

Bower's voice.

I turned and saw him, paused in his approach to the lodge. He must've just gotten off the boat. The bridge of his nose and his cheeks were red from the sun. He needed to turn his hat the other way around—it would both protect him from the sun and make him a lot less…attractive.

Crap. Less than a minute seeing him and I was already getting distracted by how hot he was.

I stiffened, saying, "This is the week I'm always here."

Bower made a humph sound before continuing toward me. He wore a light-gray T-shirt today. It had questionable smears of goo on it, like he'd been fishing and had to wrestle a northern into the net.

I deflated quickly. This wasn't going at all the way I'd wanted it to. I licked my lips, bolstering my courage, then said, "I was hoping we could talk—"

"Hey, I need a little help!"

I peeked around Bower to find the cutest little boy, not more than seven, with round glasses and blond hair that had missed several haircuts. He was carrying a net twice the size of his body with a fish that probably weighed close to his own weight. Bower turned around quickly, taking the net from the boy with ease.

"I caught it myself!" the boy told me, his wide smile showing off several missing teeth.

"Did not!" another boy shouted, coming up behind them. He pointed to Bower. "He had to help you cast and reel and lift it out of the water." The boy with glasses shoved him. They looked like they could be twins, if there weren't six inches of height separating them. Definitely brothers.

"Hey, why don't I meet you over at the fish cleaning table and I'll show you how to gut it?" Bower directed the boys to the fish-cleaning station up past the lodge.

"With a knife?"

"Yep." He nodded.

"Will we get to see the guts?"

"Of course."

The boys ran ahead, thrilled at the opportunity to decapitate a fish. Bower stood there with the net in his hand, the fish still dripping water from the lake.

My jaw dropped at the exchange. He had acted so paternal. It had been nine years since I'd seen him, and the boys looked to be about seven and five. It was totally feasible he had children—

"They're guests, Mia. I took them fishing," Bower said, cutting into my thoughts, reading my mind like he always had.

"Of course they are," I said, pretending like I hadn't thought anything else. He'd make a great father, but that wasn't the point.

"I've gotta go gut some fish." Bower walked by me, passing close enough that I got a good look at his tattoos in the daylight. One of his arms was a full sleeve of swirls and loops. I couldn't help but notice how the veins in his forearms bulged under the weight of the fish he was carrying. I turned, watching him walk away.

I took a deep breath. This wasn't going to be easy.

He'd poured his heart out to me two weeks ago, told me to give him a chance. I'd gotten drunk and hidden from him instead of confronting what I'd felt between us.

That was before. Now I was here, sans fiancé, ready to give us a chance.

Bower continued to walk away. He didn't even turn around to check if I was still standing here.

But that was okay. I wasn't a quitter.

I had a week here to figure out if Bower was the same guy I'd fallen for when I was younger. Plenty of time at my disposal. He couldn't be fishing with adorable children all the time. I could use this week to become his shadow. It wouldn't be hard; I knew this resort like the back of my hand.

There's no hiding from me, Bower Hanson.

Chapter Nineteen

Bower

I was shocked to see Mia back here. She had a fiancé back at home. If I was engaged to her, I wouldn't let her out of my sight.

The vibrations from my axe splitting the log traveled up my arm, shaking my shoulder. I'd just sharpened the blade, and it cut through the dry oak logs like butter. The firewood stockpiles were chockful, but I needed to do something physical to keep my mind off her.

It'd taken me a week to recover from seeing Mia wearing that bachelorette outfit. It'd gutted me, knowing that someone had been waiting for her back home. A fiancé. Someone she'd said yes to marrying—someone she'd agreed to spend the rest of her life with.

Another log split into two pieces, falling onto the grass. I picked up the pieces and threw them onto the pile I was creating. My muscles cried out as I picked up another log to split. *Good.* I welcomed the pain—it meant I was getting somewhere, thinking of something other than Mia.

Ruby had made it seem like I had a chance. She wasn't a fan of Mia's fiancé, that was for certain. I'd fucking laid it out there with Mia, become more vulnerable than I ever had. She reciprocated by getting drunk. So drunk that I'd had to carry her out of the bar and back to her cabin.

Not that I'd minded it. She'd felt good in my arms and even smelled good after a full night of drinking. I'd tucked her in, hoping she'd wake up ready to take a chance with me, agree that there was something between us.

But she hadn't.

I took a breath in, swinging the axe up and around, my hands sliding together as I brought the axe down—completely missing the log.

Shit. My muscles were fatiguing, but they weren't tired enough to be missing the log completely. I couldn't remember the last time I'd missed like that. I lifted my hat off my head and ran my fingers through my hair. She was getting to me.

Mia had left without saying goodbye. Just as I'd done to her all those years ago. I couldn't help but notice the irony. I'd left her for nine years, whereas Mia had left me for two weeks. But it didn't kill me any less. The not knowing had been brutal. How Mia had done it for nine years, not knowing what had happened, I'd never know, but now I understood why she was so mad. I'd sent her small packages over the years, but she'd never responded. I wasn't sure I would've either if I were in her position—but unfortunately, now there was nothing I could do about it.

Another log split in two. I threw the pieces onto the pile. It was getting too tall—the logs on the side tumbling down each time I added new ones to the top. I laid down the axe and got to work rearranging the pile so it would continue to support my diversion. I wasn't anywhere close to being finished.

During the second week after she'd left, I'd rebuilt my walls. I was good at that. I had Fort Knox built around me. It protected me, kept me from falling apart, showing those broken parts of myself to people.

So when I'd seen her standing there yesterday among the towels on the clothesline, I'd felt ready. Ready to protect her from me. She didn't need to deal with me and all my broken parts. She had a fiancé at home to take care of her. Someone who she must've been happy with if she'd gone back to him after everything I'd said to her. I wasn't enough. My words hadn't been enough for her, and I needed to get over it.

I sucked in a breath as a wood sliver pierced through my palm. I brought my hand to my mouth and pulled it out with my teeth.

Now she was here, expecting to see me—expecting that I'd want to talk to her after I'd laid out my heart and she'd run from it. Mia hadn't said anything to me before she'd left the other week. She'd hidden in her cabin as if she was scared of me—or maybe scared that what I'd said to her was true.

I had to get through one week with her here, in my space. I could dodge her for a week. The resort was big enough that we didn't have to run into each other. I could do it.

You're not going to unnerve me again, Mia Miller.

———

"B4." Paused silence. Low grumbling. "B4."

There still weren't any bingos. This game was lasting for fucking ever. I'd turned the crank, let the little balls fall out of the basket, and called number after number. Still no bingos. It was only the first game of ten. How had my grandmother done this week after week for thirty-five years? That woman was a saint.

"O69." Paused silence. Subtle giggling. "O69."

"Bingo!" someone called out. Thank God.

A man in swim trunks brought up his bingo card, balancing the chips on the surface. I glanced down at the chips in a diagonal line across his card. Good enough.

"Clear your boards." The microphone screeched as I spoke into it, and everyone raced to cover their ears.

Caleb showed up at the lodge donning his tool belt, hammer hanging from his hip. "Dude, this is the worst bingo game ever." I'd set up bingo right outside the lodge—that way I didn't have to haul all the equipment across the resort.

"It's bingo. How's it supposed to be fun?" I covered the microphone in hopes that the few guests playing wouldn't hear. They were already grumbling about having to clear their boards.

"I went to so many bingo games with my grandma in Boca Raton when I was younger. Those games get wild. Grandmas flipping each other off. Grandpas throwing their walkers down the aisles. Shit's intense." Caleb paused, taking in the current game. "This…sucks."

"If you're such the bingo professional, be my guest." I waved Caleb over to the microphone. *Best of luck.* It was a tough crowd of twelve.

Caleb unfastened his tool belt, letting it fall to the grass. "Hello, ladies and gentlemen," he said, giving a bright grin. "I'm Caleb, and I'll be taking over as bingo caller for the rest of the afternoon."

An errant "Whoop!" came from the crowd. I snapped my head up to see who it was, but I couldn't find the traitor. Everyone sat up straighter in their seats. Caleb had their full attention with two sentences. He started calling out numbers, a charismatic quip following each one.

I was horrible at this. I knew it, the guests knew it, and Caleb and Dean couldn't stop giving me shit about my "lack of enthusiasm." I should've hired an event coordinator to run these things. It wasn't for me.

My grandmother had run all the resort activities since I could remember. Grandpa had cut her off last year when she'd mixed bleach with the dye instead of water for tie-dye T-shirts. There wasn't anyone else to run all the activities that kept families coming back year after year. Grandpa wasn't interested, Dean and Caleb were busy in their respective roles, and I couldn't put that kind of responsibility on Chloe this far into her pregnancy. It left me, struggling to run all the events my grandma had run every year with ease.

"Bingo!" a voice called out from among the bingo players.

"Can the beautiful blonde please read off her card?"

I automatically looked up to see who this beautiful blonde was. Maybe it'd take my mind off a different blonde I couldn't stop thinking about.

My eyes widened as Mia stood up from behind a guest and started calling out numbers and letters. I hadn't seen her there in the back row, hidden behind the guy in front of her.

Caleb had always been a charmer. I'd seen him flirt with the ninety-year-old grandmother who was a guest here last week. He was harmless, didn't even see it as flirting. It was his way of being friendly. Still, him calling Mia beautiful irked me in a way Caleb had never irked me before.

"B2." Mia tried to hide her smile as she read the last number of her bingo win.

"That's it, folks. Clear your cards," Caleb announced. The crowd grumbled.

"What do I get for a prize?" Mia called out. She was still standing there, looking right at me.

"Uh, what do we do for prizes, Bower?"

We usually didn't do prizes for bingo. Winning was enough for most people.

Mia wasn't most people. She knew it too. She stood there looking at me with those chocolate-brown eyes, waiting for an answer.

"A Popsicle," I said.

"Hey! I didn't get a Popsicle!" the man who'd won the last game protested. What was it with the entitlement of people on vacation?

"All the winners can get a Popsicle from the freezer inside the lodge," I said into the microphone.

A few cheers came from the crowd. I patted Caleb on the back, ready to let him take over completely. I had other shit to do that didn't involve placating the egos of resort guests.

He stepped back a few steps from the microphone so it wouldn't pick up his voice. "We're handing out Popsicles to the winners now?"

"She asked for a prize. Was I supposed to say no?"

A laugh broke out from the bingo crowd. It was Mia, laughing with her fellow bingo winner, probably gloating in their mutual Popsicle victory. My teeth clenched together. It wasn't the sound of her laugh or even the fact that she was laughing. It was that I hadn't caused that sound to come from her throat. I used to be the one that made her laugh.

"Jeez, dude. You just tensed up. Are you all right?" Caleb followed my eyeline. "The beautiful blonde, eh? Are you finally over that Mia girl?"

I'd probably told Caleb too much about Mia when we'd served together. He'd always been talking about Chloe, and when the nights had gotten long, I'd share stories about Mia. It'd become clear after the fifth, seventh, twentieth time I brought her up that I was smitten with her. There'd never been another girl I talked to him about. Caleb had only known Mia. He probably knew just as much about her as I did.

"Mia!" Ruby's voice had always been louder than Mia's. She never was concerned about who heard her. "Lunch! Mom made pasta salad!"

Mia said goodbye to her Popsicle partner and gave me a look before jogging over to her sister. She was wearing tight black bike shorts that left nothing to the imagination.

"Shit. That isn't her, is it?" Caleb asked.

I grunted in reply.

"Finally I lay eyes on the famous Mia. I feel like I already know her. You talked about her enough during our tours. Maybe I'll say hi later."

"Don't bother," I said.

Caleb raised his eyebrows. "Trouble in paradise?"

"There've been some complications." The fiancé, for starters.

"I'm sure you can work it out over the Popsicle you promised her."

Shit. She'd be back for her Popsicle.

"Start calling them numbers, Caleb!" As I slapped Caleb on the back and left him to the bingo game, I found myself wondering if we had any orange Popsicles in the freezer.

For the next half hour, I reviewed the rest of the summer's reservations behind the front desk of the lodge. Everything looked up to date. There was mail to be opened—I tore open the new boat-registration decals for the resort's fleet. I needed to go down to the marina and put them on the boats.

I glanced over at the nearly spotless front counter, noticing a stray cabin key. I picked it up and opened the safe we kept the keys in. A few were on the wrong hooks. I got to work reorganizing them.

Through the windows, I saw the grass needed to be mowed, the tips of the long strands waving in the breeze. The mower was sitting right next to the lodge with a full tank of gas.

I glanced down at one of our freezers.

The frozen treats looked low. I found the box of Popsicles and packaged ice-cream treats and restocked the few empty spots and pulled the orange ones to the top. Who liked orange anyway? It was arguably the worst flavor.

The screen door slammed into the doorframe.

I turned from the freezer and saw her. She was still wearing those fucking bike shorts and a tank top that I already knew didn't have tags to irritate her skin.

"I'm here to collect my prize," Mia said.

It took a minute for my ears to register her words—my eyes were too busy taking her in. I slid open the lid to the freezer, thankful for the cool air that rushed out. It was suddenly hot inside the lodge.

I picked out a Popsicle—an orange one from the top—and handed it to her. She left me hanging there for a minute, with my arm outstretched, Popsicle in my hand, before she finally took it from me. Her fingers touched my hand briefly, and I quickly pulled away, putting my hand inside the pocket of my shorts.

Mia ripped open the wrapper and pulled out the Popsicle. "You remembered," she said before she put the Popsicle to her lips. They were full and a dusty pink color. They had been soft that night when I had wiped off a bit of that blow-job shot her friends had ordered for her.

She held the Popsicle there, against her pursed lips, before she opened her mouth, slowly sliding it inside. *Fuck. I shouldn't be watching this.* I turned around and walked back to the safety of the front desk. Behind it, I could hide what was rising in my pants. Over what was happening to a Popsicle. This was ridiculous.

The screen door slammed shut again. I stood up, surprised to see my grandma out and about. Usually about now she started sundowning, a term I learned in my research about dementia. Late afternoons and evenings were hard for her. She became unsettled and agitated. Chloe was behind her. She raised her arms, mouthing *I don't know* to me.

"Mia! Is that you?" Grandma shuffled over to where Mia was standing, sucking on her Popsicle. She released her hold on the orange ice, a popping sound coming from her mouth. I paused, taking in what was happening in front of me.

Grandma had just remembered Mia.

"Yes, it's good to see you again, Betty. Yesterday when I saw you—"

"I've got something for you, Mia." Grandma walked over and took Mia's hand in hers. "Wait, let me go get it for you." She made her way across the lodge through the door marked *Private.* It was the entrance to her and my grandpa's cabin.

"What in the world?" Chloe said, looking at Mia. "Betty recognizes you?"

"Of course she does. I've known her for most of my life." Mia popped the Popsicle back into her mouth, rolling it over her tongue.

"No, I mean…she hardly recognizes anyone anymore. Not even her husband or Bower." They both looked at me, confusion splayed across both of their faces, for different reasons.

"Chloe, this is Mia, and Mia, this is Chloe." Both girls glanced over at each other as I introduced them.

"*The* Mia?" Chloe waddled over to Mia, pulling her into a hug as close as the baby in her belly would allow. "I feel like I already know you."

Mia pulled back and raised an eyebrow at her.

"From what Caleb told me, of course. This one doesn't tell me much." She motioned back at me.

Mia looked confused as ever. Her lips were a mix of orange from the Popsicle and their natural pink color. Like a sunset over the lake.

I shook my head quickly. "Chloe's husband, Caleb, works for the resort," I said.

"And they served together for five years. Don't let her think you divulge your love life to random employees, Bower."

A sudden look of amusement flashed through Mia's features. "His love life, huh?"

Ah, fuck. What had Caleb told Chloe? She looked between me and Mia a couple of times before answering. Maybe it was the way I was clenching my jaw, but she seemed to pick up on the tension.

"Caleb's told me stories Bower shared about you and him growing up here," Chloe said quickly. "It sounded magical."

"You have no idea." Mia was responding to Chloe but looked at me when she spoke. "They were the best weeks of my life."

It was suddenly quiet in the lodge. The hum of the coolers and the distant sounds of laughing children were the only noise in the room.

"Um, I should go check on Betty," Chloe said. She waddled over to the door Grandma had gone through moments before.

"Is Betty coming back?" Mia asked.

"No, Mia. I don't think so." Chloe made her way through the doorway, turning her head back toward the lodge. "It was nice meeting you," she said before the door latched behind her.

"Is something going on?" Mia asked. "I don't mean to intrude, but something's off."

I took my hat off my head and ran my fingers through my hair, letting my fingernails drag across my scalp. With my hair pulled back, I replaced the hat on my head.

I hated explaining what was going on. I had to do it occasionally with guests who'd known my grandma for years. The reactions I got were worse than finding the right words. Some were sympathetic, which was depressing for everyone. Some reactions weren't realistic about the situation, and they'd say things like *Just stay positive! It could be worse.* Or the worst one of all, *Things happen for a reason.* For what reason would my sweet grandma and everyone around her have to suffer through the throes of dementia? *Let me know when you find the fucking reason,* I wanted to say in response. *I'd love to know what it is.*

"My grandma's sick," I started. "She has dementia. Middle stage right now. I'm surprised she recognized you."

"Oh my god, Bower, I had no idea." Mia leaned over the desk, putting her warm hand on top of mine. I kept my hand still, hoping she wouldn't remove hers. "That must be really hard." It was hard. Mia looked at me with her big brown eyes, giving me their full attention.

"It's been the hardest on my grandpa. She hardly recognizes him anymore."

"Ugh, poor Gill." Mia squeezed the top of my hand with her fingers. "I'm here for you guys, no matter what."

With a twist of my wrist, I flipped my hand over underneath hers. I needed to feel her hand in mine.

Mia looked down at our hands, our palms touching. Eyes wide, she looked back up at me, not knowing what to say. She didn't need to say anything else. She'd reacted to the news of my grandma's illness better than I'd expected. Actually, I should have expected nothing less from Mia. She'd been through hard times herself. Mia knew what to say and how to say it in a way that wasn't sympathetically dismissive or lacking empathy. A skill gained from growing up with parents who didn't fully accept her and her differences.

It seemed like Mia had made it through the worst, though. She looked good. Put together. Did her fiancé have something to do with it? She was even wearing sandals, which was shocking.

"I should apologize." Mia looked down at our hands before she lifted her head up and looked into my eyes. "I remember everything you said that night."

That night outside the bar—the one I couldn't stop thinking about.

"I was so overwhelmed…I didn't know what to do."

I wrapped my fingers around her hand. It fit perfectly in mine, just like it had when we were young.

"I should've found you the next day. I shouldn't have left without saying goodbye," she continued.

Holding hands felt right, just as it had all those years ago. My thumb grazed over her bare fingers. Then I realized I was holding her left hand. *She's not wearing her engagement ring.*

"The chance, Bower…" she said. Her voice wobbled a bit. She waited until our eyes connected. "I'll take it."

Her words flooded my body, drowning me and my voice. I let out a few garbles from my throat before coughing to clear it.

Mia pulled her hand out of mine and handed me her used Popsicle stick for me to dispose of. She winked at me—she fucking *winked*—before turning around and walking out the door of the lodge.

I stood there, dumbstruck, for a couple seconds before the screen door slammed, breaking me out of my stupor. This was the same girl who'd left me without a response two weeks ago, now telling me she wanted to take a chance?

The same girl who'd been engaged two weeks ago, ready to marry someone else.

Her forwardness was very unlike someone who was engaged…and she wasn't wearing her ring. Had she left her fiancé? Maybe she was just resting her finger. That ring had to be heavy to wear every day.

If she was now single, I couldn't imagine what'd happened in the last two weeks to change her mind. Not that I even wanted to think about her with another man. I wanted to live in this bubble —the one where Mia took a chance with me, went all in. If she really was single now, we had the week to live in the bubble… until Saturday, when it would pop.

Mia had always had this effect on me. It was so easy to get wrapped up with her—she was one of the few people that knew me—had known me before everything went to shit. If she was giving me a chance, I'd take it, but I didn't want her to see everything I was now. Fort Knox was still standing strong, although it was beginning to crumble in a few locations.

Chapter Twenty

Mia

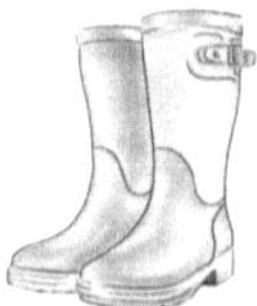

It was a new day. Same mission: shoot my shot with Bower. Today was Kids Camp—Betty's favorite day, but if I could guess, Bower's worst nightmare. All the parents were welcome to drop off their kids from ten until two for activities and games. It was fun for the kids but more to give parents a much-needed break from their children.

It was a little after ten in the morning, and I could hear the kids yelling before I laid eyes on the lodge. I rounded the corner and saw Bower in the middle of complete chaos. I stood there and watched for a second, reveling in how uncomfortable he was with all the kids. Bower was always so calm and collected. I liked seeing him sweat a little.

Eventually I felt bad and made my way over to the group of kids. They were playing with a giant parachute, every physical education teacher's worst nightmare. The excitement of the kids, running wildly underneath the parachute; the kids who inevitably let go and ruined the dome for everyone else… It was a bold choice for Bower. He probably hadn't known any better.

The kids had taken over the activity, running around the flat grassy area in front of the lodge. Bigger kids yanked on the parachute, pulling smaller ones to the ground who refused to let go of their handle. There was screaming, yelling, and laughing. Never a good combination.

"Hey, guys!" Bower yelled while trying to grab the parachute from one of the especially aggressive older kids. "If you want to play, we all need to listen!"

I could barely hear his voice over the chaos. If I couldn't hear him, I bet the kids couldn't either. The little boy with glasses who'd been fishing with Bower was being pulled around by an older boy hellbent on ignoring any adult supervision. The older boy yanked the parachute hard, and the sweet little boy fell face-first to the ground, still holding on to the handle. His glasses fell off his face and bounced a few times before stopping at my feet.

I picked them up before he started crying and went over to where he lay on the ground, the heels of his hands and knees covered with streaks of dirt. "Hey, buddy, let me help you," I said as I lifted him into a sitting position. I didn't see any blood.

"Stupid Jared. He knocked me over," he sniffled.

"Yeah, I saw what happened. Kids can be mean sometimes." I cleaned off his glasses with my shirt and handed them back to him. He put them back on his face, carefully tucking the rounded temple tips behind his ears. He tilted his head sideways once his vision became clear.

"Hey, aren't you Bower's friend?" It was a loaded question, something I wasn't about to discuss with a seven-year-old.

"Yeah, buddy, I am."

Bower came running over with the bunched-up parachute tucked under his arm. "Gavin, are you okay?" He crouched down next to Gavin, looking him over, checking him for serious injury. When he determined Gavin was okay, he brushed the dirt from his knees.

My insides warmed as I watched.

"Yeah, Bower. Your friend found my glasses for me," Gavin said. Bower looked at me, startled. "She sure is pretty."

Kids and their diarrhea of the mouth. I didn't know why I was blushing after a compliment from a seven-year-old. Bower's cheeks were a little red as well. Though the blush on his face probably came from having run across the field to check on Gavin.

"Go play tag with the other kids while I figure out what to do next," Bower said, patting the boy on the back.

"Jared better not push me to the ground again."

"Yeah, I'll keep an eye on him."

Gavin ran off to join the rest of the kids, already playing a violent game of tag. The tags looked more like pushes, and the younger kids were constantly being railroaded by the older kids, who weren't paying attention to where they were running. A little girl sat in the middle of the field crying, snot dripping out of her nose while the chaos continued around her.

"Fuck," Bower said.

I crossed my arms and popped my hip as I stood next to him. "So, how's it going?" I asked.

"Just as expected," Bower said. "Horribly, with many injuries that will result in scars."

"Souvenirs from Agate Harbors." I had a few of those on my skin. Courtesy of climbing rocks and jumping off the splintered dock.

Another girl with red curly hair fell to the ground in a heap, her wails loud enough to be heard by the resort next door. Jared ran away from her, looking to check if Bower had seen what he did.

Okay, that was enough. My inner first-grade teacher broke through.

"Hey!" I yelled at the wild youths. My teacher voice broke through the pandemonium. Everyone knew a teacher voice when they heard one—loud, demanding, and not to be ignored.

I suddenly had dozens of eyes on me, waiting for my next move. This was where I shined. I had their attention. Now I just needed to prove I was crazy enough that they wouldn't try to cross me. Control was a fine line for a teacher, especially for older kids. You had to be fair yet unhinged enough to keep them on their toes. They should never be able to guess your next move.

I clapped a familiar rhythm. *Clap, clap, pause. Clap, clap, clap.* Everyone mimicked me robotically. Teacher mode was in full effect.

"I want you to get in a line from youngest to oldest. This is going to require you to talk to one another. Ask each other for your ages. Young ones to the front, oldest to the back." Like good little soldiers, the kids scrambled to line up. Bower stepped in to help the younger ones sort out their order.

It only took a minute, and they were in a straight line from youngest to oldest. The little curly redhead stood at the front of the line, her tears now dried salt stains down her cheeks. The oldest was Jared. He looked on the cusp of puberty.

Bower joined me back up at the front to the line. "How do you know how to do this?"

"I'm a first-grade teacher," I replied. "You've got to be loud, emit a sense of authority."

He nodded. "I can do that with adults, but with kids…"

"You just have to act like this is the most fun thing you've ever done in your life. They'll follow right along."

Bower grunted.

I elbowed his side. "You're having fun, Bower…"

He grunted again, but I swore I saw the corners of his lips twitch.

It took little time to split the line into two groups for red rover, my favorite childhood game. It was dangerous enough that it was fun. I purposely put the younger half of the kids into a separate game from the older ones to minimize the casualties. I didn't need Jared blazing his way through two five-year olds holding hands. Bower watched over the little kids' game, and I managed the older kids. I liked that I didn't need to tell him what to do, that he'd welcomed the help and jumped right in.

After a few games, the little ones had had enough and sat down with Bower in heaps along the side of the big kids' game. It was brutal out there. Some boys were getting very into the game, backing up and getting a running start before crossing no-man's-land and barreling through the opposing teams' arms.

"Bower, you and your friend should play," Gavin said. His face was red from running. He sat next to the girl with curly red hair. They must have bonded over their mutual dislike of Jared.

"Yeah, come on, Bower and Mia! You can even be on the same team," one of the older girls agreed. She let go of her partner's hand and shuffled to the side, making a gap for Bower and me.

Bower looked at me from where he sat on the grass, his arms hanging off his bent knees watching the game.

"Yeah, come on, Bower," I taunted. "Have some fun." I grabbed the girl's hand who had asked us to join and wiggled my fingers of my free hand.

"Go on!" Gavin pointed to my hand. "My dad said when a pretty girl asks you to do something, you just do it." He stood up and went behind Bower, pushing his shoulders, trying to get him to stand.

Bower sat there, stoic for a moment before the other kids egged him on, telling him to play. He stood up smoothly from the seated position and walked over, his eyes boring holes into me. Bower hated every minute of this. I, on the other hand, loved it. Why was watching him squirm so enjoyable for me?

He grabbed my left hand, holding it tightly, encompassing my palm completely, and the game began. Jared came running at us, nostrils flared, chin down. At the last moment, right before Jared crashed into us, Bower released my hand and wrapped his fingers around my wrist, turning our hands so that his knuckles took the brunt of the hit. Jared was effectively clotheslined at the bottom of his sternum, landing flat on his back, his eyes wide. It took a couple of seconds before he gasped for a breath, the wind knocked out of him. I'd feel bad if I hadn't seen what Jared had been up to today. All the littles on the side cheered, especially Gavin. He was jumping up and down, his arms above his head.

I saw Bower's face from the corner of my eye. He was looking at me, and I didn't know what to do. We were still holding hands among a sea of children cheering for us.

The kids began to chat among themselves, and I looked at Bower. His eyes weren't on my face anymore. He looked down at our hands as he let go of my wrist, flipping his hand underneath mine so our palms touched. His thumb reached around and brushed against my ring finger—the one that had supported the monstrosity of a diamond for the last months. It wasn't there anymore. I'd taken it off, along with the diamond earring studs Archer had given me and left them back at my parents' house in the ballerina jewelry box I'd gotten for Christmas as a kid.

Bower looked back up at me, his brows furrowed.

I looked away. It was suddenly awkward between us. I didn't want to talk about ending my relationship with Archer with him. It didn't seem relevant anymore now that I was here. This was a different world. One that didn't have Archer in it. Just Bower. It was scary that it'd always been just Bower.

I crossed my arms, hiding my hands under my elbows. I'd been so confident coming here, taunting Bower when he'd been under the impression that I was taken. The engagement had been a fallback, something that I'd known was there if Bower wasn't everything I'd remembered. But now that it was effectively gone, I felt naked. Him knowing that I didn't have a fiancé anymore made me feel vulnerable. I had no alternative. It was either Bower or no one. I'd never felt so exposed.

"The kids sure seem to love you." I immediately grimaced at my words. Now *I* had diarrhea of the mouth.

Bower shook his head. "They barely listen to me."

"They did…" I laughed. "Eventually."

"I didn't know you're a teacher." He looked at me with a certain softness in his eyes.

"First grade. It's some reading and math—nothing too hard." I cleared my throat. I was babbling again. "Nothing like the Marines."

He crossed his arms in front of his chest. "Don't dismiss being a teacher. It's one of the most important jobs—"

"And being a marine isn't?" I playfully smacked him on the arm with the back of my hand.

Bower took the slightest shuffle back.

I immediately tensed. I'd done something wrong.

He cleared his throat. "You help kids—you get to help them grow. My time in the Marines wasn't about helping people."

"I'm sure you helped—"

"No, Mia," Bower interrupted. "I promise I damaged a lot of things during my time in the Marines."

Shit, I'd said the wrong thing again.

His eyes darted around my face before I looked at the ground.

I bit my lip. "Sorry—I'm making this weird. I can go." I didn't know what else I could say. I was doing everything wrong.

I turned away from Bower and started walking back toward my cabin. I'd been so forthright but now felt so reserved. I'd just unsuccessfully tried to flirt with him, and now everything was so uncomfortable. Maybe he didn't feel the way he'd felt two weeks ago. Maybe since I hadn't given him an answer that night outside the bar, he'd cut any hope of us being together loose. I couldn't blame him for that—I'd been illusive and indecisive.

"Mia!" I heard Bower's voice.

I stopped walking but didn't turn around.

"We weren't done talking," he called out.

My breath stopped short in my throat.

"You know you just signed yourself up to help me with Kids Camp for the rest of the week."

I turned my head just enough that I could see him out of the corner of my eye, standing there with his hands in his pockets.

"And don't even think about bailing on me," Bower added. "I know where you live."

A smile pulled at my lips. Maybe all was not lost.

Chapter Twenty-One

Bower

"Was that Mia out there helping you the other day?" Grandpa asked.

Yesterday Kids Camp had ended not a moment too soon. How did parents do it? Four hours with the hooligans, and I was exhausted. I couldn't imagine what twenty-four hours was like.

"Yeah, she was helping." She'd been good. Really good. The kids had actually listened to her. Mia had used that teacher voice, something I hadn't heard from her before. It kind of turned me on. So authoritative and demanding. Even Jared had listened to her.

"She should work here at the resort. She'd be good for the kids," Grandpa said.

I couldn't tell if Grandpa was teasing. There was a seriousness in his tone that caught me off guard.

Just in case, I told him, "She's a teacher back home."

"Oh?" asked Grandpa. "Did you catch up with her?" He gave me a look that said he saw right through me.

I shook my head. I'd hardly call any of our recent conversations catching up. They'd been lust charged and flirty—at least from what I'd felt on my end. But there was no way she normally ate a Popsicle like that. It could've been considered lewd conduct. She had to be feeling just as sexually charged as I was.

Grandpa dropped the conversation about Mia. Luckily. I wasn't in the mood to talk about Mia and my emotions. Or lack thereof. Besides aroused, I didn't know what I was feeling.

She wasn't wearing a ring on her finger anymore. We still hadn't talked about that. What did that mean? Was she not engaged anymore? Did she just take it off for the vacation? Surely that thing got snagged on everything. I couldn't imagine it was comfortable for her to wear. Something that size and cut had to have bothered her skin every day. I knew that about her. How did her fiancé not know? Or did he not care?

No more thinking about it, I reminded myself. "I'm headed out to pull the weeds from the south end of the shore." I pulled down the key ring for Agate Harbor's only pickup truck. The wheel wells were rusted, and the paint was peeling off the hood, exposing the silver shell. It started up on the first time only half the time, but it always purred like a kitten once it got going.

"You don't need to do that," Grandpa said. "We pulled weeds in the spring—that area should be good until fall."

I squeezed my fingertips into my palm, the metal teeth of the keys I held in my right hand biting my skin. I was familiar with what it took to maintain a resort like Agate Harbors—I'd gone through the file cabinet of invoices and seasonal checklists as soon as I'd returned.

The weeding had already been done in the spring, but I needed something physical to do—something with my hands. Sleep had been evasive since Mia had arrived. I found myself unable to be still for any amount of time before she crept into my thoughts. It wasn't just how beautiful she'd gotten in the nine years I'd been gone; it was just *Mia*—the way she took up space in a room, the way she looked at me—like I was a prize. It was addicting to be around her.

Being stationary meant thoughts of Mia—and that I couldn't have. The only time I saw her was when I ran into her around the resort, and the way my brain was addicted to her, wanting more and more of her time, I realized I needed to do something to distract myself.

I was going to distract myself from Mia with weeds.

Grandpa took one look at my clenched fists and nodded. "Go take care of those weeds."

The truck was right outside the lodge, and I hopped in, holding my breath, hoping that it'd start on the first time. Ever since I'd been back home, loud noises made my heart race and my mind turn into a sack of shit.

The flashbacks started once I'd gotten home and had been happening with increasing frequency. I liked to call them immersive experiences. One minute I was in reality, and the next I was immersed in parts of my past.

I hadn't realized that my service had affected me so deeply until the first Friday night back at Agate Harbors. We always did a little firework show for the guests, and the loud explosions had sent me down a deep spiral. They'd brought me back, the firework noises reminding me of the gunshots I'd heard day and night while serving in and around combat zones. Dean had found me huddled up inside one of the walk-in freezers at the bar and made me promise I'd go back to my cabin to escape the noise the next Friday.

I did just as he'd asked—and I was fine, perfectly fine, a contributing member of society. I just couldn't do fireworks, and I prayed every time I started the old truck that it wouldn't backfire and pop. I didn't need another breakdown. The first one had been embarrassing enough.

The engine roared as soon as I turned the key, and I let out a sigh of relief before driving it over to the building near the steps of the marina. We kept all our maintenance equipment in there, hidden away from the guests and locked up. We didn't need any guests—or now my grandma—getting ahold of any of the mowers or power tools inside.

What I needed was on the other side of the building, where all the tools hung on hooks and the mowers were parked in a neat row. I pulled a weed razor and a weed rake from their hooks on the wall. From one of the shelves, I grabbed a blue tarp that I'd use to put the wet weeds on to dry. Pulling weeds from the depths of the lake was a time-consuming process that today I was going to fully enjoy.

With a single toss, all three of the supplies I'd gathered landed in the bed of the truck. I brushed my hands off on my jeans as I walked over to the driver's side. I was ready for some hard, manual, Mia-forgetting labor.

"Whatcha doing?"

Long legs with black bike shorts and a small white tank top leaned against the driver's side of the truck. Mia. Her hair was in a ponytail, as it always was, and her freckles had gotten more pronounced since I'd seen her a day ago. Agate Harbors brought out the best in her.

So much for forgetting about her. I couldn't unsee who was leaning against the Agate Harbors truck.

I coughed into my elbow, trying to clear the surprise of seeing her from my throat. "I was going to go out and weed today."

"Oh." Mia twisted her finger around the end of her ponytail. "I'm sorry to bother you. I guess I'll leave you to it..." She pivoted away from the truck, her back to me as she walked away.

"Wait—"

She turned around, her ponytail swinging with her, settling on one of her shoulders.

I blinked a few times. My mind raced and then went blank. I

wanted her to stay—I needed her to help me with something, anything. "Hey!"

Mia took a step back. "I'm right here. No need to yell."

Shit. I was flustered and apparently incapable of controlling myself. I looked back at the building, trying to remember what was inside. Nothing. I was drawing a complete blank.

"Can you lend me a hand?" I asked eventually.

"Depends on what my hand's going to be used for…"

I laughed. Probably too loud, motioning her to come over to the building I'd just walked out of. I punched in the keypad again, the bolt sliding open. The building illuminated with the motion-activated lights. I glanced around looking for something, anything that she could help me with.

A generator. It was a standard one, weighing in at about a hundred pounds, just heavy enough that she might not question whether I could handle it myself. I didn't need one for weeding, but she didn't need to know that. I just needed her to be around me for a little while longer.

"Can you help me carry this out to my truck?" I asked.

Mia looked down at the square generator. "Do you want me in the front or the back?"

I blinked, my brain short-circuiting.

"Bower?" Mia asked. "Do you want to carry the front or back?"

I shook my head. *Snap out of it.* "The back—I'll take the back."

She nodded, bending with her knees, grabbing hold of a set of handles.

I hurried around, grabbing the other set. With a nod of my head, we both lifted at the same time and began carrying the generator toward the truck. I tried to keep my hands low so that our height difference wouldn't cause her to carry more of the weight. This was all entirely unnecessary. We were only carrying this generator because I wanted Mia to be around me at all times.

We lifted the generator onto the tailgate, and I pushed it back into the truck bed, closing the tailgate now that I had all the "necessary" supplies.

Mia backed up, her face and neck flushed the most perfect shade of pink. There was no way I was letting her leave.

"Say," I began, "I'm gonna need help unloading the generator once I'm down at the shoreline. I can call Dean to meet me down there…" A lie, a complete and total lie. I could lift the generator myself—and fuck, I didn't need the generator to begin with.

"Oh!" Mia jumped. "I can help!"

"Really?" I took off my hat and watched her bite her lip between her teeth as I ran my fingers through my hair. "We might be down on the shore all day…"

"I'm on vacation, Bower," she said. "I've got nothing but time."

I brushed past her on my way to the passenger side of the two-door truck, yanking at the door's handle a few times before it opened. "Hop in."

I gestured to the ripped fabric seat that probably smelled like the lake. This wasn't what she was used to—not with a fiancé who could afford a rock the size I'd seen on her finger two weeks ago—but this was what I had to offer. A seat in a run-down truck that could bring you anywhere within Agate Harbors' property lines.

I held my breath until she sat down, and I shut the door. My fingers flexed as I rounded the front of the truck to the driver's side.

As I climbed into the truck, I was enveloped by her smell that'd already permeated the cab. *Fuck.* I needed her to stay near me as long as possible.

Once again, I paused before I turned the key I'd inserted into the ignition, this time holding my breath too, knowing Mia was right beside me for this.

The key turned smoothly, and the engine roared to life.

My body relaxed, and I drove the truck back to the lodge—to my grandparents' house, where I knew there'd be food.

"I forgot something…" I said before I threw the truck into park, left it running, and ran inside. The less I said the better. Around Mia I had a problem of saying too much of the wrong thing.

Chloe was sitting at the table with Grandma, both enjoying a cup of coffee. They stared at me with matching surprised faces as I grabbed a cooler from the pantry and started throwing in dry food and then moved to the refrigerator, adding cold food too.

"Is everything okay?" Chloe asked.

"It's great!" I yelled before I slammed the cooler on the table, shaking both their cups of coffee. It took me three tries to zip it closed and four steps to make it back out the door.

Mia was still inside the truck, peering through the windshield, watching me. I stopped for a moment, willing my heartrate to slow and my shoulders to drop. This was my chance to impress her, show her what she was missing with that fiancé of hers.

I might not have been able to give her a ring like his, but I could provide her with a whole lot more than a sparkly diamond. I had the shores of Agate Harbors—memories that'd outlast a silly ring. Like Ruby had said, I just had to remind her.

Chapter Twenty-Two

Mia

After I helped Bower unload the bed of his truck, I watched him throw the torture device, which he called a weed razor, out into the lake. He stood on a rock near the water, methodically throwing the razor and yanking it back in sharp, short pulls to slice the tops of the weeds.

I stood back, away from any splashes, just watching. His muscles strained every time he yanked back the razor, which looked like a regular rake, but it had cut-up pool noodles zip-tied to its head, so it floated on the surface of the water, and tiny razor blades between its prongs. Once he'd snipped enough weeds from the lake, he used a different rake to scoop them from the surface of the water and dump them onto the tarp he'd brought. His hands were gloved, and he looped the excess rope each pull made around his upper arm. Lake water dripped off the strands of the rope, wetting Bower's shirt.

He looked hot weeding the lake, all his muscles rippling beneath his shirt. Maybe if he got heated enough, he'd take it off.

Suddenly a loud popping sound echoed across the lake. I glanced out to see a Jet Ski had stalled out, but to my surprise the weed razor clattered onto the rocks, right next to the rake Bower had set down beside him. My breath caught as I watched him fall to his knees, his hands gripping the rocks he'd been standing on.

"Bower!" I yelled. I tried my best to get over to where he was bent over while staying as far away from the water as I could. "Are you okay?"

Bower's eyes were closed, and I could see his ribs moving up and down as he breathed. "Yeah—I'm fine," his voice labored. He blinked several times before his eyes fully opened, immediately locking into mine. "Sometimes loud noises trigger me, but that wasn't bad. It was just a Jet Ski. I'm fine."

I nodded. Bower had spent years serving overseas. I understood that he had triggers; after what he'd gone through, anyone would.

He stood up slowly, grabbing hold of the rake lying on the rocks next to him. His hand shook as he lifted it, bringing the handle close to his chest.

I stayed on the rocks, balancing as I watched him recover. I didn't know what to do to help him. I didn't want to seem too overbearing, smother him when he'd already told me he was fine. But as I watched him stand there, his eyes closed and his chest visibly moving up and down as he breathed deeply, I couldn't help but feel I needed to do something.

"Come here," he directed, his hand gesturing toward the large rock next to him.

I jolted at his curt tone. He'd never talked to me like that. A shiver racked my body, starting at my neck and ending at the tip of my tailbone. He was still recouping; the Jet Ski had really startled him. I shook off the feeling the best I could.

I scurried over to where he'd directed, his eyes following my every move. I wanted to do anything I could to help.

"I'll weed, and you can rake." He held the rake handle out to me, and I grabbed hold of it, my hand briefly brushing against his. As soon as I did, I froze, pulling back as fast as I could.

Immediately, I regretted everything. There was sand on the

handle, and the grains dug into my skin. If I'd looked at the rake instead of at him, if I hadn't been so keen on helping him, if he hadn't looked at me like *that* as I'd climbed over the rocks toward him…maybe I wouldn't be standing here with the sandy rake in my hand and my face scrunched up like…

I forced the muscles in my face to relax.

"Here." Bower pulled off the gloves he was wearing and offered them to me. He was still talking in that tone…the one that made my entire body flustered.

I looked down at my hands, at the grains of sand sitting on top of my skin. Bower grabbed the hem of his shirt, pulling it away from his body, offering it to me.

I kept my eyes down as I rubbed my hands on his shirt, the grains falling to the ground. As soon as my hands were free of the sand, Bower offered the gloves again. They were heavy, wet with either lake water or sweat. I sucked my lower lip between my teeth.

Bower reached for the gloves. "Shit, I'm sorry. I forgot—"

"No, no," I lied, "they're fine." My fingers trembled as I pulled the warm, wet fabric over my hands. Bower had just been through his own triggering experience on the rocks—he didn't need to worry about me. I could handle the gloves.

If Bower could take a deep breath and manage his anxiety, so could I. I breathed in through my nose. It was fine. They were just wet. I blew the air out of my mouth. I could handle it.

It wasn't so bad once I'd lifted a few piles of cut weeds and dumped them onto the tarp Bower had laid out on top of some flat rocks. My fingers went numb, and I could no longer feel the sweat or the warmth inside them.

Bower cleared his throat. "I like the boots," he said as he nodded toward the black rain boots I was wearing.

"Thanks," I said. "You gave me the inspiration all those years ago."

He tilted his head to the side, lifting his chin as if he was interested—like he wanted more.

"I've helped a few kids over the years," I offered.

Bower nodded, like he was listening.

"There were a few kids who had similar sensory issues to me at my school. I mentioned to their parents that they might enjoy a pair of rain boots—an accommodation for the tight sneakers or sandals they usually wore."

A proud smile, like mine, grew on Bower's lips. He'd offered me that accommodation all those summers ago. His kindness had changed my outlook on the challenges I faced. There were accommodations for everyone—we just needed to be patient enough to find them. Those rain boots had helped me enough to where I was now able to offer the same kindness and patience to my students.

The sun beat down on me as I raked and scooped the weeds after Bower cut them from the lake. This section of the water was almost completely clear of lake weeds by the time Bower called it.

"I think we've done enough," he said as he pulled the weed razor from the lake.

I looked at the pile of weeds I'd piled onto the tarp. There weren't as many as I thought there'd be based on how many times Bower had thrown his weed razor into the lake, but I was sweaty and hot, and that felt good. It felt like I'd done something to take care of the lake I loved.

"We can leave the weeds here," Bower said. "I'll pick them up once the sun dries them out and they don't weigh as much." His eyebrows raised in the slightest way. "They'll be great kindling for bonfires."

He was still that boy I knew—obsessed with fire.

And I was the girl feeling the fire between us.

"Wait here." Bower motioned for me to stay.

I stood there, my knees locked, watching him leap from rock to rock back toward his truck.

It only took a minute for him to return, bounding down toward me, with a cooler in one hand and a gray wool blanket in the other. As soon as he was close, he skidded to stop, small rocks tumbling down from the larger rock he'd stopped on. "Do you think you can make your way up here?"

I nodded. It was only a few large rocks away, and he had food. I picked and chose the rocks I stepped on to make my way up to him.

He had already laid out the blanket and was in the middle of unpacking, laying out meats and cheeses, crackers, and a few sides like pickles and olives.

I sat down on one of the rocks near the food, pulling off the gloves and laying them on the rock next to me. As I turned, my elbow bumped into a package of wipes Bower held out. "For your hands," he said.

I couldn't suppress my smile as I took the wipe and cleaned off every bit of sweat between my fingers.

Bower held out his hand, and I sheepishly kept the dirty wipes in my palm.

"Give them here, Mia," he directed. "You have to eat."

I placed the used wipes in his hand and glanced down at the food before selecting a cracker and adding a slice of cheese on top.

He tucked away the dirty wipe into one of the side pockets of the cooler, turning back toward the food between us. "So...come here often?" he asked.

I looked over, smirking. "Only every summer."

Bower grinned back, looking back out onto the lake. He sat with his feet on the ground and his bent knees relaxed in front of his chest. His forearms rested casually on top of his knees. "Silence is comfortable with you," he said.

I watched him stare out onto the lake; the worry lines on his forehead had flattened and his jaw had unclenched. This was the first time I'd seen him relaxed since…since we were kids.

"It's always been like this," I said. "It's always been comfortable." Besides these last two weeks, I couldn't remember anything different. It'd always been easy with Bower. There'd been no pressure, just a calm understanding between us.

Time passed as we ate, watching the few boats and Jet Skis that passed by.

It wasn't me who reached out, but somehow the fingers that we stretched out behind us, like a kickstand for the top halves of our bodies, touched. I kept my fingers there just for a second, long enough that Bower felt them and didn't move away. He kept his pressed against mine just hard enough that it couldn't be a mistake.

I looked out on the lake. The clear water seemed to go on forever. It was so different than the lakes in the Cities. The same was true with Bower—he was so different from the men I'd met there.

Here we were, touching fingers, eating together, looking out onto the lake. And it hit me.

This was a date.

A fucking date.

We'd never used the generator I'd help load into the truck, I'd raked a small number of weeds to consider this a "day's" worth of work, Bower had brought lunch…

I yanked my hand away from his and pushed myself off the wool blanket, finding my feet beneath me. "Bower Lee Hanson. Did you just trick me into a date?" I glared down at where he sat looking up at me, the corners of his lips pulling up.

"You know I don't like my middle name." With a single hand, he pushed himself up to standing.

I brushed the stray hairs that'd escaped my ponytail off my sticky forehead. "Your idea of a date is putting me to work?"

He smiled. "But it's so fun making you sweat."

"*Bower!*" I used the heels of my hands to shove his shoulders.

Unfortunately his shoulders were unnaturally strong and unaffected by my shove. The imbalance of his strong shoulders and my weak wrists sent me completely off-balance, my feet stumbling over the uneven rocks beneath them.

I only stopped once two hands gripped hold of my waist, pulling my entire body close to his.

So close to his.

"Is this what you do to your dates?" Bower asked. "Push them and then fall over so they'll put their hands on you?"

I moved toward him. It was all too tempting—his heat and the way his voice was suddenly several octaves lower.

"I had to get your attention somehow," I whispered. We'd been together in tandem for so long—hours without anything physical happening between us.

"I was waiting," he whispered back.

A shiver ran down my spine. "For what?"

In the distance, a boat blasted its horn.

Bower flinched, his arms wrapping even tighter around me.

I looked up at him, and at the same moment he looked down at me. My thighs were pressed against his, my chest pushing against his stomach with every one of my rapid breaths.

"I'm sorry. I didn't mean to grab you like that." Bower quickly removed his hands from my waist and bent over to gather what was left of the picnic we'd just shared. "We should get back for the crayfishing contest," he mumbled.

That wasn't what I wanted. I hadn't wanted him to let go.

I looked at the rocks surrounding us—plenty of tripping hazards. Maybe I should fall again, just so Bower would catch me.

Chapter Twenty-Three

Mia

The sun was high in the sky, and I was sweating. Bower had been so generous as to bait my hook for me with a slimy leech for the crayfish since I still couldn't bear to touch them. There was stiff competition this year. Jared and two other boys were dominating the field, their five-gallon buckets already half full of crawling crayfish. I used my crayfish-catching technique (patent pending) to catch as many as I could, but they just weren't latching onto my fishing line. I also kept getting distracted by the errant parent coming up to me, wanting to tell me how much fun their child had had yesterday and asking if I would be here next year.

Bower wasn't helping my concentration either. He stood there leaned against the marina hut, his arms crossed, watching. I liked to think he was watching everyone as the referee, so to say, but every time I looked at him, his eyes were on me. I felt like I was underneath a microscope, my every move being noted.

"Looks like you lost your touch!" Ruby stood there with a five-gallon bucket a third of the way full of crayfish. I was behind—that was for sure.

Dean stood on the dock, catching crayfish a few feet away from my sister. I couldn't help but smile when he rippled the water, making the crayfish scuttle away from where Ruby leaned over the dock with her hand in the water. She said a few choice words to him before moving away.

"Five more minutes!" Bower's voice brought a frenzy to the marina.

Everyone a part of the contest moved quicker, more feverishly, trying to catch as many crayfish as possible before time was up. I walked along the dock, peering into the water, willing there to be a crayfish. My bucket was precariously low. I refused to be embarrassed as a previous crayfish champion.

There! A huge crayfish scurried out from under a rock and across the sandy bottom of the lake. It was a little farther out, but if I threw my line just right, the bait would land right in front of his pincers. I stood with my toes hanging off the side of the dock, the line in my hand. With a flick of my wrist, I threw the line out into the water. The baited hook sank down right in front of the crayfish. *Perfect.*

The crayfish skittered out to investigate this gift from the heavens. A nice juicy leech, just what a crayfish liked. "Go ahead, big guy," I cooed. "Latch onto my line." I leaned over past the dock, watching, willing it to take the bait, and then—

Shit! Oh, shit!

The cold water enveloped me as soon as my body hit the lake. Fishing line forgotten, I pushed my way to the surface, finding my footing against the silty bottom of the lake. Sand and other lake debris squished between my toes. It felt like quicksand the way my feet sank into the lake floor.

The grainy texture of the sand against my skin mixed with the slimy algae that lived along the bottom sent waves of pain straight into my teeth. I clenched my jaw, willing myself to be calm. It was okay. I was okay. I could rinse off my feet once I got out of the water, I tried to tell myself.

Water from my hair dripped down my forehead and along my closed eyelids. Maybe this would all be a dream. I'd wake up warm in my twin bed, with Ruby snoring in the bed next to me.

Nope. I opened my eyes to find the entire crayfishing contest staring at me, Bower at the front of the crowd. I didn't know what was worse: the audience or the sand pulling my feet into its murky depths.

"Mia, here!" Bower held out his hand to me. A lifeline out of this hell.

Like at the red rover game yesterday, his grasp was tight. He pulled me close to the dock before extending his other hand. I gladly gave him my free hand right before he pulled me up and out of the water like I weighed nothing. My bare feet hit the dock, my sandals now sacrificed to the lake bottom. It had been a stupid idea to try wearing them anyway.

"Are you okay?" Bower asked, still holding both of my hands in his.

"Yeah, I'm fine," I lied. There was sand still stuck to my feet. I could feel the grains rubbing against my skin. It felt to me like I was standing on jagged, uncooked rice. My tactile senses magnified. This was why I never went into the lake.

Water dripped off me, the slight breeze chilling my wet skin. Why had I worn a white tank top today? The black bike shorts I was wearing were fine, but everyone could see my bra through the wet tank top. I let go of Bower's hands to cross my arms across my chest, my poor attempt to cover what everyone had already seen.

"Mia, are you okay?" Ruby asked, coming to stand next to Bower. She looked down at my sand-covered feet. She knew what this was like for me—someone else could laugh it off, brush themselves off and carry on. That wasn't an option for me.

"I'll make sure she's fine," Bower said. He kept his eyes on me, his gaze traveling from my feet up to my waist—quickly moving up to my face.

Ruby smiled, that older sister *I told you so* smile that she still loved to give me.

My body shook as a particularly strong breeze hit me. Goose bumps popped up all over my skin. Suddenly I was too cold and miserable to worry about what my sister might've thought she was seeing.

Bower's grip on my forearm tightened just as another set of shivers made my body convulse. "Fuck, Mia, you need to warm up." He pulled my torso against his. Warmth was practically radiating off his body. I found myself snuggling into his side, his grip tightening on my waist, his fingers digging into my obliques.

"Come here." It was his only warning before he grabbed tighter onto my waist and lifted me up so his other arm supported the back of my knees. I was suddenly cradled against him as he began walking. "You don't have any shoes," he said.

I wiggled my bare toes, feeling the sand particles between them. Immediate tooth pain. I clamped my mouth shut, squeezing my teeth together, hoping to alleviate the discomfort. This wasn't some romantic moment between us. I didn't have shoes, and the ground wasn't pleasant to walk on without them. This was practical, Bower carrying me. *Don't get any silly ideas, Mia.*

"Where are we going?" I asked. My family's cabin was in the opposite direction.

"My cabin," Bower grunted. He walked with a purpose, one foot in front of another. Like he was on a mission.

Bower had his own cabin? I'd just assumed he still lived with his grandparents. Another silly idea. He was a grown man. I could feel it all along the left side of my body. He was all man. Hard muscle rubbed against my ribs, moving up and down with every step he took. I hadn't been this close to him since…ever. Bower even smelled like a man. Maybe that was just DEET. But there was also a scent about him that was unique, the scent I associated with Agate Harbors and how I felt up here. Safe, assured, protected. Like a cedar closet that protected sweaters from moths. Cedarwood—he smelled like cedarwood. I resisted burying my nose into his neck and taking a deep inhale, holding it in my lungs for as long as I was able.

Bower set me down on my feet in front of the wooden door of a smaller studio cabin. It was one of the older cabins and had thick stacked logs on the outside, with green moss growing between them.

He turned the handle on the door, opening it and waving me inside. No one locked their doors up here. I stepped inside tentatively, not knowing what I would find. Four windows, one on each side of the house, illuminated the space. It was clean. Tidy. A king-sized bed was pushed to one corner of the room, and a round table with a single chair sat in the L-shaped kitchen. A door on the other backside of the cabin probably led to a bathroom.

I stood on the rug in the entryway, not wanting to track any of the lake water dripping off my body or the sand stuck between my toes onto the clean floor. Bower dug through an armoire next to his bed, coming out with a plain black T-shirt and dark green gym shorts. I'd have to roll the waistband several times to keep them on my hips, but I appreciated the gesture.

"Come in," Bower said, waving me into the cabin.

I stood there awkwardly, moving my weight between my feet. "I shouldn't. My feet..." I gestured down to the sand already collecting.

"You're going to make me put my hands on you again, aren't you, Mia?" Bower asked this as less of a question and more of a challenge.

"I'm just trying to be nice and not spread sand all over your cabin."

"All right, you asked for it." He stalked over to where I was standing on the rug and lifted me into the same cradled position he'd carried me here in, then brought me over to the bathroom and set me down on the rug next to the shower that barely fit me. There was no way I could bend over inside without my ass hitting one of the side walls.

Wait, why would I be bending over? Snap out of it, Mia.

Bower turned on the shower, keeping his hand under the spray until the temperature was to his liking. His eyes stayed on me as he did. Despite being fully clothed, I felt naked when he looked at me. I kept my arms crossed against my chest, protecting him from a personal wet T-shirt contest. It wasn't long before steam filled the bathroom, signaling the shower was ready. He opened a small linen closet and pulled out a fluffy bath towel, which he sat on top of the closed toilet next to the shower. He tucked the clothes he'd pulled out from the armoire underneath the towel.

"Just leave your wet clothes on the floor," he said gently. "I'll pick them up when you're done."

With that, Bower flipped on the overhead fan before exiting the bathroom and closing the door, giving me privacy. I stood there for a minute. My mind was just as cloudy as the room was becoming. Being cradle carried twice by Bower had done something to me.

I shook my head, snapping myself out of the fog I was in. Slowly, I stripped out of my wet clothes, leaving them in a neat pile on the ground, then ducked under the flow of warm water.

It felt glorious. All the sand washing off my feet and down the drain. My skin warming from the cool lake water. I took stock of Bower's shampoo selection: Basic drugstore fare. A three-in-one shower product marketed toward men.

I squeezed a bit of green shampoo onto my palm and lathered it into my hair, the smell of cedar mixing with the fog of the shower. This was what he smelled like. There was something exciting about covering myself in his scent. I scrubbed my legs multiple times—they were itchy from the lake water. He didn't have a rag or loofah in here, so I used my hands. Not that I'd use his loofah. Too many scary bacteria stories from the internet for that. Plus, that felt like a total violation of his privacy. Who knew where he would've rubbed it. *Ugh, stop thinking those thoughts!*

The water was now lukewarm and beginning to cool. I turned the faucet handle to the left, stopping the flow of water. The curtain rings screeched against the rod as I pulled the curtain aside, reaching for the towel Bower had left me. I wrapped it around me, drying myself quickly. The T-shirt Bower had left me was far too big. It hung down almost to my knees. The shorts, as I had thought, were no different—way too big. I rolled the waistband four times before I felt they wouldn't fall off my hips. I towel-dried my hair the best I could before I opened the door of the bathroom, steam billowing out into the cabin.

"Better?" Bower asked. He was sitting on the single chair at the round table in his kitchen, waiting, like he had nothing better to do than to wait for me to be done showering.

"Much better," I said. There wasn't the sand between my toes anymore. My ankles didn't have dried sand flaking off them with every step I took. I was back at my baseline.

My legs were itchy, though. I bent down to scratch my shin, barely holding back a moan. That felt so much better.

"Ah, shit," Bower said. "I thought if I got you to a shower in time, you wouldn't get them."

"Get what?" The itching was spreading. Now my other leg itched, right behind the knee. I used both hands to scratch both of my legs. Was I losing my mind? I couldn't stop.

"Chiggers," Bower said casually. Like it wasn't a big deal.

Chiggers? The little microparasites that burrowed into your skin and caused an allergic reaction that made little red bumps that made you itch like crazy? Those chiggers?

I whimpered, letting those little sounds come from my mouth

travel to Bower's ears. I couldn't help it. There was no acting brave and faking it in this situation. There were parasites under my skin. I could feel them. All of them digging in, burrowing, making me their home. I scratched harder, my skin breaking beneath my fingernails. My fingers glided over my skin, now slick.

"Mia, stop." Bower grabbed onto my wrists as he had done before, this time his grasp was tighter. I looked up at his face, his eyes locked onto mine. "You're hurting yourself."

Glancing down at my legs, I saw they were covered in red bumps, blood streaked up and down my calves. *Shit.*

Bower lifted my hands from my legs and pressed them together. "Hold them just like this," he commanded.

He entered the steamy bathroom and emerged with a wet rag and white tube of ointment. Grabbing onto my elbow, he guided me to the chair he had been sitting on when I came from the shower. I sat compliantly, my hands still clutched together like I was praying. Maybe I should be praying for the parasites to leave my body and rid me of the incessant itching.

Bower wiped the blood off my legs before he flipped open the top of the tube and squeezed a pea-sized amount of ointment onto his fingers. With sure hands, he worked the medicine into the red welts on my legs, blending the white cream into my skin with his fingers moving in slow circles. One by one, he massaged each welt, taking time to make sure the ointment was absorbed before moving onto the next one.

Slowly, the itching subsided. I didn't know if it was because of the ointment he was rubbing into my skin or the fact *he* was rubbing my skin, making nerves in different parts of my body fire, distracting me from the itching.

He moved me to stand with my back to him, his fingers rubbing the ointment into a spot on the back of my thigh. When his fingers left my skin, I felt a rush of air against the back of my legs as he stood up behind me, his breath hitting the skin behind my ear, causing my hair to brush my cheeks.

Involuntary shivers went down my spine. My hair was down. I hadn't tied it up again since I'd showered. I brought my hands up to my hair, pulling it back into a ponytail. A large, calloused hand covered mine, wrapping his fingers around the thickness of my ponytail. Another hand took hold of the hair binder I kept on my wrist and pulled it over my hand. I lowered my hands to my sides, breathing deep breaths.

With him standing behind me, I couldn't see his face. I felt blindfolded, waiting for him to make the next move. His fingers dragged across the crown of my head, smoothing the hair, sending ripples of pleasure down my body.

I tried to keep still and not tilt my head back, letting him know how much I was enjoying it. I shouldn't have been enjoying it as much as I was. There were chigger bites all over my legs, and I had just fallen into the lake. He was being nice by doing my hair. That was all.

When the top of my head was smoothed, Bower took the hair binder and expertly wrapped it round my ponytail twice before giving it a gentle tug to secure it. He spun me around, examining his handiwork, tucking a tendril that he had missed on the side of my head behind my ear. I couldn't help but lean into his hand and close my eyes as he did. Even the smallest touches from him were potent. Bower kept his fingers moving, tracing my jaw and stopping underneath my chin, his index finger hooked beneath it.

I fluttered my eyes open, taking a moment to look at his face. I couldn't remember a time that I was as close to him as I was now. His breath hit my face. He breathed rapidly, as if it was in time with the fast beat of my heart. There were crease marks on the corners of his eyes that deepened every time he smiled. There were even a few stray freckles I had never noticed before. He looked as he always had to me, all those years ago. He was Bower, just older, with a bit more maturity in his features. What did he see on my face? Stress lines on my forehead from trying to be the perfect daughter? The mass of freckles that Archer found juvenile?

I tilted my head toward the ground, preferring my feet to his judgment. Bower was quick to correct me, using his finger to guide my face back to meet his.

There was something understood between us. The silence had never been awkward. We thrived in quiet, the time we spent to be introspective while still being around each other. We knew each other so well. Like right now I could tell Bower wanted to do something that would change the course of our entire relationship. I could tell this by the way he was breathing, how his eyes darted to my lips before reconnecting with my eyes. The worried look on his face as he pondered the same thing I was: Should we do this?

I saw the thought flash through his eyes before he acted, reaching behind my head, cradling the back of my skull with his palm. His other hand wrapped around my lower back and pulled my body into his, the soft parts of my body hitting the wall of muscle that was his. He stared into my eyes, asking for permission. Like he didn't already have it.

"Oh, yes, this is a family resort," a voice was saying, suddenly coming closer from outside. "Isn't it beautiful?"

Bower and I held our breaths, still staring at each other. His movements paused, his hands still cradling my head and gripping my lower back.

"It's so beautiful here. I get why Mia loves coming here," a male voice said.

I froze. My vision waning, the sounds meeting my ears suddenly inaudible. What? No. He couldn't be here.

"We love having her here." That was Betty's voice. What was she doing with Archer? What was Archer doing here?

Three knocks sounded on Bower's front door. They echoed throughout the cabin and my head. They sounded like the last ticks of the clock before Cinderella's carriage turned back into a pumpkin. Like the perfect moment I was just experiencing was about to expire.

"Bower, you there?" Betty's voice infiltrated the cabin. "We're looking for Mia!"

I pulled away from Bower quickly. He looked at me for a moment with those blue eyes before turning around and opening the door.

Betty stood in the doorway, Archer peeking his head around her round frame behind her, looking into the cabin. His eyes locked onto me, and a look of surprise came over his face right before he took a couple of steps backward, almost tripping over his feet.

"Oh, Mia! I just met this man." Betty smiled at me before she turned around and looked at Archer. "Remind me, what's your name?"

"Archer," he said. The surprised look on his face washed away quickly, anger replacing it for just a moment before he smoothed out his features. "What are you doing here, Mia?" he asked. He seemed to have regained his footing as he walked casually back toward the cabin.

"I'm on vacation with my family," I said from around where Bower stood in the cabin's doorway, blocking most of the inside from Archer's view.

"You're not with your family, Mia. You're in a cabin with a hick," Archer said. He puffed up his chest, trying to make himself look bigger.

Bower stood there stoic, not letting Archer's insult affect him. He had probably dodged bigger shots overseas during his time in the military.

Archer knew nothing about Bower. He wasn't a "hick," as he called him. Just because he didn't live in the city or drive a fancy car didn't mean he was any less educated than Archer. In fact, Bower had spent more time learning and training than Archer ever had. Not everyone got lucky on their first venture. Archer lived in such a privileged bubble, he forgot that.

"We're on a break, Archer. Why are you here?" I tried to keep my voice level. I didn't want him to get the upper hand.

Archer laughed, only for a moment, before smiling at me with that cocky grin I hated seeing. "You're right—you did say we were taking a break, but I didn't know that meant we could see other people."

Bower turned to look at me. He searched my face for the truth. I couldn't hide from him. What Archer said was technically true. I'd called it a break, but with every intention of cutting ties when I'd gotten back. After I'd explored things with Bower.

I looked down at my feet. I was an idiot. Such an idiot. My two different worlds were colliding right in front of me, and I was in the middle of the crash.

"Bower, are you okay, dear?" Betty, forgotten along the side of the house, poked her head in the doorway, clearly having already forgotten what she was doing here.

He immediately softened. It had been a long time since she had recognized him. "Let's get you back home," Bower said, linking his arm into his grandmother's.

"Bower," I tried to say, "please just wait, let me explain—"

"You can stay here, Mia. I'll let you have time with your… fiancé." He didn't look back as he guided Betty away. He left me in his cabin, wearing his clothes, with my ex—soon-to-be ex— glaring at me like I was the devil reincarnate.

Archer shook his head at me as he stalked over to the doorframe.

I took a couple of steps back as a precaution. I'd never seen Archer mad before. It was scary.

"You told me you needed a break so you could go fuck that guy?" he yelled.

My body scrunched down defensively, folding itself in. "I didn't… We never…"

"Here I was back at the house you were supposed to move into, all alone, racking my brain trying to figure out why you needed a break after your bachelorette party at your favorite place in the world. Somewhere you never shut up about," he ranted. "Only to find out that the reason you wanted to come here at all was because you had some guy squirreled away. It was the perfect cover really— the resort your family always vacationed at." He sneered. "I didn't think anything of it. Not until I found you here. Looking like… that." Archer looked me up and down, taking in my appearance.

I opened my mouth to argue, to say something in my defense, but no sounds came out. I didn't know what to say.

"It's over, Mia. I saw all I needed to see. Forget me paying off your student loans. You can stay here with the hicks. His grandma is clearly on meth or something. She couldn't even string a coherent sentence together." Archer spit onto the ground next to where he was standing. "You belong with them. Crazy— you're all crazy. Good luck." He turned around and walked away.

Tears welled in my eyes, slowly spilling down my cheeks. I let them fall, not wiping them away. I deserved to feel the way I did. My tears weren't for Archer. They were for Bower and the way I had disappointed him. I didn't deserve him.

Archer was right. I was fucked up. Bower would spend our whole relationship taking care of me, accommodating me in ways that he shouldn't have to. He had his grandma to worry about and care for. He didn't need me, an extra responsibility.

I picked up my dripping-wet clothes from the bathroom floor and tucked them under my arm, letting the water from the clothes soak into the shirt I was wearing. On my way out, I slammed the door to his cabin, feeling the entire structure vibrate. I was suddenly out of breath. My body slowed for a moment before allowing air to fill my lungs. I let it out, loudly, into the pile of wet clothes in my arms. The cry burned my throat and shrunk my lungs.

This was all my fault. I needed to explain—not to Archer. Bower. I wanted *him*. But he was furious with me, and he had every right to be.

I'd ruined everything between us.

Chapter Twenty-Four

Bower

Mia hadn't been wearing her ring, but she was still attached to that guy. The one who'd showed up in clothes that cost more than the salary I could pay Dean. She hadn't fully ended it with him, stringing him along as a backup—for what? If things didn't work out between us?

She wasn't all in like I was. There was no one else for me. I had laid it out there the night of her bachelorette. When she'd showed up this week without her ring, I'd let myself believe she was all in too.

I pushed the pool vacuum down the bottom of the deep end of the resort's pool. Just another of the way too many jobs I took on here. But at least it gave me something to do while I thought through this mess with Mia.

It felt right having her here at the resort. In my cabin. Taking a shower in my bathroom, where it had taken an enormous amount of willpower not to join her.

And the way she melded into my body when I'd pulled her close? She had wanted me to kiss her.

At that, I shook my head. Yesterday I'd almost kissed an engaged woman. Thankfully we had been interrupted. I didn't kiss engaged women—married or taken either. It had never been my style. Growing up watching my grandparents' devotion to each other made the thought of breaking up a union unforgiveable.

Why would Mia put me in a situation like that?

A child screamed from one of the cabins near the pool. I looked over at the clock that was zip-tied onto the fence that surrounded the pool. It was early, but soon families would descend, parents ready to get their kids into the water and out of their hair. I picked up my pace but still made sure to go slow enough not to cloud the water.

The whole situation with Mia was just as cloudy. Was she up here, testing the waters, trying me out to see if I would be boyfriend material? I would never share a girl with any other man. The thought of *that* man touching Mia, whispering sweet nothings into her ear, proposing marriage… It made me sick. The whole situation made me sick.

And if she hadn't fully ended it with him before coming here, did that mean that was the type of guy she wanted—clean cut, rich, asshole? Maybe she had changed in the last nine years. I was the boy from years ago, a childhood crush, that she had to see one more time just to make sure she was making the right decision.

I guess I hadn't passed the test.

I'd left Mia and Archer at my cabin to let them figure out whatever was going on between them. They could ride off into the sunset together for all I cared.

Well, I did care, but her test run, or whatever this was, was over. I wasn't going to be jerked around by Mia anymore. If I wasn't her choice, I'd have to live with that.

And if she eventually brought her and Archer's kids up here? Maybe I'd sell the fucking resort.

———

It was late afternoon, and I hadn't seen Mia for nearly two days. I could avoid her and her fiancé for the next two days before they left on Saturday, that'd be great. I wasn't sure I could handle seeing the two of them together in any capacity.

My phone rang, and I flipped it open, seeing that Grandpa was calling. He was out fishing. Probably ran out of beer or bait.

"Hey," I said. "Need more Bud Light?"

"Uhh, Bower—" *Background noises, muffled talking, twangs of country music.* "Imma need you to pick me up. I got the boat docked at—" *More muffled noises, cheering, shuffling noises. Silence.* The phone beeped three times, showing a dropped call.

Cell service was terrible up here on a good day. *Fuck.* Where was he? I didn't mind picking him up—better that than him getting a DUI or crashing the boat—but there were several bars he could be at. So many bars and restaurants up here had docks you could just pull your boat up to.

I tried to call him again, but it immediately went to voicemail. A dead phone or no service. Best to start checking off bars one at a time.

His usual haunts were close together toward the middle of the lake. The drink specials were great—all the restaurants and bars competing for business. Many of the locals bar hopped by boat from one to another.

I jogged down the stairs to the marina and grabbed a key to one of the resort's motorboats from the lockbox Caleb had just installed and headed to the boat.

Our boats were a mix of older vessels and newer ones we liked to save for guests to rent. I'd picked an older boat that I knew was still in good condition. Like every time I turned a key, I held my breath, bracing my body for any sounds that might trigger me. The key turned smoothly, and the engine started right up—the only sound was the soft purr of the motor.

I puttered out of the marina and into the bay. *No Wake* buoys floated every hundred feet, so I kept the speed to a minimum.

There were huge houses with sandy beaches built around the bay. Every house was a cookie cutter of the previous one, complete with Adirondack chairs circled around a firepit.

Taxes were high up here because of these big houses. They weren't the small cabins at Agate Harbors, although the owners probably spent as much time up here as any of the guests at our resort. Their docks housed multiple Jet Skis and hundred-thousand-dollar pontoons with big motors and fancy lighting.

I stood, keeping my head above the boat's windshield, scanning the bay. Tiny ripples broke the surface tension of the water when a turtle's head poked above the surface before diving back under. The lake was alive but quiet, with so much going on under the surface that we couldn't see.

Larger ripples, more than just a turtle's nose poking through the surface, hit the hull of my boat. I glanced in the direction they were coming from. A paddleboat, one of the resort's, floated nearby, its exposed rudder tangled in green weeds. Its operator, obviously frustrated, rocked the boat from side to side, trying to dislodge it. It wasn't any use. I could see the weeds wrapped around the rudder. We would need to bring a knife out here to cut through them.

I turned the wheel of my boat to steer toward the guest who'd gotten in over their head. It wasn't the first time. Overzealous guests from the Cities always thought they could navigate the lake. Often they ended up lost in the chain of lakes or bottomed out on an unmarked sandbar. The closer I got to the paddleboat, the faster my heart started to beat in my chest. I recognized the back of the guest's head. The blonde hair that was a little too blonde. The frustrated tension in her shoulders—her *bright red* shoulders. How long had she been out here, stuck?

My boat's wake sent waves to shore, rocking her paddleboat unnaturally. She looked over her shoulder quickly before turning around and curling her body in, trying to make herself smaller.

There was no hiding on this lake. This was my stomping ground. I knew every lily pad and every tree.

"Mia!" I called out. I saw her body freeze, tense, and then slowly turn toward me. I killed the motor, letting my boat drift toward hers. "Are you stuck?"

"Bower?" Her nose and cheeks were red with sunburn. She never wore sunblock because the feel of it on her skin made her uncomfortable. Mia must not have thought she'd be on the lake long.

A part of me liked seeing her like this, helpless, without her fancy fiancé to save her. I was the only one with the boat. Without me, she'd be stuck out here until someone else was kind enough to ask if she was okay. Judging by the empty beaches of the mansions behind me and the boats still up in their lifts, it wouldn't be anytime soon.

My boat floated right behind Mia's paddleboat, nudging it with its tip. She squealed at the jolt, slightly falling forward.

"Where's that fiancé of yours?" I asked.

"He went home."

My jaw dropped. Archer wasn't here? What did that mean?

"Hop in," I said. Regardless of how weird things were between us, I couldn't leave her stranded in the sun. I left the steering wheel and came to the bow of the boat, extending a hand.

She stared at me in surprise. "Aren't you—aren't you mad at me?"

"Mad?" I asked. Annoyed and upset, yes, but I wasn't mad. I wasn't sure I could ever be mad at Mia.

"I thought since you didn't come looking for me yesterday…" She looked down at her feet. "I wanted a chance to talk to you—to explain everything."

I hadn't searched her out because I'd thought she'd been with her fiancé—that she'd chosen her fiancé over me. But here she was, no fiancé in sight. If she wanted to talk, I'd hear what she had to say. Though first, we needed to look for my grandpa.

"Well, here I am," I said. "Jump in my boat."

Mia looked like she might choose to stay out on the paddleboat, sunburn and all.

"Come on, Mia. Come with me." I stood at the side of the boat, extending a hand to her. Her fiancé might've gone home, left her up here all alone, but I wasn't going to leave her.

My boat rocked as waves crashed toward the shore. I only had a minute before I'd have to back out the boat so I wouldn't get stuck along the shoreline myself. "It's okay if things feel weird after what happened the other day. I get it—it's weird for me too."

Mia glanced up at me before looking back down at the water.

"Look, the situation is shitty. We can be upset with each other later," I said, "but we've got to get going. I've got to find my grandpa."

Her eyes widened. "He hasn't wandered off too, has he?"

I chuckled. "Only to his favorite watering hole. We need to go pick him up. Can you help me?" I made the decision that we'd get this whole mess figured out, but first I needed to get her to talk to me. If it took using my lost grandpa as an excuse, I'd take it.

Mia looked up at me from the paddleboat that sat low in the water. She let out a final breath of defeat before looking at me, those brown eyes surrounded by the pink of her sunburned skin.

She stood up in the paddleboat, the boat wiggling beneath her feet. Her hand met mine, our fingers interlocking. Mia stepped onto the side of the boat, my arm pulling her up and in. Once her feet hit the carpeted bottom of the boat, she pulled her hand out of mine and brushed it off on the black bike shorts she was wearing.

I motioned for her to come behind the windshield toward the back of the boat, but she sat down on the seats near the bow, her face pointing toward shore. So I took the hat from my head and set it on top of Mia's, making sure the bill blocked the sun from her face. She turned and looked up at me, the bill directing my eyes right down into hers. She looked away once she realized I was staring.

Finding my way back to the captain's chair, I drove the boat past the no-wake zone and pressed on the throttle. Standing above the windshield, I let the wind hit my face. Mia grabbed onto the side rail—and to the top of the hat on her head as the boat picked up speed, bouncing over waves and other boat's wakes. Her blonde hair flew behind her, escaping the tight pony-tail she kept her strands in. She'd wanted to sit in the front of the boat. I hoped she knew how to hold on.

Chapter Twenty-Five

Bower

People were already packed into Jo-Jo's. It was Thursday after all, never mind that it was in the middle of the day. The weekend started early out here.

I maneuvered the boat into a free slip before cutting the engine and tying the stern to the dock. I looked to the front of the boat, where Mia was already tying up the bow. You couldn't take the lake out of a city girl. Not here in Minnesota.

Mia made it onto the dock before me, standing there waiting with her arms crossed in front of her while I put out the boat's fenders. I didn't expect to be here long, but boats were always coming and going.

I stopped myself from staring at where she stood on the dock with sunburn on her nose and along her cheekbones. Her hip popped out to the side; I almost expected her foot to be tapping against the weathered boards of the dock. She'd removed my hat and must've retied her hair. It was tied back again, none the wiser to the windy boat ride. Mia handed me my hat, and I put it back on my head.

I led the way along the dock and up the two sets of stairs to where the bar sat up on a hill. Jo-Jo's had a bunch of lawn games that were popular for day drinkers.

"Where's Gill?" Mia asked, popping that hip again.

"His phone died mid-call. He's one of three places on the lake—this is the first."

"Three places? Bower, I thought you knew where he was!" Her cheeks turned redder than her sunburn. "I don't have time for a scavenger hunt."

"You're on vacation. You have time for everything."

Mia let out a sigh.

"Come on, Mia, you love following me around." Technically she did. This was like old times, me driving the boat and her tagging along on all my adventures every summer.

"Let's go find Gill." She marched past me and toward the bar. Several people playing giant Jenga and ladder golf stopped and waved at me as I passed. I waved back quickly, trying to keep up with Mia.

Inside was just as busy. All the tables were full, and the bar was packed. Country music played loudly over the speakers, and Christmas lights hung from the ceiling as year-round decor. If only Agate Harbors could have a lakeside bar like this—we'd finally be in the green.

Mia wove through tables, looking at everyone's faces. A quick scan of everyone in the small space told me that my grandpa wasn't there. Someone would've flagged me down by now, letting me know Gill was here. He knew everyone around the lake.

"Hey, man!" A hand landed on my shoulder, squeezing it. I turned around to see Jack, a local who worked at a marina on the lake. "Let me buy you a shot." He flagged down the bartender and looked at me, waiting for my order.

"I'll pass, but you could buy one for her." I gestured to Mia, who was still weaving through tables examining faces like she was part of the FBI. I hadn't drunk alcohol for nine years. It wasn't even tempting anymore—but the people up here wouldn't take no for an answer, not when it came to veterans.

"Of course, man. Anything for you."

Jack ordered a shot of tequila. It came with a salted rim and a lime wedge stuck to the edge of the glass. I thanked him, and he patted me on the shoulder twice before returning to the conversation he was having at the bar.

I brought the shot glass over to Mia, who was finishing her search.

"He's not here," she said. I could've told her that within five seconds of walking into the bar, but it was fun to watch her comb the place.

"No, he's not," I agreed, handing her the shot.

"What's this?" Like she didn't already know.

"Tequila."

"No, thank you." Mia tried to hand the shot glass back to me.

"You'd refuse a shot that was so kindly bought for you by the nice gentleman at the bar?" I raised the glass at Jack, who saluted me and smiled at Mia. She glowered at me.

Within the next second, she stuck out her tongue, twirling the shot glass against it, letting the salt granules melt into her tongue. I swallowed, feeling my Adam's apple bob in my throat. Why was I staring? She tilted her head back, letting the liquor slide down her throat. It didn't even look like she swallowed. Mia brought the lime to her lips and sucked the juice from the fruit. My cock twitched in my pants. Had tequila shots always been this sexual?

Mia dropped the lime into the shot glass and set it down on a table next to us. "There. You happy?"

I sure was. Maybe that shot of tequila would help open her up, dissolve some of the uncomfortable tension between us.

Mia left the bar and made it to the dock before I did, her

blonde ponytail bouncing against her upper back, then turned around suddenly when we got to the boat. The dock bobbed as I stopped in front of her and crossed my arms.

Her nostrils widened as she looked down at my chest. She took a step back, her arms uncrossing. "Shit, Bower, this isn't us. We don't communicate like this. I don't like it."

My arms loosened, falling to my sides, and I nodded. I didn't like it either.

"I'm sorry I ruined everything. I didn't think Archer would come up here."

I rubbed my hand over my face—I didn't like to hear his name on her lips. "I thought you'd ended things with him when you told me you wanted that chance. You made it seem like it was over with him." I glanced down at her left hand. "You haven't been wearing your ring."

"No, we were done. I would've completely ended it before I came, but..." Mia paused for a moment, her cheeks turning redder again. "I've never broken up with someone before." She looked down at her sandaled feet, wiggling her toes. "I felt bad. He made me feel bad about...everything."

"You shouldn't feel bad about breaking up with someone who makes you feel like shit." I took a step closer to Mia, the dock shaking. "We only have so many summers. Why waste them on someone like that?"

"Well, he isn't wasting my summers anymore."

My heart slowed, each beat waiting for her next words.

"He's gone. For good."

I took another step closer to her, the wobbly dock forcing our bodies together. She put her hands on my chest, stabilizing herself. As soon as her hands touched me, she gasped, her eyes looking up at mine. I stared down at her, frozen, as if her touch had left me calcified.

"We should go check the next place." Mia removed her hands from me and jumped into the boat.

Cold air rushed to fill the space where her hands had been.

"Right," I said hastily, "we should go."

Maybe now we could get back to solving the growing tension between us.

213

Chapter Twenty-Six

Mia

I let the boat's rumbling motor fill the silence between Bower and me as I sat behind the windshield this time. I'd felt something on the dock just now. Maybe this could still work between us. The thought made me equal parts nervous and excited.

Bower was everything Archer wasn't. He'd proved that again and again, and now *again*. He wasn't mad at me—at least not in the same way Archer would've been. I would've gotten the silent treatment for days, whereas Bower had rescued me. I'd caused the drama the other day, and still Bower hadn't held it against me. He might've still been upset, but he wasn't about to take those feelings out on me. We could talk like grown adults, like we'd always been able to talk, even when we were younger.

"Hold on," Bower said from the driver's seat. I tried not to look over at him too many times on the way to the next bar. The way he stood at the steering wheel, one hand on the wheel and the other on the gas, his eyes scanning the horizon. He was very much in his element, and it had every molecule in my body buzzing.

I stood up to watch his landing. He was steering straight

toward the shore of a sandbar in the middle of a lake. There were boats already beached in a line, their passengers presumably at the straw-covered tiki shack in the middle of the small island. I put my hand on the dash in front of me, bracing myself as Bower drove the boat straight into the sand. Our bodies lurched forward before they rocked back, the boat losing its forward momentum.

Bower fell back into his captain's chair right as I put too much weight on one foot. I tried to correct myself by crossing my other foot in front, but I'd already lost balance, my body making momentum of its own. My legs twisted underneath me, my knees bending.

"Ooph!" My ass hit something hard and warm. I could smell him again. Cedarwood. I opened my eyes that had closed while I'd been falling. *Stupid reflexes.* If I had fallen just a little to the right, I could have avoided his lap all together and fallen on the bottom of the boat behind his chair. It would have been more painful but less embarrassing.

Bower had his arm wrapped around my waist. It was just a reflex to catch me. The hard length growing against my back was also just a reflex. I was a girl sitting on a guy's lap. This was bound to happen. It was a natural response.

I sat there frozen for a second, feeling his tense body underneath me, his shaft still expanding along my hip. It still wasn't done rising?

I stood up, brushing off my shorts that weren't even dirty. Another reflex. A nervous one. I hadn't meant to land on his lap. I hadn't meant to make him feel that way, feel…*that* against me.

"Sorry," I said, wincing. It felt like I'd invaded his privacy somehow, even though his body had welcomed me with an erection.

"That should *stick* for a little while." Bower turned off the engine and pulled out the key. He had an amused look on his face, like he was reveling in my embarrassment. He adjusted himself in his shorts before he stuck the key into his pocket, looking along the sandbar we'd just pulled up to. If he could pretend like that didn't just happen, so could I.

The music was loud but good, a mix of classic bar songs and pop songs that were fun to dance to. People were dancing on the beach, celebrating that it was Thursday and it was sunny. What other excuse did they need? Like Bower had said, we only had so many summers.

The bar setup looked like a tiki bar with palm fronds on the roof and teakwood used to build the structure. The entire bar looked like it could be rolled away. It probably was during the winter months, carried away on a pontoon, but for now it was a perfect summer bar. Chairs lined the beach, almost every one of them filled with people with drinks in their hands, an inordinate amount of piña coladas being served.

"Gill hangs out here?" I asked. It looked nothing like the bar we'd just left.

"The drinks are supposed to be good." Bower shrugged before he leaned over and opened a compartment under the seats in the back of the boat.

I threw one leg over the side of the boat, ready to jump onshore and begin the search. Gill had better be here.

The crashing waves halted me. It was shallow water over here, but still water nonetheless, with sand just below. I watched the grains move back and forth with the pull of the water. My sandaled foot dangled over the edge. The likelihood of me jumping off the boat was becoming smaller and smaller.

"Here." Bower held out a pair of yellow rain boots—the same type of boots from nine years ago that had protected my feet from the sand.

"How do you still..." I held them in my hands. The moment I touched them, it was like a vault had opened, all the memories of Bower rushing into me through the boots. He knew what I needed without being prompted. I never had to ask. He just knew. He knew me.

"Put them on," Bower said.

I eagerly kicked off my sandals and pulled on the boots.

He jumped off the boat, water splashing as he landed. I leaned over the edge, anticipating the jump I'd have to make. The water was shallow, but was it shallow enough that it wouldn't flood over into my boots? Bower waited for me, his arms extended.

I sat on the side of the boat, my boots hanging above the water, and let him help me. He grabbed me under the arms and lifted me into the water. My body crashed against his as he slowly lowered me down to the sandy bottom inch by inch, letting me feel every ridge and valley from his chest and down his torso. I held my breath as I realized he could feel all my ridges and valleys as well. I watched our bodies move against each other's, my shirt riding up as I got closer to the ground. Bower set me down gently, like I'd weighed nothing, my boots completely protecting my skin from the water and sand. I pulled down my shirt quickly, looking away from Bower.

The bass of the speakers was thumping, vibrating my bones. Girls danced on the beach in string bikinis and cutoff jean shorts. The guys hung back, seated at the bar, a single elbow resting on the bar top as they turned to take in the view. A large sign above the palm roof read *The Sand Bar*, an obvious name.

"Bower! Come over here!"

A male voice caught Bower's attention. He grabbed onto my wrist, like he always did, and pulled me over to the bar, toward the voice that had called his name.

"I heard you were back. How come we haven't seen you?" the man asked. He sat at the bar shirtless, in swim trunks and thong sandals. His tan skin told me he spent a lot of time in the sun, probably drinking at this bar.

"Hey, Josh. I've been busy with the resort," Bower said. He was still holding my wrist.

I broke free of his grasp, pulling my wrist through the weakest point of his grip, between his thumb and fingers.

"Looks like you could use a drink," Josh said. He called over the bartender before I could argue. Why was everyone buying us drinks? Bower tried to wave the bartender away, but Josh insisted on ordering us piña coladas. "What are you doing with Bower?" he asked me.

"He's making me work on my vacation," I said.

Bower rolled his eyes, using his entire head. "Hardly. Mia has enjoyed following me around since we were young." He looked at me with a light in his eyes that wasn't usually there.

The bartender delivered our piña coladas in plastic cups with a cherry on top. I took mine and greedily took a sip through the straw. It was cold and icy. Perfect for a hot day on the lake.

Bower left his drink on the counter of the bar. "We're looking for my grandpa. Have you seen him?"

"No, I haven't seen him here today," Josh said.

We both let out a collective sigh.

Bower grabbed my wrist again and pulled me away from the bar. Josh held up his glass of beer toward us, and I did my best to do an "air cheers" as Bower was pulling me away.

"Who was that?" I asked.

"A friend," he grumbled.

"Do all your friends buy you drinks?"

"Most of them do."

"Mr. Popular," I taunted.

Bower grunted an unintelligible response before he picked me up and set me on the bow of the boat. I held on to my drink, keeping it upright as I landed in the seats. The cherry in my drink bobbled slightly. I took another sip once my rain boots hit the bottom of the boat. Bower was right—they did have good drinks.

I lifted my boots onto the seat across from me, crossed my ankles, and leaned back, feeling the warmth of the sun on my face. The resort was tie-dying T-shirts today—probably right at this very moment—all the cute kids running around with bottles of dye, their parents chasing them. For once, I wasn't sad I'd miss a resort activity. This was not where I expected to be when I'd taken the paddleboat out. I'd thought I'd paddle around the bay a few times, burn some of the guilt I was feeling out of my system.

It had never crossed my mind that I'd end up here, reluctantly hiding that I was having a great time with Bower, but now this was exactly where I wanted to be.

I took another sip as I watched Bower fling himself over the edge of the boat after he pushed us off. He quickly made his way to the wheel, inserted the key into the ignition, and then paused. I watched his jaw clench, accentuating his cheek bones, his chest stilling as he turned the key. My toes spread in my boots as I prepared to go over and check on him. I paused when, as soon as the boat started, Bower relaxed.

I was extra sensitive after Tuesday's confrontation—I didn't want anything to go wrong. I snuck back into the passenger chair before he backed out, trying to preserve my hair and my drink.

———

I could hear the untuned guitar and the singer's twangy voice from across the lake. Boats pulled up alongside us as we cruised toward a whitewashed building with dozens of boats parked in front of it. Large letters raised with two-by-fours spelled out *Paddle Point*. The sign was big enough that I could easily read it outside the no-wake zone around it.

As soon as we passed the orange-and-white buoys, Bower killed the engine and the boat puttered toward the bar, the other boats floating along with us. A few people from other boats waved hello to him. I wasn't sure if it was just lake etiquette or if they actually knew him. Probably the latter. The lake was small, and Bower seemed to have merged right back into the lake community in the couple months since he'd been back.

Paddle Point had a large docking system that packed the boats in. If Agate Harbors had something like that, they could really be pulling in the dough. Bower could find better musicians too. The off-tune music was already making my ears ring.

I helped Bower dock the boat. A bowline knot was something I still remembered from all those years ago. I tied the bow of the boat to the dock, and Bower tied up the stern, both of us working in tandem, like we'd done this for years. Technically we had, just many years ago.

I hopped onto the dock as soon as my knot was tied and waited for Bower to finish up. He popped a couple of fenders along each side of the boat to protect it from getting hit by the dock or other boats. This dock was a lot more solid, made from metal. It creaked under my rubber boots, but at least the boards didn't bow under my weight, threatening to give out.

Bower hopped out of the boat, the dock wiggling back and forth. "He's got to be here," he said. "It's a big place. We should stick together."

I looked up at the bar that was slightly uphill from the docks. There were two sets of stairs before you got to the deck of the bar that overlooked the lake. Bower walked past me and made his way toward the stairs. I followed, watching my footing as the dock shook after every one of his foot falls.

The band got louder as we got closer to the bar. The stair treads were abnormally short, and my calves were burning. Once my feet hit the top, I breathed a sigh of relief. The deck at the top was massive, with people milling about along high-top tables with beer-branded umbrellas. The view from up here was amazing. I understood why it was such a popular bar. People would flock here for the view even if the music was mediocre. You could almost see to the other side of the lake from up here. The sunsets had to be amazing.

Bower weaved through tables, patting people on the back and shaking hands. Every time he stopped at a table, I scurried to catch up to him. I didn't know if he actually wanted to talk to these people or if he was going slow, waiting for me to navigate the crowds that so easily moved aside for him. He was like a bull, the crowd parting for him. I was a mouse, squeaking through cracks and holes, trying to find my way.

I caught up with him right as he had finished talking to an older couple sitting at a high-top table. Both were tan, obviously enjoying the lake life.

"Who's this?" the woman asked. Her eyes sparkled as she took in Bower and me standing next to each other.

"This is Mia." Bower grabbed my hand and pulled me forward, introducing me. I waved at them awkwardly with my free hand, while his grasp on my other hand stayed tight.

"So nice to meet you, Mia." The woman looked at the man sitting next to her before back at us. The two exchanged a knowing look. "Bower's been such a blessing for Betty and Gill. It sure is nice that he gets a break once in a while."

She looked down at our clasped hands, still together. I let my hand fall limp, signaling Bower that it was okay to let go, but he held fast, doubling down on his grip.

"We keep trying to get Bower to come work for us, even part-time." The man grabbed onto the woman's hand. They must've been a couple. "We want to retire within the next decade at least." They both laughed.

"I've got my own resort to run," Bower said. He was smiling when he spoke. This wasn't the first time he had this conversation.

"Here are your drinks, Mr. and Mrs. Peterson." A red-haired server set down two margaritas in front of the couple. They looked delicious, like they had been made with fresh juice and good tequila.

"Do you want one, Mia?" Mrs. Peterson asked. I pursed my

mouth, ready to say no, but it was like she read my mind. "Sarah, bring another margarita, please." She tilted her head in my direction. "On the rocks?" I nodded. "And a glass of water for Bower."

Sarah left to fulfill the drink order. Bower pulled out his wallet and laid a twenty on the table to pay for the drink.

Mr. Peterson pushed the bill away. "What's the point of owning a bar if you can't buy your friends drinks?" He winked at me, and I couldn't help but blush.

"I'll get you next time at Agate," Bower said.

Sarah brought my margarita and Bower's water over in record time. Faster than any drink I'd ordered at Agate Harbors. No wonder the resort's restaurant was struggling—they just couldn't compete with the fast service and craft cocktails the other restaurants on the lake were offering.

"You didn't want a margarita?" I asked Bower.

"Bower doesn't drink," Mr. Peterson said.

I looked at Bower, my head tilted to the side. He'd had his friend buy me a shot at Jo-Jo's, he'd left the piña colada on the beach bar melting in the heat…

"Haven't in nine years," Bower said while he looked at me, a glass of ice water cradled in his palm.

I tried to do quick math in my head. That would put him at sixteen? Seventeen?

"Let us know if you need anything," Mr. Peterson said. "I'll keep an eye out for Gill."

"Thanks," Bower said before dragging me away.

We weaved through tables and people, many of whom knew Bower and greeted him with open arms. He always introduced me, pulling me forward, not letting go of my hand. Most people hadn't seen Gill, which wasn't surprising due to how busy the bar was. There were a few who'd seen him "about twenty minutes ago" they thought, give or take thirty minutes. So he really could be anywhere.

The entire time we circulated, my hands were occupied. One with a drink and the other enclosed in Bower's hand. It took the pressure off meeting everyone, not having to be awkward with my hands or touching someone's unfamiliar palms.

Part of me thought this was Bower's doing, his way of accommodating me. I didn't want to be touching a bunch of sweaty people who spoke too loudly and too closely. One of my hands was tucked into Bower's dry hand and my other hand was around the cool glass of my drink. I could give a friendly nod, and that was enough.

"Let's go back outside," Bower said. He pulled me by the hand outside the bar, the loud music leaving my ears, replaced by the live country singers.

Bower put his water on the drink rail and hopped up onto the seat of one of the wooden benches that looked out over the lake. Keeping my hand in his, he helped me up onto the wooden bench so I was standing next to him. From up here, we were high enough to see over everyone's heads.

Still no Gill sightings.

I slurped my empty margarita obnoxiously, trying to suck up the last drops.

Bower turned to look at me. "Stop," he said, his eyes going dark.

"What?" I tried to pull my hand free from his, but his grip was too tight.

"Stop sucking on that straw. It's giving me too many ideas."

I let the straw fall out of my mouth, and he grabbed the glass from my hand, bending down to place it on the ground beneath the bench. The entire bench wobbled as he moved.

"Shit—we probably shouldn't be standing on this." Bower let go of my hand, only to move his to my waist, lifting me down to the ground. His hand immediately returned to mine the moment my feet touched the deck.

From the corner of my eye, I saw the lake. It was right

behind us as we stood on the bench. The sun was setting, the golden globe hovering halfway underneath the horizon. It looked like it was bobbing in the lake, spreading its majestic colors in the sky. Pinks, oranges, and yellows surrounded us. The trees along the lake looked black in the looming darkness. They were silhouettes framing in the sunset. Absolutely breathtaking.

Bower leaned his elbow along the drink rail, his other hand encapsulating mine. I didn't try to remove it. It felt safe. I wouldn't lose him as long as my hand was in his.

My shoulder brushed against his as I leaned on the railing, taking in the view. Why were the Petersons looking to retire? I could live on this deck until I died. Drinks and sunsets? Perfection.

Bower's free hand wrapped around my shoulder. Like we were friends admiring the sunset. I'd do this with a girlfriend. It was very platonic.

The sun sank lower, and so did Bower's arm. His hand slid down my shoulder blades and bumped along my ribs before settling on the curve of my waist. I sank into his body. Maybe I was pulled closer by Bower? It didn't matter; it felt right. The sides of our bodies were touching from our chests down to our toes.

I stood there, trying to admire the sight. It was beautiful, but all I could focus on was all the points Bower and my body were touching. The side of my body was aflame, feeling every movement of muscle beneath Bower's skin and every breath he took.

I needed something to drink. I reached over for Bower's water, the cold condensation on the outside of the glass calling my name. He turned just enough that when I reached over for his water, the fronts of our bodies came together. There was a bit of distance between us, our frames only touching when we both deeply inhaled at the same time. My breasts to his chest, his abs to my…not-so abs.

We were both breathing heavily. Maybe it was because of

how fast I was drinking his water. I swallowed gulp after gulp with every inhale I took. Bower locked eyes with me as I drank, every pull from the straw making my cheeks sink in. He swallowed as he stared, making his Adam's apple bob up and down. The water ran out, my pulls from my straw making loud slurping noises.

Bower's mouth fell open. "I told you not to do that, Mia."

The straw left my lips as I opened them, my body frozen against the railing.

"It gives me too many ideas of what you could be doing with that mouth of yours."

I tried to set the glass down on the railing, but it slipped out of my hands, wobbling back and forth, threatening to fall over the edge. "I've never…" I trailed off, immediately regretting my word choice.

Had the straw sucking been too sexual? After a day on the lake with Bower, the water had tasted really good. But according to my friends—who weren't really my friends—I didn't know how to take a blow-job shot, much less give an actual blow job that involved sucking and…

"Shhhh…" He brought his fingers to my lips, letting them fall, pulling my lower lip with them. "Don't get in your head."

Bower let go of my hand, my palm suddenly cold without him there, and wrapped his around the back of my head, cradling the bottom of my skull. "You don't know what you do to me, Mia." He pulled me in close against him, letting my stomach feel the erection in his shorts. It nestled in against me, warm, pulsing ever so slightly.

My breath hitched. I looked down between our bodies before looking back up at his face. It was trained on mine, studying it, looking for signs that I was okay.

I had his full attention, wrapping my hands around the back of his neck, letting my body fall into his. This was what I wanted.

"I think I know," I murmured. I tilted my head ever so slightly, an invitation that Bower readily accepted.

The word "Fuck" left his lips before they crashed onto mine, his hand on the back of my head keeping our mouths pressed together. Bower tilted his head slightly, his tongue pressing against my closed lips, bargaining for entrance. I pulled him closer with my hands around his neck, opening my mouth, our tongues meeting, playing with one another. I sunk my teeth into his bottom lip. Bower groaned, opening his mouth to devour me whole. It could have been minutes or hours—time wasn't timing. It was just Bower and me on a deck in the dark, with a few tiki torches for light.

Steady clapping coming from the deck and getting closer met my ears and broke up the moment. Our mouths fell apart, the chilly night air stinging my now raw lips.

"Congratulations! It's about time!" Gill continued clapping as he approached, drawing the attention of the rest of the bar goers.

My face instantly flushed. I looked up at Bower to see his reaction, his eyes still locked on me, on my lips. They felt puffy and swollen. How long had we been making out? It hadn't been a sweet innocent kiss; it'd been a release of the accumulation of feelings that had been there since we were young.

By the look on Bower's face, it had only released some of the pressure inside of him. His pupils were still dilated, his breathing was still heavy. His chest pushed against my breasts as it rose and fell. There was now a pulsing between my legs, tension that Bower had built up yet hadn't helped me with. After watching him all day in his backward hat, manning the boat, holding my hand like I was his, the kiss had made it worse. I clamped my thighs together, hoping to quell the feeling. That did nothing to help me.

"Sorry—I didn't mean to interrupt." Gill held his hands up in the air like we had pointed a knife at him. Maybe my eyes were throwing daggers. The kiss had been good. I didn't want it to stop.

I revised my previous statement: All I needed to be happy was sunsets, drinks, and Bower's lips on mine.

Bower's hand found mine and gripped it with the same intensity he had all day, like he wasn't going to let me get away. He adjusted his pants before motioning to his grandpa to follow, and we made our way back to the boat.

Gill sat in the back of the boat with both of his arms relaxed across the tops of the long stretch of seats. Once we left the no-wake zone, Bower pushed the throttle, letting the boat go. I angled the passenger chair so that I was facing forward, watching the lake fly underneath us.

There were hardly any boats on the lake at this time of night. The ones that were out there were lit up just like our boat was, red lights on the left and green on the right.

Bower's boat slid over the top of the water. The lake was glassy and smooth. The stars were putting on a show tonight in the cloudless sky, letting their twinkling lights flicker down on the lake. The hum of the motor, the stars in the sky, and the wind blowing on my face hypnotized me.

"Bower! Slow down!" Gill's voice cut through the trance I was in. I looked over at Bower, who pulled his eyes away from me, pulling back the throttle and slowing the boat. No-wake buoys bobbed in the illegal waves the boat had made before he slowed down. "Keep your eyes on the lake, boy."

I looked down at my feet and tried to stop the smile that pulled at my lips. Hearing Bower being scolded like he was thirteen all over again by Gill, who was currently half the size of him, was priceless. Bower shook his head, looking over at me, a smile pulling at his lips too.

Chapter Twenty-Seven

Mia

"Be good, you two. Don't do anything I wouldn't do!" Gill called out as he slowly made his way along the docks of the marina.

Bower and I watched from the boat to make sure he didn't fall in. He'd been right to call Bower. He'd had too much to drink. I didn't think Bower minded picking him up either. It'd been fun, like a scavenger hunt, only for a drunk grandpa.

I'd won a prize too: a swoon-worthy kiss with Bower that had made my entire body tingle.

I kicked my feet up on the dash in front of me, crossing my rain boots at the ankles. Bower took his eyes off his grandpa for a moment to run them up and down my legs.

"Eyes up here, *boy*," I said, mimicking his grandpa's previous scolding.

Bower looked away, smiling, and threw the boat into reverse. The motor paused for a moment before it fell into gear and slowly backed out of the marina. "We're going out," he said. He stood up and watched the back of the boat as he turned it ninety degrees before flipping the gear to maneuver the boat forward.

"What if I have plans for the rest of the night?" I pulled my feet off the dash and planted them on the floor of the boat with a loud thump.

Bower stood at the helm of the boat, the muscles under his tattooed skin moving as he flexed his hand along the steering wheel. We were moving through the bay outside the marina where he had found me earlier today. The paddleboat was still there, stuck in the weeds, waiting to be rescued.

"I thought we went over this," Bower said. "You're on vacation. You're not busy."

I turned around and watched the lights of the marina get smaller and smaller. This time I wasn't hesitant about being in the boat with Bower. He was right. The only thing I wanted to be busy with was him. The only plans I wanted to have involved him.

My week up here was rapidly coming to an end. We had tonight and tomorrow before I had to go back home, back to pick up the pieces of my life and prepare for the start of the school year. Whatever this was between Bower and me—we had to figure it out soon.

I lived hours away and couldn't come up here on a regular basis, and I wasn't sure Bower would be able to get away from the resort. Even if we could get away to see each other once a month, we hadn't had time to build a solid foundation. It was entirely possible our relationship would crumble beneath the pressure of going long distance before it even got its footings.

But what if this thing between us went somewhere after this week? Would I quit my job and live up here? I was afraid to ask the questions because I wasn't sure I wanted to know the answers. We needed to figure it out—fast.

Once we left the no-wake zone, Bower leaned into the throttle, and I sat back, letting him and the night take me anywhere they wanted me to go.

The house Bower pulled the boat up to looked oddly familiar. It took me back to when I was sixteen and Bower had brought me to that party. The last time I'd seen him. It was the same house. Perhaps the house had been painted a different color, but it was the same one. The setup along the beach was the same too. A bonfire in the middle, coolers and people everywhere.

"Is this the same…" I asked before Bower cut me off.

"The same house, yes. Owned now by the son of the man who owned it back when we were kids." *Ahh.* The similar vibe made sense now.

Bower and I docked the boat, flipping the fenders over the side before climbing out of the boat. My rain boots clunked along the metal dock, causing people along the beach to look at us approaching.

"Mia? Is that you?" Ruby's voice rang out from the beach. She was ankle deep in the water, her flip-flops hanging from her hand. Dean was beside her, walking barefoot in the water. I waved at her as Bower reached out his hand to help me down off the dock and into the sand. It was only a six-inch drop. I took his hand anyway. His immediate grip told me he wasn't planning on letting go anytime soon.

"It's like déjà vu, isn't it?" Ruby asked.

I nodded. "It's freaking me out."

"Hey, everybody here are adults. No one's getting arrested tonight," Dean joked.

Bower's hand tensed over mine. We still hadn't talked about that night.

"Caleb and Chloe are saving spots up by the bonfire for us," Dean suggested after Bower didn't respond to his joke.

Bower grunted before leading the group up to the fire. It was tall, crackling and spitting embers surrounded by a circle of rocks. Chloe and Caleb sat on a rocking bench together, her hands resting on top of her stomach, his arm stretched along the back of the bench around her shoulders. Dean and Ruby found two Adirondack chairs and sat down in them quickly. This felt like a game of musical chairs.

"Whoops, only one chair left!" Ruby said, smiling. Bower sat down in the single empty chair before I could, an amused look on his face. My hand was still in his as he pulled me toward him, my body twisting around before my butt landed on his large quads.

He was warm on the chilly night. I couldn't help but lean back and meld into his chest. His shoulder cradled my head as I rested against it. The heat from the fire in front of me and the heat of his body behind me sandwiched me in. Bower wrapped an arm possessively over my stomach, his thumb drawing circles along my side. I shivered even though I was now warm.

Ruby tossed a can of beer over to Bower, who caught it before it landed in my lap. He passed it over to Caleb without opening it. "Thanks, Ruby, but I don't drink," Bower said. His arm wrapped back around me, his thumb continuing the torturing circles. I wiggled on his lap and the circles stopped, his hand now pressing hard into my side, subduing my body.

"Since when?" Ruby asked.

I glared at my sister—that was a rude way to ask someone about their drinking—but she just shrugged.

Bower didn't seem to mind the brazen question and answered without pause. "Since nine years ago on this beach."

I stilled and turned to look back at Bower.

"When you got arrested?" Ruby asked.

I twisted my head back to her. "What the fuck, Ruby?"

Bower nodded. "I never wanted to put someone I loved in danger ever again."

I hadn't been in danger that night—he'd saved me from getting into trouble, saved me from the wrath of my parents. I'd felt terrible that night, especially because I hadn't known what to do. I'd been a sixteen-year-old girl in way over her head.

Was that what he thought I'd felt that night? That he'd put me in danger?

I twisted around to Bower and put my hand on his face. His

hand moved to my lower back. "I was never in danger," I whispered. "You put me on that boat—you saved me."

"If I hadn't been drinking, everything would have been different. I could've been faster getting you on that boat. I could've had quicker reactions—maybe I would've had time to get on the boat. I would have been there the next summer and the next."

"You don't know that," I said. I rubbed my thumb along his jaw. The stubble from his beard was rough.

"I do, Mia. You only get so many summers. I've wasted so many of mine already." Bower looked down at my lips.

I sucked in a breath, ready to be pummeled by his mouth again.

His hand left my lower back, catching something behind me.

"Get a room, you two," Ruby said from across the fire.

Bower was holding the bag of marshmallows she had thrown at us. My eyes lit up. *S'mores.* This night was total déjà vu. There were supplies for s'mores tucked next to the chairs—chocolate, graham crackers, and roasting sticks.

I got to work making my favorite summer treat. I sat perched on Bower's lap as I leaned over, tucking my marshmallow into a cavern of embers near the base of the fire.

His hand slipped beneath my shirt, right between the gap of my shirt and shorts that revealed the skin of my lower back. Goose bumps peppered my skin even as the heat of the fire scorched me. His fingers traced the bumps of my vertebrae, following the peaks and valleys of each knob, first traveling up to the bottom of my bra and then back down to the waistband of my shorts.

Each time his fingers grazed my shorts, I held my breath, squirming against his lap, wishing his fingers would continue their journey lower. Bower let out a quiet groan each time I squirmed, only loud enough that I could feel the vibration of his low voice travel through his body and against the back of my legs.

"I didn't know what s'mores were until I moved up here," Chloe said.

"Really?" Ruby asked. "They aren't a thing in Florida?"

"I mean, I guess they are. They just aren't as common as they are up here."

Bower's fingers found their way to my waistband yet again. I couldn't help but wiggle against his thighs. His fingers sent tingles down between my legs. Bower's other hand gripped my hip, his fingers tucking between the fold of my bent body, between my upper thigh and stomach. His hand grasped me tightly, putting pressure on my body to still my movements. He squeezed me tightly for a moment before releasing, his hand still close to that area of my body that was pulsing.

From then on, every time his fingers brushed my waistband and I squirmed against him, he squeezed me with his other hand on my hip in retaliation. His fingers traveled closer and closer to my core with each squeeze. My body throbbed for him, wanted him to keep reaching lower and lower. My bike shorts were thin. I could feel Bower's rough skin right through them.

"I'm due in about a month," Chloe was saying. I was only vaguely following along to the conversation around the bonfire.

"It's a girl," Caleb said proudly, giving her belly a rub.

I smiled, trying to act like nothing was happening underneath my shirt or between the fold of my body. I watched my marshmallow go from a perfect golden yellow to a brown color. I didn't want this game we were playing to end, damn my marshmallow.

His fingertips met the edge of my waistband again, my body full of sexual energy. He had built that energy up every time his fingers dragged up and down my spine. I adjusted myself against his thighs, trying to get comfortable. I could no longer sit still, letting him torture me like this. There was something innate about how my hips needed to move.

Bower's hand reached lower, still over my shorts, pushing between my legs. His wrist caught between my pelvic bone and the top of my thigh right as his fingers brushed over my center. I must've been radiating heat; I was practically panting, bent over on Bower's lap. His fingers pressed down, right on top of my clit.

The sounds from the party became fuzzy. The bike shorts I was wearing felt warm against me, the fabric pushed between my folds. I was wet from the teasing and touching Bower had been putting me through—he was feeling that with his fingers.

I froze.

Bower stopped moving his fingers and slowly pulled them from between my legs, wrapping his arm around my hips. He used the arm he'd been tracing my spine with to wrap around my collarbone, pulling my back flush with his chest. My back hit something hard, long, and warm, lying against Bower's stomach. Oh my god, he was hard. I could feel his warm breath against my ear and the scratch of his chin against my neck. I shivered against him.

"I've had enough. We're leaving," he whispered into my ear.

Bower lifted us to a standing position, keeping my body in front of his, obviously trying to hide the monstrosity in his pants. "We're headed out," he announced to the group.

Everyone went quiet, abruptly ending their conversations.

"Okay…I guess I'll see you back at the cabin…" Ruby said.

I gave the group a wave before Bower's arm slipped down, wrapping possessively around my waist, his erection grinding into my lower back with every step.

At this point, I would follow Bower wherever he would take me, so long as he promised to help me relieve the pressure that he had built up inside of me.

Chapter Twenty-Eight

Mia

Bower finally let go of me and helped me climb into the boat. I sat in the passenger seat, looking anywhere but at the beach. I didn't want to lock eyes with Ruby—or anyone who'd watched Bower herd me toward the docks.

He made quick work of the ropes and started the boat, this time not pausing as long before he turned the key. The engine vibrated the seat I was sitting on in a way I had never noticed before. I squeezed my thighs together, crossing my ankles, and only looked up once Bower pushed down on the throttle, signaling we were out of the no-wake zone.

Bower was driving the boat with a look of determination I had never seen on his face before. He didn't even glance over at me while he was driving, the moon and stars lighting the way. There were even fewer boats on the water than when we'd arrived at the party. Lights from the docks of the houses along the lake had already flickered out, assuming that boaters were done for the night. There was an uncanny stillness about the lake at this time of night that was both spooky and enchanting. It had all my nerves standing at attention.

Bower pulled the throttle back, slowing the boat. Where were we? He sat down in his seat as the boat puttered through a bay. At least I assumed it was a bay. The surrounding foliage was getting denser, and trees leaned in closer to the water, their branches dancing along the surface of the lake. They began scratching against the side of the boat, bending, flicking water once the boat passed. It continued to get narrower and narrower the farther the boat went.

Bower's eyes met mine for just a moment before returning his attention to steering the vessel. It was so tight that one wrong twist of the steering wheel could mean beaching the boat. It was hard to tell with the poor lighting, but I thought I saw a smile on his lips.

Our boat barely fit through the arch of trees and branches surrounding the waterway. Just when I thought we might get stuck, wedged between the branches of trees, the foliage opened, releasing the boat from its grasps. We squeezed through, and I could finally breathe again.

The circle of open water sparkled beneath the starry sky above us. Trees surrounded us, not a cabin in sight. Bower killed the engine, standing up holding a yellow anchor with rope attached to it. He tossed it overboard, lowering it to the bottom of the lake before tying the rope to the side of the boat.

The boat floated in the bay he'd driven us to, and looking up at the sky, I saw why he'd brought me here. There were no trees above us, just the night sky in all its glory. There wasn't any light pollution like where I lived in the Twin Cities. It was quiet. Crickets chirped alongside frogs, creating a melody that, along with the occasional hoot of an owl, made my blood pressure instantly decrease. I let all the air out of my lungs before drawing in a fresh breath. It even smelled good out here.

"Remember this place?" Bower asked. He stood at the bow of the boat, glowing beneath the moonlight. The shadows created from the light above him made the muscles in his arms look even more defined. I looked around in the dark bay, trying to orient myself. "It's my secret fishing spot."

I looked at Bower and smiled. I didn't know if he could see my mouth, but he was right. It was the place he'd brought me for fishing when we'd been young. It was secret, secluded, and ours. No one would venture in here unknowingly. The passage was too tight.

"I widened the channel a little since I came back," he explained. "I still come here, you know, to fish."

"Do you think about me while you're fishing?" I asked, then immediately regretted my brazen question. But I wanted the answer.

Bower took his hat off his head and ran his hand through his hair before replacing the hat. "I think about you all the time, Mia. But especially here."

I stood up and walked over to where Bower was standing on the bow. I needed to touch him, to feel him against me. Once I was within arm's reach, he grabbed my wrist and pulled me against him. He wrapped his arms over my upper arms and down my back, gripping my waist. I pressed myself against his body, relishing in the warmth radiating from him.

"I think about you all the time too," I whispered, looking up at him as he looked down at me. I'd never forgotten about Bower. There hadn't been a day that went by without Bower somehow working his way into my thoughts. A commercial about camping or a billboard for an up north escape would bring flashes of what Bower and I had back into my head.

"You were just engaged, Mia," Bower said. "I doubt you thought much about me at all."

All the air exited my lungs. "Sure, I was engaged, Bower, but for all the wrong reasons. I thought Archer was the safe choice—the money, and my parents loved him…"

He scoffed.

"What I didn't realize is how safe you make me *feel*," I continued. "Archer paid for things and kept my parents happy, but I never was myself around him. I was always walking a fine line—I always felt like one misstep and I'd become a disappointment."

Bower took a piece of blonde hair—the hair that Archer had wanted blonder, longer, styled down on my shoulders—and tucked it behind my ear.

"I never feel like that around you. I can be myself."

"When you left that weekend, I didn't know if you'd be back," he whispered. "You had that ring on your finger and all your asshole friends with you."

I looked down at my feet. So many things about that weekend had gone wrong…

"Once you came back, I didn't know what to do."

Oh, Bower. He didn't know how bad I had it for him.

"I'll always come back, Bower," I said. "I come back every summer."

I tilted my head and pursed my lips, giving him warning before I pushed myself up on my toes to meet his lips.

Bower kept his lips still for a moment before pulling my body against his, weaving his hand around the back of my head, cradling my skull. It was as if both of us needed to prove to one another how badly we'd always wanted each other.

I bit down on his lower lip, eliciting a groan from deep within Bower's body. I moaned against his mouth. He swallowed every sound, sucking my tongue into his mouth, rubbing it against his own. My hips slammed into his body, my body in need of friction. I'd never felt like this before, so out of control and sensual. His massive erection pressed against my stomach, pulsing whenever I pushed against it.

"Bower…" I moaned. I was rubbing myself against him. My body acting of its own accord, seeking relief.

For the first time, I wasn't embarrassed or shy about the reactions I was having. This was Bower. He'd seen me at my worst. I had a feeling this would be my best.

This was a new side of me, someone who didn't hesitate when it came to sex. Before, I'd always held back, never comfortable enough to make that big step. I'd even told Archer that I wanted to wait until we were married. He'd assumed it had to do with religious views, but really, I just hadn't been looking forward to that part of being married to him. I'd been trying to hold him off—hold any other guy I'd dated off because I just hadn't had those feelings. I hadn't felt comfortable enough with them to let them have all of me.

There'd always been something I felt was missing. I could never put my finger on it, never give it a name…but now I knew what it was.

I'd been waiting for Bower. He was my safe spot, my comfortable place.

Bower pulled away from my lips, panting, his forehead still pressed against mine. "Give me a minute," he said before letting go of my body.

I slumped over as he did, cold without his touch. He started lifting seat cushions on the bow, flipping them up and pulling out boards with attached cushions that made the front of the boat into a giant triangle-shaped bed. Bower grabbed me around the waist, pulling me in for another deep kiss before pushing me over onto the new bed he'd made. My knees hit the edge of the pads and I fell backward, letting my arms land splayed alongside my head.

"Fuck, Mia. You're so beautiful." Bower stood over me, adjusting himself in his pants again before crawling alongside next to me, pushing his body against mine.

I lifted my head to let his arm snake under, laying it back down against the muscles there that cradled me softly. With his other hand, Bower grabbed my jaw, pulling my lips over to his, kissing me as our bodies turned to face each other, like we were magnets snapping together. Our mouths continued to touch and explore while Bower's hand left my jaw and felt its way down my neck. It traced my collarbone, moving along the bone before dipping into the notch above my sternum. His finger circled the hollow there before following down to the softness of my belly. He had to have felt how fast my heart was beating and how rapidly I was breathing.

Bower didn't stop, though. He continued down toward my shorts, dipping between my legs, feeling the wetness that had only soaked further through my shorts. My arm shot out and grabbed his hand, stopping it from traveling any further.

"Is something wrong, Mia?" Bower pulled his face away from mine, looking at me with those big blue eyes like he'd done something to hurt me.

"No, no. Nothing's wrong," I said. "I…"

I didn't know how to explain this in a way that wasn't a turnoff. Bower probably expected me to be experienced—I'd been engaged earlier this month. But the truth was Archer and I had done nothing other than kiss.

I was completely new to all of this, all the feelings I was experiencing with Bower. I didn't know what I liked or didn't like. What Bower would like or wouldn't like. If I would even be good at sex. I had planned to ask Ruby for some tips and tricks before the wedding but hadn't gotten around to that yet.

"I don't know what I'm doing," I blurted out eventually. I breathed in deeply a couple of times, catching my breath from lifting the weight of that confession.

"What do you mean?" Bower asked.

Of course. Now I'd have to explain that I'd never done anything sexual with my fiancé. Today most people found that off-putting. Like I was a prude.

"I never did anything with…him."

"Never did…anything?" Bower pulled himself up onto an elbow, leaning over me with a confused look on his face.

Oh god, I was blowing it. The virgin completely turning off the experienced man. I tilted my chin up and looked up at the sky. Anywhere but Bower's face. "I'm sorry I led you on by wiggling on your lap earlier, but it felt so good—"

Bower put the tips of his fingers over my mouth, silencing my words. "You're a virgin?" he asked.

I nodded, his fingers still over my mouth.

"You're all mine?"

My eyes widened, and I lowered my head to see his reaction. Bower looked happy. No, he looked ecstatic.

"I didn't think…after all these years…" Bower dragged his eyes down my body, following the curve of my breasts, the flare of my hips, the muscles of my thighs. My entire body quivered as he looked. His face shot back up to mine. "We don't have to do anything if you don't want to."

I couldn't pull his hand off my mouth fast enough. "I want to, Bower, I want to."

Bower smiled, leaning into kiss me. "We'll go slow, I promise," he said.

I nodded eagerly.

"Let's start with a kiss." Bower leaned in and kissed me deeply. I kissed him back, my tongue wrestling with his.

"Can I touch you?" he whispered, motioning toward my breasts.

I nodded. He placed his hands gently on my shirt, feeling my breast through my clothing. My nipples responded to his touch, instantly hardening, poking through the fabric. Bower groaned as he watched the peaks appear beneath my shirt.

I watched him bite his lower lip as his hands rubbed them. I was getting turned on, watching his face and his reactions to exploring my body.

"Can I take your shirt off?" He helped me sit up and lifted my shirt up over my head. Cold air hit my stomach, causing goose bumps to pop up on my skin. I was wearing a sports bra, nothing sexy or enticing. I covered myself with my arms. Bower pulled my arms away from my body, shaking his head. "Don't cover yourself up, Mia. Let me see you."

I let Bower guide my arms away from my body, his hands holding my wrists at my sides. My nipples poked through my bra. Luckily it was dark so Bower couldn't see the deep blush I felt underneath my skin.

"So…fucking…beautiful." He looked up and down my chest, licking his bottom lip. "Can I?" He motioned to my bra.

There was no one here. Bower had made sure of that. It was just me and him.

I nodded, suddenly feeling brave. I pulled my wrists from Bower's grasp and crossed my arms in front of my body, gripping the bottom band of my bra and lifting it up and over my head. I felt my breasts bounce down once they left the fabric of the bra.

Bower let out a groan before I could get the bra up and over my head. As soon as the fabric pulled away from my eyes, I saw his face. He was enamored, and I felt powerful. Like I had the same hold over Bower that he had on me.

His hands clenched and opened at his sides as he stared. He was holding back. For me. I grabbed his hand and brought it to my breast. It was an invitation that was welcomed immediately, greedily.

I found myself flat on my back, Bower on top of me straddling my hips. His length pressed between our bodies, pulsing as his lips met the soft skin of my breast. He kissed each one before sucking my right nipple into his mouth. I gasped, arching my back bending into his mouth. His tongue licked my nipple circling it and teasing it.

"Does that feel good?" he asked, pulling off my breast.

"Yes," I said, looking down at him. So fucking good.

"Can I go lower?"

"Yes," I said again. My hips lifted to meet his. Another invitation. My center brushed against his length, only for a second before I gasped, dropping my hips back down to the bed.

Bower lowered himself, pressing his erection into me. "So willing. It's like your body knows exactly what it wants," he said.

I gulped, taking in his size as it pressed against me.

"Don't overthink it, Mia. I'll help you get ready." Bower left a line of kisses from below my breasts to the waistband of my shorts. He looked up at me from between my legs, asking permission before he peeled the shorts down my hips, revealing what was underneath. He pulled the shorts all the way down my legs, removing my boots before dragging the fabric off my feet and tossing it aside.

Bower bent my legs at the knee and propped my feet apart from each other, so I was on full display. I looked up at the sky, not wanting to see the look on his face as he took me in.

"Mia." His voice was commanding. My eyes snapped to his. "Look at me. You're beautiful. Perfect. I can't believe you're mine."

Bower leaned down and planted a kiss right in the hollow between my thigh and folds. I gasped, the feeling of his breath and lips so close to that area. "I'm going to touch you." His eyes glanced down between my legs.

I nodded again, so eager for his touch. I could feel wetness puddling out of me, dripping between my cheeks onto the bed he'd made.

He leaned over me, lying between my open legs, his hand falling down my thigh toward my center. "Eyes on me."

My eyes shot to his, his pupils large. I held my breath as his fingers traced over my folds and into the pool of wetness between my legs. Bower sucked in a breath, his eyes closing. I slammed my legs together against the sides of his body. Fuck, was something wrong?

"Shhhh, Mia." Bower's eyes opened, his fingers still between my folds. "This is all for me?" He moved his fingers up along my center, stopping at the top. I sucked in a breath, my back involuntarily arching at the sensation. "You're so wet." Bower let out a breath. "It's a fucking dream."

It was the reassurance I needed to continue breathing. His fingers pushed onto my clit, spinning tight circles against it. His rough fingertips massaged the spot until I was writhing against his hand, pushing the pace of his fingers faster, harder.

I was seeing black spots in my vision. The stars suddenly disappearing from the sky above me. "Ahh...*fuck*...Bower..." My voice wasn't my own.

"Yes, Mia, let it happen. You look so fucking good underneath me."

Something snapped inside of me. I blacked out, unaware of my surroundings, just pulsing with pleasure. If this was sex, why hadn't I had any sooner? My body deflated, like it had been holding that hostage for years.

Bower's face pressed against my neck as I recovered, his hand still between my legs. "Fuck, you look so hot when you come for me," Bower whispered in my ear.

I wiggled beneath him, his fingers moving between my legs, rolling them in the wetness I'd just created.

Bower stood up and pulled his shorts down with his thumbs, kicking them and his shoes to the side of the boat. He grabbed my thighs, pulling my body to the edge of the bed, then got onto his knees, his head poking between my legs. "You're so messy."

His face disappeared; I could only see the top of his head as he bent over between my legs. I scooted back when I felt his warm tongue parting my folds. Bower grunted impatiently as his hands reached up and planted on either side of my hip bones, pulling me back into place. They held me there, legs splayed open as Bower once again slipped his tongue between my folds. My body tensed, and the hand grip on my hips tightened.

I found myself holding my breath as he licked me from

bottom to top, teasing my clit with his teeth. I'd never felt anything like it before. The wet warmth of his mouth meeting the wet warmth between my legs. A moan left my lips when he let my clit pop out from between his teeth. He reassured me he was still there by sucking it into his mouth again, teasing it with his tongue.

Bower taunted me, using the suction of his mouth against the most sensitive part of me until the black dots started appearing again in my vision. My insides clenched like they had before. It was happening again. I dug my shoulders into the padding of the boat, arching my lower back from the cushion.

Suddenly Bower pulled his mouth away from me with a popping noise from breaking the suction.

I sat up on my elbows, the aching between my legs worse than ever. "What the heck, Bower?"

"You liked that, didn't you? You were almost there again." He stood up again, looking down at me, wide open just for him.

My eyes fell down to his shaft, still fully erect, with glistening drops of moisture on its tip. The size was shocking. Maybe it was because I've never seen one up close before. Maybe he was average. Although I highly doubted it.

"I want your next orgasm to squeeze my cock inside of you."

My breath hitched. This was it. The big moment. I wasn't scared; I was just nervous. Nerves were good. They meant that you were doing something that was important to you. Anything with Bower meant something to me.

"I don't have any condoms on the boat," Bower said.

"You don't keep a box handy for all your boat hookups?" I was teasing, mostly. I hoped he didn't have any boat hook ups.

"No, Mia, I don't hook up on boats. Not until tonight." Relief washed over me.

"I have an IUD," I offered. I'd had one since I was eighteen to combat the crazy period cramps I used to get.

"I got tested as soon as I got back this summer, and I haven't been with anyone since I came back home," Bower said. His hand grasped his erection, and he pumped the shaft a couple of times, creating new beads of moisture on the tip. I watched, fascinated.

Bower looked down, following my eye line, and smirked when he saw what I was looking at. "Eager, aren't you, Mia?"

My eyes shot back up to his. "I think I'm ready, Bower." I lay back, looking up at him. The man I'd compared every other man to since I met him. No one compared.

Bower put his hand on my inner thigh, waiting for my permission. When I nodded, he slipped his fingers between my wet folds and pushed one inside of me. I felt my body squeeze around his finger as it pushed deeper and deeper.

I looked down between our bodies, at his hand between my legs, his erection inches away. How was this going to work?

"Fuck, you're tight," Bower said as he withdrew his finger.

"Sorry," I said. I looked back up at his face, trying to read it.

Bower paused, his eyebrows furrowed. "What are you sorry about?"

"That I'm so tight and I don't know how this is going to work." I gestured toward his erection, bobbing between his legs.

"You're about to give me the best night of my life, and you're worried about being tight?" he asked.

I nodded. It seemed like a problem.

"Mia, look at me." Bower paused, waiting for my eyes to meet his. He brushed the hair from my forehead and tucked it behind my ear once they did. "It's going to work. Your body was made for me. I'm going to show you exactly what your body can do."

He leaned in and gave me another one of those kisses where our tongues battled between our mouths. We only separated when we were too out of breath to continue.

"Are you ready?" Bower asked.

I nodded. I didn't know how I could be any more ready.

"It's going to feel wet, maybe uncomfortable for you," he said.

I wasn't worried. There was no way I could feel any more uncomfortable than I already was. My body was buzzing with anticipation, begging to be released.

"I'll try to make the first part as painless as possible, but it's going to hurt for a second or two," Bower warned me.

My hands gripped his shoulders as he bent his head down and palmed his erection, guiding it toward my center. I felt his tip against me, pushing, stretching me open to accommodate his size. Nope, this wasn't going to work. Like he said, I was tight.

"Take a deep breath," Bower instructed. He grabbed the top of my thigh, using it to brace himself before he pushed his tip into me, stretching me. I sucked in a breath as he continued to push, the tip fully inside me.

He waited until I nodded, letting him know that I was ready. He gripped my thighs tighter before he plunged the rest of the way into me.

I gasped. I hadn't expected *that*. Tears crowded the corners of my closed eyes.

"Breathe, Mia. Give me a couple of deep breaths." Bower's voice brought me back, and I blinked open my eyes. His face was right in front of mine, his eyes searching my face for clues as to how I was feeling. "I'm sorry, baby. Sometimes it's best to just dive in the first time. It'll feel good soon."

I breathed in and out through my nose, trying to take in the new sensation that overwhelmed my entire body.

"It'll help if you try to relax around me." His hand moved from my thigh to my side, his thumb massaging the space below my belly button, trying to relax the muscles that had clenched at the unfamiliar intrusion.

I closed my eyes for a second, willing myself to relax. I felt everything loosen, slowly, then all at once. I could feel him inside of me, but it was no longer uncomfortable. The burning had subsided.

I wiggled underneath him, testing the new feeling between my legs.

Bower groaned. "Baby, you can't be doing that unless you want me to blow in the next thirty seconds." I froze underneath him. "I know you don't know what you're doing, but that felt fucking amazing."

"It did?" I asked. I wiggled my hips a couple more times.

"Every time you move it feels good," he said. "Let me help you feel good too."

Bower stood up, his shaft still inside of me. He lifted my legs up into the air, placing each of my ankles on his shoulders, my feet framing his face. *Oh. Oh fuck.* His tip hit something inside of me that felt—*oh.* He started moving, pulling out slightly before pushing back in, rubbing against that spot over and—*oh...*

"I can't—" Bower took my ankles from his shoulders and wrapped them around his waist, bending over and climbing onto the makeshift bed. He covered my body with his, nuzzling his nose into the side of my neck. "I can't be that far away from you."

I wrapped my arms around his chest, holding him close as he continued to move in and out of me. I reveled in every warm breath against my neck, every press of his lips against my skin, every word of praise he whispered into my ear.

You're taking me amazingly well, baby.

Just like that.

You have no idea what you're doing to me, do you?

"Bower," I moaned.

"Mia." He was panting, the veins in his neck large.

"Is it—" I swallowed some air, trying to take a breath. "Supposed to feel like this?"

"Feel like what, baby?"

"Like—" I couldn't breathe. My toes curled, and my stomach

tightened. I closed my eyes as my body shook. I could hear Bower groaning above me, his body slamming into mine at a fast pace.

Warmth filled my insides as Bower's shaft pulsed, my walls constricting around him. I twitched, quivering, like aftershocks of an earthquake. I blinked a few times, bringing myself back, my eyesight coming back into focus.

Bower hovered on top of me on his elbows, his warm breath against my cheek. "I've never come so hard in my life," he whispered into my ear, his breathing still labored.

I'd never had sex before, and now, after having sex with Bower, I knew I wanted it again—with him. I wanted to feel him near me, on top of me, moaning my name. It was addicting, the feeling of having Bower so close.

But soon he wouldn't be close. I'd be back home, spending the rest of the summer living in my parents' house preparing for the beginning of the school year. He'd be here at Agate Harbors, running the resort.

My vacation was ending, but I didn't want what Bower and I had started to finish.

Chapter Twenty-Nine

Bower

I hadn't said it just to inflate her ego. I'd never come that hard in my entire life. I'd seen stars, not unlike the ones in the sky above us. Mia had been amazing. This had been her first time, and as much as I'd tried to make it special, once I'd gotten inside of her, I'd barely been able to hold it together. Any move she'd made, her breasts bouncing along, had sent fireworks through my cock. She'd been *tight*. She'd told me she was a virgin, but shit, she'd fit me like a glove. I'd stretched her to my exact size, and I didn't want her to be resized by another man, ever.

She lay there beneath me now, trying to catch her breath. I knew she had come with me inside of her. I could feel her walls squeezing me as I'd come right along with her. *Shit*. I'd finished so hard there had to be a crazy amount of come inside of her right now. As soon as I pulled out of her, it would all leak out onto her skin. I rose above her, admiring her breasts on the way up.

Mia whimpered as my warm body left hers. I pulled my shirt up and over my head, tucking it between our bodies, underneath my cock.

"I'm going to pull out," I said, giving her a warning. Sometimes that was as jarring as the first time it went in.

She nodded, and I pulled out slowly, allowing her body to adjust to the emptiness. As soon as I was all the way out, I pushed the shirt against her, hopefully catching anything that would slip out of her.

Mia reached down and grabbed the T-shirt, holding it against herself as she sat up on her elbows, watching me.

"What?" I asked. I looked around the boat, trying to find our clothes.

"Sex is amazing," she said, her head cocked to the side. "What was I waiting for?"

I stopped looking for our clothes and stalked over to Mia. She sat up straight, her breasts bouncing at the sudden movement. I hadn't expected that confession from her. She'd been engaged. I'd assumed she test drove the goods before committing, but for whatever reason, she hadn't. *Thank God.*

I took her jaw in my hand and lifted her head so she could see me in the moonlight. "Me. You were waiting for me," I said. It meant something that I'd been Mia's first. And hopefully her last.

"I was," she whispered.

That was all I needed to hear. My lips crashed onto hers, our tongues playing in a way that made my cock start to rise again. No, I told myself. We couldn't again. It had been Mia's first time. She was probably sore and still working through the aftereffects.

I ended the kiss, pulling her forehead to my lips. Soon. Very soon I would be deep inside her again, listening to her call out my name.

I tossed Mia her clothes, and we both got dressed. I picked up my soaked and crumpled T-shirt we'd used to clean up and wiped down the bed I'd made in the bow of the boat. Chances were high Mia had bled a bit during sex, and I didn't want her to feel embarrassed if she spotted it.

After a quick wipe, I threw the shirt into the foot space beneath the driver's side and put the boards back beneath the seats. Mia watched me, trying to help, but I put her back in the passenger seat where she belonged.

I pulled up the anchor quickly, slapping mosquitos that landed on my bare back. The anchor had a bunch of weeds wrapped around it as I threw it onto the floor of the boat. I decided to leave it be. I didn't have time to pick it off before I became a buffet for the local mosquito population.

The key was still in the ignition. I turned it, expecting the engine to come alive. Nothing happened. I turned the key again, still nothing.

"Ah, fuck," I said aloud. The resort boats were old, and while we kept them in good condition, they could be finicky. Not what I needed right now.

I gave it another turn, and the motor sputtered to life, growling underneath us. I let out a sigh of relief. That would have been a tough phone call to make. Talk about a walk of shame.

Just then there was a loud pop, and the boat tremored beneath my feet. My ears rang with the loud noise, the sound echoing again and again inside my head. My knees fell to the floor right before I felt the bottom of the boat hit my face.

Then sand.

There was sand against my cheek. Hot sand. I had to keep my face pressed against it, keep my body low to the ground. The chin strap on my helmet dug into my skin, but I didn't dare move. Helicopter blades whirled in the sky above, more pops of gunshots in the distance.

"We're taking fire!" Gus yelled through my headset.

More gunshots over the radio. I clenched my teeth, my body tensing at each one. We had to do something, help our squad. I made a move to get up.

I felt a heavy hand on my shoulder. "We've got to follow orders. Stay down," Caleb said, lying in the hot sand next to me.

"It's fucking Gus!"

"I know, but we're no help if we're dead."

Caleb was right. I slumped back down into the sand, the errant pop of a gun getting less and less frequent.

We lay there waiting for the all-clear call on our radio. That had been close. Luckily the militants had moved in the opposite direction of Caleb and me. We'd been out scouting with no backup.

A staticky voice came in, stating the all-clear and asking for everyone to check in. We all did.

Gus's radio was silent.

We all knew what that meant.

I saw yellow rain boots when I opened my eyes, a warm hand rubbing my back. My back that was covered in cold sweat. I'd been back in the desert, in the sand, reliving the worst memories of my life. They hadn't felt traumatic when I'd experienced them. The constant adrenaline flowing through my veins had made it easy to brush it off and continue to the next stressful experience.

It wasn't until I'd come home that they'd started to hit me.

I was home, I remembered then. On the boat. With Mia.

I pushed myself up into a seated position. Mia's concerned face came into focus. I wiped the sweat off my forehead, my body still shaking from the episode. They always took a toll on my body. The amount of adrenaline flowing through my veins for even a few minutes wrecked my nervous system.

"Are you okay?" Mia asked, putting a hand on my shoulder.

I'd probably scared the shit out of her. It gutted me that she'd seen me like that. Not after what she'd just given me. I was supposed to be the one taking care of her, not a puddle on the bottom of the boat, shaking like a blithering idiot.

"I'm fine," I said, pushing her hand off my shoulder and standing up. I leaned against the steering wheel for a minute. The boat was still running. It must've misfired, creating the popping noise.

Mia held her hand to her chest like I'd bitten her.

"Let's go home," I said.

She stood and looked at me for a minute before sitting down in her seat, looking forward through the windshield.

I was ruining everything. We'd just had this magical moment under the stars. She'd given herself to me, and now I was fucking everything up. Well, I'd already fucked everything up the moment my body had hit the floor.

She was probably regretting giving me this chance—regretting any thought she'd had that we could be something together.

I was someone who people saw for a week and then didn't think about for a year. Everyone who came to Agate Harbors was transient, coming and going. They came for a break of fun and then left to return to their real lives. This wasn't Mia's real life. She had a life, a job in the Cities. What had I been thinking? That she'd leave her job, her friends, the only life she'd known to come up here and be with me?

She didn't need to deal with my issues. I'd had them mostly under control this week. My focus had been on her, and she'd placated my mind until tonight.

I'd come back broken from my time in the Marines. I knew that. I should've never allowed us to get that close. I'd taken her fucking virginity. But our chemistry was too strong. I'd let that get in the way of reality.

And now she was seeing my reality—what happened to me at any given time when there was a loud, unexpected noise. She'd never experienced this side of me, and I didn't want her to.

I'd probably just ruined everything we'd built together this week.

Chapter Thirty

Mia

My mind and body were still reeling from last night. Or early this morning, if we were being precise. Bower had dropped me off at the marina and let me find my way back to my cabin on my own. At that point the sun had started to rise, bathing everything in an orange glow. We hadn't exchanged a word since he'd driven us out of the secret bay. He wouldn't even look at me. I could tell his flashback had embarrassed him.

When he'd hit the floor of the boat after the engine had popped, I'd immediately known what was happening. I'd never seen one in person before, but I had read about them in my psychology classes in college.

I wasn't close to an expert, but Bower had all the telltale signs. He'd spent many years in the military. He hadn't shared much about his time overseas, but judging by the way his body had tensed and sweat had bubbled up from his skin, it hadn't been easy.

I wished he would feel comfortable opening up to me, explaining what was going on in his head, but he hadn't said anything, and I didn't want to push. I didn't like it when people poked around at me, asking me questions about why I was the way I was. I wasn't about to make him explain what was going on in his head to me. And I knew that sometimes somethings were just unexplainable.

I rolled over in bed. My body ached in the most delicious way. Bower and I had had sex last night. I was no longer a virgin. The clock next to my bed read three o'clock.

I'd finally fallen asleep at six this morning, after I heard my mom start the coffeepot. Ruby must've been keeping my parents away for the day. No way they would let me sleep until three in the afternoon otherwise.

Bower had been weird last night, but anyone would act differently after a panic attack. They needed time to decompress and recover. I understood Bower needed that. Hopefully ten hours was enough for him, because I already needed to see him again. Needed to feel his lips on mine.

If he thought one flashback was going to set me back, he had another thing coming. He'd accepted all my sensitivities, and I was more than ready to accept his. Knowing that he faced challenges like me made him more appealing, more interesting. It made me feel more connected to him, like I didn't have to push myself to be perfect either.

My feet hit the floor as I sat up, stretching my arms above my head. I felt that stretch between my legs. I was sore, but in a way it felt good—a reminder of last night, Bower pounding into me, my eyes rolling to the back of my head. Part of me was mad I had waited so long to have sex. I'd been missing out on so much all these years. But the other part of me was glad I'd waited. Bower had made it special, an experience I wouldn't have gotten with anyone else.

I was still wearing the clothes I'd come home in. They smelled like bonfire smoke and lake water, but I didn't have the energy to change last night.

I felt like a new person. Something about how Bower and I

had connected last night made me hopeful that we could make this work between us. There was something between us that neither of us could deny, and it had me thinking of what our relationship could be—our future together. Maybe it could be here, in my favorite place in the world…maybe it'd include fishing and kids and time spent on the lake.

I made quick work of changing clothes, throwing the smokey ones into a pile in the empty closet with my other dirty clothes. I pulled out a clean outfit from my suitcase and got dressed, tying my dirty hair up into a bun.

The cabin was quiet when I emerged. Hopefully I could grab something to eat and escape the cabin and my parents, who would no doubt want to know why I'd been out so late last night. I heard their muffled voices from the deck, through the sliding glass door.

I grabbed a muffin left over from breakfast sitting on the stove and drank some stale coffee right from the pot. Who was I? In one night, I'd lost my virginity and a need for cups.

I tiptoed through the cabin, sneaking out the front door, closing the screen door slowly so it didn't slam.

"You little tramp." I froze. Turning to find Ruby, standing in the grass just outside the cabin, a canned beer already in her hands. I guess it was past three, after all, and we were on vacation. "I had to tell Mom and Dad you weren't feeling well so they'd let you sleep."

"Thanks, Ruby," I said. I took a bite of my muffin and tried to act casual.

"You look different…" she said, her eyes narrowing.

"Whatever do you mean?" I asked as I took another bite, although my mouth was already full.

"I'd say it was the ten hours of sleep you just had, but I think it's something else…"

I swallowed the dry muffin, letting it scratch my throat on the way down.

"You had sex with him, didn't you?" she hissed.

I looked anywhere else but at Ruby. She knew me too well; my eyes would give me away in an instant.

"Look at me, Mia." On reflex, my eyes met hers. "You did!" Ruby jumped up and down, clapping her hands.

"Shh!" I threw my half-eaten muffin at her. She yelped as she dodged the blueberry confection. "Mom and Dad are right around the corner!"

"Heaven forbid they know that their middle-aged daughter had sex!" Ruby lowered her voice to a whisper-yell.

"First of all, I'm not middle-aged. Second, shut up." This time I dodged the muffin Ruby picked up from the ground and flung at me. The muffin hit the cabin, falling to the ground like confetti around me.

"Congrats, sister. You're finally grown."

I rolled my eyes and bumped Ruby's shoulder as I walked past her.

"Can I buy you a drink?" she asked before she tilted her head back taking the last sip of her beer. "As a congratulatory gift?"

I looked around the space in front of our cabin, standing on my tiptoes, hoping I'd see a tall man with a backward hat roaming around.

Ruby smirked. "You're looking for him, aren't you?"

"No, I'm not," I lied, crossing my arms in front of my chest.

"Someone's in *loooveee*," she sang.

"Stop it, Ruby."

"Can't go more than ten hours without getting your fix, huh?" She came up beside me, squeezing her hand beneath my bent elbow, pulling me toward the lodge. "Come on, lover girl, I'm buying you a drink. I'm sure we'll find your boyfriend on the way."

———

The entire lodge was decorated in red, white, and blue. I'd forgotten it was the Fourth of July. Arguably the most festive weekend up north. Your first time having sex would do that to you. I was thinking of little else other than the sex with Bower and the breakdown he'd had last night.

As soon as we walked into the restaurant, I looked for him, my search coming up empty. My shoulders dropped. He wasn't here yet. He'd show up—he had to. It was my last full day here.

The bar had pleated fan flags hanging on the U-shaped counter, and someone had hung rope lights along the ceiling of the bar that alternated between red, white, and blue bulbs. The folded chalk board signs advertised the drink special tonight as *Firecrackers*.

"Mia, Ruby!" I turned to see Chloe waving at us from a table with Caleb and Betty. They already had a basket of fried cheese curds steaming in the middle of the table. *Fuck yes.* I'd eat while I waited for Bower to show up.

My sister and I walked over, sitting down next to Caleb, and I dug into the basket without asking permission. Greasy food hit different after a late night. Never mind that this was basically my breakfast, at a time when it was nearly dinner for everyone else.

"I was just reminding Betty that next year I get to dress the baby up in a cute red, white, and blue outfit!" Chloe said, rubbing her hands over her baby bump.

"The baby…all this broad talks about is the baby," Betty said with a sigh, mostly to Ruby.

I tried to hold in my reaction. Bower's grandma had never talked like that before. Betty with dementia was sassy.

"It's more interesting than what you like to talk about, Betty," Chloe clipped back. "Walking uphill to school both ways."

I tried not to smirk. Oh, Chloe was a worthy opponent for Betty's sass. That must've been why she watched Betty so often.

"It was the snowstorm of fifty-seven, and the icicles were a foot long," Betty said. "We had to walk around with our eyes to the sky so we wouldn't get impaled."

"That sounds morbid," my sister said.

"That's a tame one. Stick around—Betty has some zingers," Chloe said, winking at Ruby.

Betty turned and looked at me, her face blooming into a big smile. "Mia!" she said. Everyone at the table froze, looking between the two of us.

"Hi, Betty," I said, smiling back. I didn't know why she always seemed to recognize me, but it made me feel special. Like I had back when I was having Popsicles with her.

"Stop by the cabin later. I have something for you," she said.

I nodded at her before she turned away, her face drooping, the lucid Betty retreating into herself, lost again. Everyone watched, sadness sweeping over the table when she was gone.

"It's the strangest thing that she recognizes you," Chloe said. "She hardly recognizes Gill anymore."

"Yeah, I don't know," I said between bites of cheese curds. "We've always had a connection when I was growing up, but I don't know why she would recognize me over her husband."

"Firecrackers for the table!" Dean brought over a tray of drinks from the bar.

It was the perfect distraction. Bower wasn't here, and it'd hurt to see that Betty wasn't aware of who she was sitting at a table with, besides me for that short moment. It was the Fourth of July—my favorite holiday. Part of me wanted to compartmentalize my worries for a little while, distract myself until Bower showed up and we could talk.

Dean set the drinks in front of us—it didn't slip past me he served Ruby's drink first. "Mocktails for the ones who are celebrating this holiday sober." He placed drinks in front of Chloe and Betty that looked identical to mine. "You guys ready to order?"

I put the last cheese curd in my mouth before I ordered everything fried from the menu.

———

Bower showed up to the bar right as I stuffed the last of my burger into my mouth. My stomach finally stopped growling at me, and I was on my second firecracker. I watched him check in with Dean and stop to shoot the shit with the regulars sitting around the bar. He didn't once look at me or our table.

"There's your man," Ruby whispered, looking over at him.

"I'm going to go say hi," I said, standing up. He must not have seen me yet. The bar and restaurant were busy. It was a holiday after all.

I stood at the edge of the bar, waiting for him to notice me. Dean saw me first, winking at me before tapping Bower on the shoulder and pointing at me. Bower wrapped up his conversation with a customer and came over to me, his face void of emotion.

I smiled at him as he put his hands on the bar and leaned against it, his short-sleeved Henley showing off his tattoos.

"What can I get you?" he asked. Like I was a customer, not the girl he'd just had sex with last night.

I frowned. Was he okay? Physically, he looked fine. He had his hat on backward, like usual. The scruff growing on his face looked a little longer than it had last night—like maybe he hadn't trimmed it this morning.

"We stayed out late last night," I said with a forced laugh, trying to sound laid back. "I didn't wake up until three this afternoon."

Bower looked at me, only blinking a couple times. We stared at each other, long enough without exchanging words that alarm bells rang inside my head. Something was wrong. Was he still suffering from the flashback? Was he having a hard time recovering? After what had happened last night, both the sex and his breakdown, he needed to talk to me—but he just stood there, waiting for me to tell him what I wanted to drink.

"What's the matter with you?" I asked.

A pained look briefly crossed his face, a twitch so slight that anyone else would have missed it. "Do you want another fire-cracker?" Bower asked.

I looked at him, dumbfounded. My jaw might have hinged open.

Was this the same man who'd called me "baby" multiple times last night while we'd been naked? I wasn't some sixteen-year-old girl with hearts in her eyes, and Bower wasn't some teenage punk who'd just wanted to get off. He was a grown man, and I was a grown woman. What we'd had last night wasn't some one-night stand. No matter what had happened last night, there was history between us. He couldn't just brush me off.

Someone across the bar called out for Bower, and he waved at them before turning back to me. "Let me know if I can get you anything." He looked at me for another second before turning around to tend to the customer.

Someone could've sunk a knife into my stomach and I would be in less pain than I was in now. What was going on? This wasn't Bower. What had happened between last night and now to make him act like this? Minus the flashback, he'd been fine. Quiet but fine.

I hadn't expected him to sweep me off my feet, bend me over, and kiss me in the middle of the bar, but a smile or a hug would've been nice. Any acknowledgment of what had happened last night.

I walked back to the table and fell into my seat, my butt hitting the chair with a thud. The entire table, minus Betty, looked over at me.

"He wanted to know if I needed another drink," I said by way of explanation for my loud return to the table.

"What?" Ruby asked.

"He asked if I needed another firecracker."

"Wait, I'm so confused."

"So am I," I said. "We had such a nice night, and now he acts like he doesn't know who I am."

"Did something happen last night? You know, besides…" Ruby wiggled her eyebrows at me.

"I mean, the boat misfired on our way back and he had a panic attack," I said. "I helped him come out of it. I thought we were fine, more than fine, but now he won't talk to me."

Caleb's entire body language changed. He tensed up, and his legs started bouncing under the table, making the entire tabletop shake.

"Caleb?" I asked. He obviously wanted to say something.

"It's not my place to say anything, but I might have some insight for you," he said. He glanced at the bar, looking at Bower, who was elbows deep in the ice well.

"I think it's time to go home and have some tea," Chloe told Betty, standing up, pushing the chair out from the table. "She gets temperamental in the evenings," Chloe whispered to the table. "Well, it's been a fun night. So nice to see everyone."

"If that's your idea of a fun night, I feel sorry for you," Betty grumbled, walking alongside her toward the door.

I watched them leave before turning back to Caleb. Everyone was acting so weird tonight.

"Chloe always gets uncomfortable when I talk about my time over there." Caleb waited for her to leave the bar before he continued. "We all brought home a lot of baggage. Chloe's seen what I've been through since I've been back. It affects all of us differently. I can only tell you my perspective."

He let out a breath, his hands rubbing his face. "Bower and I served together in the same platoon over in Syria. We'd go on daily patrols around the city. We were meant to be there, visible to the citizens, backing up our Syrian partners who'd eventually fully take over the daily patrols," he said. "Every day we'd dress for battle—we had to be prepared for the worst-case scenario, but of course that didn't happen every day. We'd be out there day after day for months patrolling, staying vigilant. We'd walk for hours waiting for something to happen. For someone to shoot at us, for an explosive to drop. Usually nothing happened, but we always knew it could. We were always 'on,' prepared, anticipating something horrible happening to us. We listened to gunshots take out our friends." He paused. "Losing Gus was the hardest."

Caleb took another moment and a deep breath. "Day after day, we would wait for something to kill us. Luckily nothing did, and we left the service physically unscathed. But I still feel like I'm waiting. I haven't been able to turn off that switch. I'm constantly on edge, waiting for something terrible to happen."

"That sounds miserable," Ruby said.

"I mean, it can be, but I've got Chloe to lean on. She's been there through my transition back to civilian life. It's getting better. The job Bower gave me keeps me busy."

"Who does Bower have to lean on?" I asked.

Caleb shrugged. "I'm here if he ever wants to talk. He hasn't said much about our time serving since we've been back. He's been closed off about the whole thing, not wanting to bring attention to it."

"Well, shit, he must be dealing with some stuff right now," Ruby said.

"Like I said, everyone brought something home, some sort of baggage. For me it's sand. I can't feel that fucking stuff on my skin. It brings me back to places I don't want to revisit."

"I get that," I said, smiling knowingly at Caleb. "The sand bothers me too."

He smiled back. "Maybe you can get Bower to talk to you about it?"

"I'd love to," I said, "if he'll talk to me about something other than what I'm drinking…"

"When I got back, Chloe did a bunch of research and found some good veteran organizations that would point him in the right direction if he decides he needs help," Caleb said. "I could pass those along to you."

I nodded. Sure, if I could ever get Bower to talk to me again. I looked over at the bar. Dean was the only one standing behind it.

———

It was dark again. The resort was still awake, everyone waiting for fireworks to begin.

I needed to find Bower and shake him, hug him, whatever would make him talk to me. I wasn't going to let him go, get away without talking to me about what was going on. His cabin was the first place I'd look.

"Where are you going, Mia?" Chloe's voice startled me. I turned to see her and Betty on the rocking chairs on the porch outside the lodge. "Fireworks are about to start—wouldn't want to miss them." She motioned to an empty chair next to her. "Come sit with us. We have the perfect view."

"Thanks, Chloe, but I'm actually looking for Bower."

"It's that time, isn't it?"

For the fireworks show? I nodded absentmindedly, walking closer to the porch. Mosquitos and moths hit the outdoor lights repeatedly, trying to get closer to the warm bulb. I turned and waved, walking in the direction of his cabin.

"Mia?"

I stopped and looked back at Chloe, who'd gotten up from her rocker. "I don't know if you're going to like what you see."

My steps hastened, breaking out into a jog. What was Bower doing at his cabin? A loud pop filled the air right before red sparks filled the sky. The beginning of the firework show.

Bower's cabin was dark. Not even the outside light was on. I knocked on the door twice, waiting for an answer.

Tentatively, I tested the door handle, and it opened. The main room of the cabin was dark. Only the green light from the digital clock on the stove lit the space.

I stepped inside, letting my eyes adjust. It was even darker in here than it was outside. Another firework popped, the sparks crackling in the sky as they disappeared.

The sound of running water filled the silence after the explosions of the fireworks faded. I took a quick look at the sink, but it was off.

Stepping further into the cabin, I followed the sound. I pressed my ear against the bathroom door, hearing the shower running, streams of water steadily hitting the fiberglass sides. If someone was taking a shower, there would usually be breaks in the stream of the water as they washed themselves, loud splashes coming off their hair and body. Something wasn't right.

I twisted the handle of the bathroom door, and just like the front door, I met no resistance. It was even darker in here without the lights from the appliances. The overhead fan roared, trying to keep up with the fog the hot water created in the tiny bathroom.

My hand felt the wall for the light switch, flipping it up as soon as I found it. The bathroom was full of steam from the shower, the mirror completely fogged over. Three dull pops sounded from outside, more fireworks. The bathroom was empty. The only place left was the shower.

I grabbed the fabric of the shower curtain, taking a deep breath and exhaling before I pulled it to the side. A wet, curled-up Bower sat over the drain. His knees pulled up to his chest, his arms wrapped around his shins. He was soaked, still in his Henley and blue jeans. His hair was sopping, streams of water dripping off it down his face. His eyes were closed, his eyelashes clumped together. Rapid pops of fireworks made Bower flinch, his arms pulling his knees even closer to his chest.

"Close the door!" he shouted, water spraying from his lips.

I reached behind me and swung the bathroom door shut, letting the steam engulf me. I didn't know what to say or what to do. Did he do this every week?

I reached out to touch his shoulder. The water was warm, but for probably not much longer. Bower flinched as I set my hand on his wet shirt. I pulled my hand away quickly, not wanting to cause him more distress than he was already in. Caleb had warned me about this, how he and Bower were different since they'd gotten back, but I hadn't realized how bad it was for Bower. He'd given me very few signs he suffered this deeply, other than the misfiring boat last night.

I crouched down next to the shower. "What can I do to help you?" I asked.

"Leave," Bower said.

"I'm not going to do that, Bower."

"You're leaving tomorrow anyway, Mia. You won't be back for another year. Just leave now and save us both the misery."

"I can come back to see you," I said. "You could visit me once the season dies down. It doesn't have to end tomorrow."

"You don't fucking get it, Mia! Look at me! Look at me!" Bower turned his head toward me, eyes bloodshot, water streaming down his cheeks, mixing with tears.

I looked at him, right in his eyes. They didn't have that twinkle that I was used to seeing. He looked broken and exhausted.

"We don't have a future together. I could never marry you, never have kids. Think fireworks are bad? Imagine me with a crying baby. I'd probably fucking jump off a cliff or shake the baby to make it stop."

I reached out again, pausing before I made contact, my hand hovering in the air between us. Bower was thinking long-term for us. Marriage. Children.

I set my hand on his shoulder. "It wouldn't be like that, Bower. We'd figure something out, get you help."

"There's nothing that can help me, Mia. Even you can't fix what's wrong with me. I've got PTSD that's never going to go away." Bower shrugged my hand away. "I'm wrong for you in every way. The boat last night made me see that. It's not fair to you to be stuck with a man like me. Can't even deal with a boat misfiring without going into a full-blown panic."

"That was one time—"

"One time in one week. How many times in a month? A year? A lifetime?" Bower looked back at the shower floor, watching the water fall down the drain. "I shouldn't feel like this." He wiped his nose with the back of his hand. "I got out of there intact. Others didn't. I'm lucky."

"Caleb said he knows places that can help you," I told him. "Let us help you."

"No one can help me," he said. "Don't try to be a martyr for me, Mia. Don't give up what you want out of life for me. I saw you with the kids the other day. You're so good with them. You'd be such an amazing mother. I can never give that to you. It would kill me every day I was with you to see you give up that part of your life. You deserve children, Mia. Happiness."

"Then get help, Bower. Find something that works for you so you can give me that. I want you—all of you. I couldn't imagine doing that part of my life without you. I want our kids to grow up running around the resort, growing up like we did."

"I can't, Mia," he said. "No one can fix what's broken inside of me. Just leave. Please."

"I'm not going anywhere."

"*Fucking leave, Mia!*" Bower roared.

I couldn't hear the fireworks or the water hitting the walls of the shower over his voice. He'd never talked to me like that before. There was a level of hatred in his voice that I wasn't used to.

My eyes closed on reflex. I didn't want to see him like that. That wasn't who he was.

I slowly opened my eyes, watching Bower sink back into himself. The water from the shower had to be cold by now, but he didn't show it. He sat there like a stone, letting the water flow off him and down the drain.

"Is this it, Bower? Is this the end?" I asked, knowing I wouldn't get a response. He was too far gone, retreated within himself with no escape route.

It killed me he'd thought about our future—marriage, children—and already counted himself out, unworthy or unable. He'd had all these conversations with himself instead of with me. That wasn't fair. To him or to me.

I'd imagined myself with him before, what our future would be. Our children running around the resort, growing up knowing how to fish, playing in the sand, maybe with rain boots on.

He'd dismissed everything tonight. Every notion that'd we'd have a future together. It was him giving up on us, not me. If he wanted me to leave, then I would.

I stood up, looking down at him, still huddled in a ball under the water. I wanted to hold him and sit under the water with him until he was okay, but he didn't want that. I knew enough about anxiety that I respected that. I was very much uneducated in everything PTSD-related. When I thought of someone with PTSD, I assumed they were constantly suffering, unable to go about their daily lives. For Bower and Caleb, PTSD reared its ugly head at the most inopportune times.

I was sure Bower would much rather be helping Dean at the bar right now than sitting in his shower with his clothes on, trying to drown out the noise of the fireworks. I was sure Caleb would love to spend time on the beach with his wife and soon-to-be daughter, building sandcastles and enjoying the water. PTSD had stolen that joy from them, their freedom.

And now, it seemed, PTSD was going to steal Bower from me.

Chapter Thirty-One

Bower

Last night I'd let the cold water flow over me. Part of me had enjoyed the stream of water pelting my body. It'd provided me with another sensation other than the anxiety pounding my body with every pop of a firework that had shot into the sky.

Of course, I knew they were fireworks, but that didn't make it any easier. They sounded just like gun shots, and gun shots brought me back there, to places I didn't want to go that made my heart beat out of my chest and sweat cover my body. Nothing could change this. Every Friday I was there, shower on, fan on, door closed, hiding from the noise and the memories that clung onto me, refusing to leave.

Mia had tried to help me; she'd showed up and tried to rescue me from the panic I'd been feeling.

She was trying, but I couldn't let her in. I didn't want her to get sucked into my life, no matter how badly I wanted her to be a part of it.

I wanted things with her I could never have. Things I could never give her. Mia wanted a family; she wanted a supportive partner—something I could never be. There'd always be that loud sound out of left field that took me out. I'd have to avoid fireworks for the rest of my life. No late nights at the ballpark, no Disney World firework shows or shooting off rockets on the Fourth of July with my kids.

I'd tried to explain that to her the best I could last night, and I'd ended up yelling at her. Me pushing her away was what was best for Mia. She was leaving and would go back to her real life, which differed completely from the resort fantasy life she lived once a year. She deserved her real life, not being stuck in a false fantasy with a fucked-up boyfriend.

There was a strange tapping sound. I lifted my head from my pillow. It must've been the breeze hitting a branch against my window. I laid my head back down onto the wet pillow. I hadn't changed out of my clothes after getting out of the cold shower, just climbed under the covers.

"Bower?" Mia's voice traveled through the door. "I know you're in there."

I lay there frozen. I was both embarrassed about last night and embarrassed that I was still lying in bed this morning, instead of going after her before she left.

"I'm about to leave, and I…I don't want to." I could hear her feet shuffling on the step. "I don't want to leave like—when we're like this."

I sat up slowly. My body ached from the way my muscles had clenched last night. "Mia…" I started.

"Bower, I just want you to talk to me."

"Don't keep your family waiting," I said.

"They're fine—"

"Mia, what you saw last night. That's me. That's my reality every Friday—sometimes other days too. Anything can set me off." I kept my eyes on the floor. I couldn't bring myself to look toward the door, where I might see the shadow of her feet beneath the threshold. "I don't know why I thought I could be with you…be normal with you."

"Bower—"

"That was my mistake, my fault. I shouldn't have taken your virginity, taken that away from you. I didn't deserve to."

I could hear Mia sniffling from the other side of the door. I couldn't stand that sound.

"I think you should go." I raised my voice. "Go home and find someone who isn't a fuckup like me."

"Do you really mean that?" Mia asked, her voice wavering.

"*Yes!*" I shouted. If this was what it took to push her away, then I would.

Something clattered across the hardwood floors, rolling and bouncing along the planks.

I stood up in my chilled, wrinkled clothes. I should've dried myself off or at least taken my clothes off before I climbed into bed last night. I just hadn't had the willpower.

The lamp next to my bed had a pull chain, and my hand fumbled to find it in the dark. When I found the metal ball, I pulled down quick, turning the light on, illuminating the room. In the middle of the floor was a red, smooth pellet—some sort of rock.

I picked it up, turning it over in my hand. An agate.

A strip of light shone from under my front door, the gap I'd been meaning to fix with rubber weather stripping. She'd slid the agate beneath my door.

The agate was red, with lots of different bands. It was warm against my skin, like it had been in her hand.

A memory played behind my eyes. Mia and me on the boat fishing, Mia and me laughing at something that really wasn't all that funny, Mia and me building cairns along the lake. Her placing the exact agate I had in my hand on top of her cairn.

She'd kept it. For fourteen years, she'd kept it with her.

Where had this rock been all these years? The bottom of a drawer? Tucked away in the back of a closet?

No, that she had it here with her on vacation meant that she kept it somewhere close. Maybe a purse. She'd carried a piece of me, a piece of Agate Harbors, with her all those years.

I stumbled toward the front door, twisting the knob, and pushing the door open. It slammed against the side of the cabin before bouncing back and hitting me in the chest. I scanned the area, hoping to catch a glimpse of her blonde ponytail swaying back and forth.

She wasn't there.

I curled my fingers around the rock in my palm, gripping it tightly in my hand, feeling the warmth of the rock that had come from her body. This was for the best. She deserved better than me.

Car engines roared as guests left Agate Harbors. It was checkout day.

The week was over.

Mia was gone.

———

"B4." I was less than enthused, and the crowd knew it. "B4."

"Bingo!" A female voice rang out from the crowd. My head shot up, as if it could possibly be Mia.

These days any female voice would do it—make me turn around, stop any conversation I was having to see if it was *her*. It never was. I deflated each time it wasn't her, shrinking further into myself.

She was gone. She had left two weeks ago and wasn't coming back. I let the agate I kept from her fall through my fingers inside the pocket of my shorts. It was the only thing that grounded me nowadays.

I handed out a coupon for a free Popsicle to the winner. We had an awful amount of orange Popsicles in our freezer. It was everyone's least-favorite flavor. Every time I restocked the freezer, they sat there as a reminder that Mia wasn't here to eat them.

"That concludes our bingo game," I said, monotone. "We'll be tie-dying shirts later today, at two o'clock at the lodge. See you all there."

I couldn't put enthusiasm into my voice. I had one tone these days: boring.

Chloe had told me I looked miserable the other day. She wasn't wrong. I was the guy who'd lost the love of his life, who had a grandmother who was disappearing before his eyes, and who had a struggling resort to run. Things just weren't going my way.

Grandma had been getting worse. She hadn't recognized me in weeks. Grandpa had been off fishing on the lake more than ever. The resort was almost entirely being managed by me. I could lie and say it was going well, but it wasn't. Thank God I had Caleb and Dean holding the resort together. Dean kept the drinks flowing, and Caleb kept the toilets flushing. Chloe had been a godsend too. She'd taken over much of the care of my grandma, even though she was due any day.

"How'd bingo go?" Caleb asked as he caught up with me on my way back up to the lodge. He had a plunger slung over his shoulder, like a lumberjack with an axe. A real Paul Plumber.

"As good as you'd imagine," I said. I carried the bingo supplies in a crate, ready to shelve them until next week.

"Bower, stop." Caleb grabbed my arm, willing me to stop my stomp back up to the lodge. "You've been moping around this place since she left."

"I fucked up, Caleb," I said. "I let everything get the best of me."

Only Caleb knew what I meant when I said *everything*. He knew what *everything* was, how it affected me daily. I knew it affected him too, just not the same way.

"Did you explain to her what was going on?" he asked. "I'm sure she'd understand."

"I did. I told her I wasn't going to be able to make her happy."

"You said *what*?" Caleb asked. "Bower, you could make her happy. You could have a wonderful life together if you got the help—"

"No one's going to be able to help me!" I snapped.

"If you're yelling at me, I think you should give therapy, a support group a try," Caleb said. His calm tone only further infuriated me. "You shouldn't be this angry, this upset. You shouldn't lose the girl over this. Mia's like Chloe. She wants to help, to understand you. It's *you* getting in the way of that."

I threw the crate onto the ground. It landed with a loud thud, the metal ball cage making the loudest screech. I hoped it broke. I hoped I never had to run a game of bingo ever again.

The lodge wasn't far away. I stomped over there, not looking back if Caleb was following me. Anger and embarrassment steamed inside of me. My friend had called me out. Everything he said was true, even if I didn't want to believe that just yet.

A gust of wind blew the towels that were hanging on the clothesline. Grandpa was standing behind them, a clothespin in his mouth. There he was, carrying on the love of his life's tradition of fresh air-dried towels, even when she couldn't.

"Bad game of bingo?" Grandpa asked as I stomped past him. I felt like I was six years old all over again, mad about something trivial yet still important to someone who was six. "Say, I thought I'd see Mia around here still."

I stopped stomping and dug my shoes into the grass. He knew Mia had left, but I'd been avoiding him for the past two weeks.

"Mia went home," I said.

"Why, Bower?"

I turned around. "Because I'm fucked up, Gill."

Grandpa paused and visibly let out a breath before tossing the clothespin he had in his hand into the basket of freshly washed towels. He walked over to me, standing before me, looking up. I had been taller than him since I was fifteen, although that never intimidated him.

Grandpa pressed his index finger into my chest. "Get help, or lose her." He pressed his finger harder. "This'll be the biggest mistake of your life, Bower. Forget getting arrested—this one will haunt you forever."

I recoiled like I'd been struck, his words hitting me harder than a hand ever could.

Chapter Thirty-Two

Mia

I'd said goodbye—it wasn't one of those good goodbyes where you got closure and felt good about leaving. It'd felt unfinished and uncomfortable. I'd knocked on the door, even knowing that he wouldn't answer. And that was okay. Bower hadn't been in a place where he'd wanted to talk to me. I couldn't help someone who wouldn't accept it. As much as I wanted to hug him and tell him everything would be okay, I didn't know if it would be.

He wouldn't let me help him or attempt to find someone that could. I knew how tough it was to ask for help, but if he wanted to find strategies to cope, he needed to ask. I might not be there when he was ready, but I knew he had Caleb and Chloe. Dean would be there too. He had people around, people he could confide in.

That no longer included me.

I'd left him with an agate—the one I'd kept in my purse all these years. Part of me wanted to leave every piece of Agate Harbors behind completely. I didn't know how I'd ever go back.

So when I left, I'd tossed the agate beneath his door and run.

The drive home from Agate Harbors had been awful. My

parents, surprisingly, had picked up on my bad mood and asked after Archer, and that was when I'd bitten the bullet and told them we'd officially ended things. There'd been no escaping their disapproval for hours.

The house had been quiet since we'd gotten back. I'd kept to myself, hiding out in my bedroom—the one I'd slept in since I was a kid—trying to avoid my parents. It was going to be my room for the foreseeable future now that the wedding had been called off.

It was mid-August, and I was back at school preparing for my new students. Beginning a new school year had always made me happy. Opening the door to my first-grade classroom had always brought me infinite amounts of joy. All the crisp notebooks, crayons that still had their paper wrapped around them, pencils that all had a freshly sharpened point. It was supposed to be a fresh start—though this year, it felt like I was stagnant, stuck.

But this summer was over. Done and dusted. Filed away with the warning tags of *Do not open. Forget this ever happened.*

I busied myself with all the tasks that came with setting up my classroom for a new school year. There were desks to arrange, name tags to write, a whole packet of information about the new statewide tests we'd be giving a couple months into the school year. Instead of invigorating, this year my to-do list felt daunting.

I spent so much of my time teaching kids to memorize so they'd do well on tests, and that wasn't why I'd wanted to be a teacher. Kids learned so much better when they could explore with their hands—playing and creating was so much more important than being able to spit out numbers and use simple recall skills.

That was why I'd particularly enjoyed helping Bower out with Kids Camp this summer. The kids were doing what they were meant to be doing: Having fun. Playing. There was just as much learning going on as there was with a pencil and paper.

Memories of Kids Camp and holding Bower's hand during red rover flooded my brain. It had been the first time we'd touched, felt that static flowing through our bodies into each other's.

I needed cobwebs over these memories, stat. Bower didn't want a relationship with me. He'd all but physically pushed me away from him.

The principal got on the loudspeaker and announced an all-staff meeting in the library and to bring the packet of testing information with us, maybe also a pen to take notes with. *Ugh.* This was bound to last at least half of the day. I'd have to stay late tonight arranging my classroom.

The library was on the other side of the school. I walked down the first-grade hallway, the empty walls soon to be decorated with colorful artwork. Chairs and tables were still stacked in the lunchroom, waiting for the janitorial staff to unstack them for the hungry kids, who would complain about how they were serving steamed broccoli for the third time this week. Sunlight streamed in through the large windows at the front of the school.

A small woman paced outside in front of the doors, pulling on the handle and jiggling the lock. I hesitantly got closer. The doors were locked for safety. All the staff had a key card to get in. Was she a new staff member who hadn't received her key card yet?

I cracked the door open a bit. The woman was already turning to walk away from the building. "Can I help you?" I asked.

She turned around, startled by my voice. I also got a surprise. "Betty?"

She looked a little older, a little more tired, but it was Betty. She looked out of place here. I had never seen her anywhere other than Agate Harbors.

"Mia!" Betty walked toward me, her shoulders back, standing straighter. She pulled me in for one of her amazing hugs.

I hugged her back, squeezing my eyes shut. Tears threatened to spill from my lids. I'd needed this hug. It felt like an apology for Bower, even though she knew nothing about what happened between us.

"What are you doing here?" I asked, my chin still resting on her shoulder. I pulled myself away and out of the haze of the hug. Wasn't someone supposed to be watching her? How did she get here, four hours away from her home?

"I-I don't know," Betty said. She looked at her feet, then around her, suddenly confused. "What am I doing here? Where am I?"

She was starting to panic. I could sense it by her body language and the way her voice raised an octave higher.

I grabbed her hands and held them in mine. "It's okay, Betty. You're here now, safe with me. We'll get it figured out."

I led her into the school, using my key card to unlock the door that had closed behind me. She gripped my hand tightly, like she'd sink down into the depths of her mind if she let go.

I brought her to my classroom. The school was quiet, all the teachers already gathered in the library. With every step we took, I heard a strange rattling noise. I paused a couple of times, looking around to see what the noise was and where it was coming from.

I walked Betty over to my desk, helping her sit down, making sure she landed squarely on the seat. As soon as she sat, the sides of her pants sank low, the fabric stretching unnaturally toward the ground.

"Betty," I said, still holding her hands in one of my own. "What's in your pockets?"

She lifted one of her hands out of mine and reached into her pocket. The same rattling sound met my ears as she sifted through it, a perplexed look on her face.

Her hand emerged closed around an object. She held her hand between us, slowly unfurling her fingers. In the center of her palm was a rock, a white one with tiny black speckles dispersed throughout. She set it on my desk, her hand digging back into her pocket, coming out with another rock and then another. I watched as she pulled rock after rock out of her pockets, lining them up on my desk. They all were so different. Some had tiny sparkly crystals, and others were matte tan and looked like sand squished tightly together.

I didn't have words as I watched her, and she didn't give me any explanation either. When her pockets were empty, she looked at me, smiling. "Mia," she said, reaching out her hands again for mine. I watched her face go from perplexed to content. "I have something for you back at my cabin." She said it like she hadn't just emptied fifteen rocks from her pockets.

"Your cabin is four hours away, Betty," I reminded her.

"I looked you up in the reservation system. This is the address it said. I took the bus and found you."

I blinked at that and then realized—the bachelorette party I'd planned. I'd used the school's address instead of my parents'. That seemed like a lifetime ago.

"You did, Betty. You found me. I'm glad you did." I tried to take a breath and release it slowly, like I'd learned to do in my own therapy. Betty was in crisis right now. Her family had to be looking for her.

"He needs you."

I stopped breathing as she said those words. Her eyes were those that I remembered. It was like looking at a glimpse of who Betty used to be. The kind, warm woman who'd accepted me when no other adult had.

"Why don't you sit here for a bit, Betty?" I said. "I need to make a phone call."

She nodded and began stacking the rocks, balancing one on top of another on the surface of my desk. I paused a moment before I walked away, making sure she was content and would stay. I opened my phone and pulled up the number to Agate Harbors.

While we waited, I let Betty stack rocks on my desk and offered her what little food I'd found in the teachers' lounge. My principal stopped by my room after I hadn't shown up to the staff meeting. She saw Betty sitting in my classroom and, after I explained the situation, gave me the rest of the day off, promising to send a recap email of the meeting I'd missed that I was sure would be just as fascinating as the real thing.

All the while, Betty didn't seem to recognize me or even acknowledge my presence. I watched her, though, not letting her out of my sight.

My phone buzzed. It was Gill, calling me to let me know he was here. It'd only taken him three and a half hours to get here, even driving through cabin traffic. I didn't want to know how many traffic laws he'd broken to manage that.

I grabbed my purse and phone before I slowly led Betty through the school and out the front doors. The rest of the teachers had called it a day, and the school was empty.

Gill was outside the doors, pacing. He rushed to Betty when I swung open the door and led her outside. She cringed, squeezing my hand tightly as her husband approached. I cringed too as Gill stopped, backing off as soon as he realized his wife was uncomfortable with him being so close. To see two people who'd loved each other so fiercely, so completely be now so inaccessible to each other was difficult to watch.

Behind them I saw a flash of blond hair. It was lighter than when I'd left a month and a half ago. Bower had come with his grandpa. It shouldn't have surprised me—of course he'd come help his grandpa—but seeing him in person again had all those feelings I'd tried to tuck away flooding through my veins. The fast drive time made more sense now too.

He occasionally glanced at his grandparents but kept his eyes on me. I tried my best not to fidget beneath his stare.

"I'm so sorry, Mia," Gill started. "Chloe had her baby, and we haven't been able to find reliable help to watch her."

I shook my head, pulling my eyes away from Bower. "It's not a problem. Really." I guided her hand toward Gill's, trying to hand her off to him.

She pulled back, stepping away. "Who are these people you're giving me to?" Betty cowered next to me, folding in on her herself, trying to use me as a shield against Gill and Bower, the very people who loved her deeply.

"I know it's hard to understand, but that's your husband and your grandson. They're going to take you home," I explained. I tried to be calm, looking her in the eyes and holding her hands in mine.

"No!" Betty yelled. "I'm not going with them!"

She pulled me back toward the school doors, letting go of my hands to yank on the locked handles. The doors rattled as she shook them.

Gill looked down at his feet, his hand coming up to his eyes. He didn't like seeing his wife like this. Unrecognizable. Someone he didn't know and someone who didn't know him.

Bower came up behind Betty, putting his hands on her upper arms, trying to guide her away from the school doors and toward the car. She swatted at him, screaming that she was getting attacked. He backed away slowly with his hands up. We all knew he wasn't hurting her, but the accusations were painful.

I felt a tear roll down my cheek. Watching this was excruciating. There was nothing Bower or Gill could do. She didn't know them. It felt to her like she was being kidnapped, being brought to an unknown destination with unknown people against her will.

"Hey, Betty?" I asked tentatively, walking toward where she stood breathing heavily, holding on to the handles of the door. Her knuckles were white, her face covered in beads of perspiration. She was so worked up. She wouldn't be leaving with either of them. Not alone. "Can I take you home?"

Betty looked up at me, her eyes empty and her lip trembling. I peeled her hands off the door handle and held them gently in mine, trying to let her know that she could pull away if she wanted to. I wasn't forcing her to do anything.

"I'd love a Popsicle," I said. "Can we have one when we get home?"

Betty cocked her head to the side, the look of recognition suddenly appearing on her face. "I'm sure I have an orange Popsicle buried in the freezer," she said.

I smiled at her, squeezing her hand slightly. "These are going to be our drivers, okay?" I gestured to Bower and Gill.

She looked at them and back at me before nodding. They both headed to the car that was still running in front of the school, pulled up in the bus turnaround.

I helped Betty into the car, climbing into the back seat with her. I made sure she was buckled before nodding to Bower, who eyed us in the rearview mirror. Gill turned around and gave me the softest of smiles.

With Betty's hand still in mine resting on top of the middle seat between us, we turned onto the highway that led us north.

Apparently my summer wasn't over just yet.

Chapter Thirty-Three

Mia

Betty clung to me the entire ride up to Agate Harbors. I sat in the middle seat next to her. Bower drove, slower this time, with Gill in the passenger seat. It was a quiet ride, a country-music station playing softly in the speakers.

I tried not to look too often in the rearview mirror. Every time I did, Bower's eyes met mine, and I had to quickly look away, warmth filling my cheeks. We hadn't talked since he'd told me to leave.

He hadn't called or anything since. Not that I expected him to. If Betty hadn't shown up here today, I wasn't sure I would have ever seen him again. After this summer, I hadn't planned on ever returning to Agate Harbors.

A wave of dread came over me as we drove under the resort's sign. I was returning to the place I couldn't get away from fast enough a month and a half ago. Everything I'd felt driving home that day surged through my body. The loss, the disappointment, the anger.

As soon as Betty was comfortable back at home, I would leave. How was I going to get back to the Cities? I didn't have a car. *Damnit.* I hadn't thought this through at all. Maybe I could use the same car service that Ruby had called all those weeks ago to take me back.

Anxiety shot through me as I visualized my empty bank account. I was still living with my parents, but I didn't have the money for a four-hour car service. Calling my parents or Ruby was out of the question. They'd ask too many questions.

Slow down, Mia. One thing at a time.

Bower pulled his car up to the lodge, and Chloe ran outside, a tiny infant strapped to her chest.

"Is she okay?" Chloe pulled open the door, looking into the car. "Thank God. Betty! What were you thinking?"

Betty grumbled something, letting Chloe help her out of the car. She let go of my hand, and I extended my fingers after four hours of my joints being bent. *Ouch.*

"I found a printout of a bus ticket receipt," Chloe whispered to Bower. I saw him squeeze the steering wheel tight, his jaw clenching. She corralled Betty into the house, Gill following close behind.

Bower exited the car, slamming the door behind himself. He stood with his back to the car for a minute. His shoulders rose and fell with every deep inhale and exhale. He was trying to calm himself.

I watched him through the passenger door, still open after Chloe had gathered Betty, and I let my legs dangle out of the car, sitting on the seat sideways. What did someone do in this situation? Betty was home. The man who was unwilling to fight for our relationship stood with his back to me, refusing to acknowledge my presence.

I pulled out my phone and started searching for bus routes. If Betty could do it, so could I. There had to be something leaving tonight, at the latest tomorrow morning. I would find a way to spring for a motel room for the night.

"Mia." Bower's voice stopped my swiping thumb.

I slowly raised my head to look at him. He stood there, his

fists clenched at his sides as if he was holding something in, trying to restrain himself. From what, I had no idea.

"Come have an orange Popsicle with my grandma. You promised."

Fuck. I had promised her. I slid off the leather seat, my feet hitting the ground. I tucked my phone away, making sure I didn't close out of the local bus line I found. One Popsicle and I was on my way. Maybe Gill or Chloe could drive me to the bus station.

Bower opened the door to the cabin, holding it for me. I walked into a Popsicle party of sorts—Betty, Gill, and Chloe all holding one in their hands, none of them orange.

"Betty insisted," Gill said by way of explanation.

I walked over to the freezer and pulled it open. I picked out one that I knew was orange and ripped open the paper. Orange flavor filled my mouth, but it didn't taste as sweet as it had this summer. It tasted like tart memories—like everything I wanted to forget.

Chloe flittered about the cabin, picking up dishes and sweeping crumbs off surfaces. All the while she had a baby strapped to her chest and a Popsicle stick poking out of her mouth. She disappeared back into the bedrooms, continuing to tidy.

"Mia," Gill started, "I wanted to thank you for helping us deal with this difficult situation. I don't know why or how Betty found you, but I'm glad she did because once you called, I knew she was safe."

"It was no problem, really, Gill. I was happ—"

"Oh my god!" Chloe yelled from Gill and Betty's bedroom. The baby strapped to her chest let out a squeal at her sudden outburst.

Gill, Bower, and I stood up, rushing to the bedroom. Chloe stood next to the bed, cradling her baby against her body, bouncing her up and down to soothe her. I looked around the room, searching for something that would startle Chloe.

On every flat hard surface, tiny rock cairns stood. Most of them were stacks of three, others stacks of four or five. The two windowsills, the nightstands, and dressers were all full. The corner of the room between the wall and the nightstand contained ripped-open envelopes lined with bubble wrap, presumably empty. Crinkled envelopes were shoved between the space, stacked, and placed on top of each other, filling the gap between the floor and the top of the nightstand.

"When did she have time to do this?" Gill asked.

Chloe pulled an empty brown envelope and tossed it to the ground. She pulled out envelope after envelope, the pile at her feet getting bigger, envelopes falling down the mountain of envelopes she made and landing in front of me.

I picked one up, curious what it was. I looked at the return address in the corner. Some sort of military base in the Middle East. And it was addressed to…me. Here at Agate Harbors.

What in the world? I picked up another envelope that had fallen to my feet. It was addressed the same way. Another, the same. Another, still the same. I started looking at the postdate. Each envelope I picked up had a different date stamped. Some from seven, eight years ago. Others were more recent.

I crouched down so that the windowsill was at eye level. At the tiny cairn erected there. The rocks looked eerily like the ones Betty had pulled from her pockets. All unique, like they were from completely different areas of the world. I picked a white one off the top of a cairn, careful not to disturb the ones beneath.

I turned my body so I was facing Bower. I could feel him standing behind me, watching me. "You," I whispered.

"I thought you'd gotten them." Bower gestured to the empty packages that now lay on the floor around the room. "Obviously you didn't."

I walked up close to him. I could feel his breath against my forehead as I looked down at the rock in my hand. "I thought you never wrote or called…all those years," I whispered. "I thought you forgot about me."

"I never did," Bower said. His hand cupped my jaw, pulling my face up to meet his. His body radiated heat. The magnetic pull between us snapped my body against his.

"You sent me rocks?" I asked.

"For eight years, so you wouldn't forget me, wouldn't forget about us."

"I never could," I whispered, looking down at my hand holding the white rock I'd plucked off the top of the cairn Betty had built.

Bower looked down too, our foreheads meeting. His hand, next to mine, unfurled and revealed the red agate I'd tossed beneath his door months ago, my last goodbye. He'd kept it. He let the red agate fall into my palm and bounce on top of the small rock already in my hand.

He put his hand on top of mine, our palms meeting, rocks between our hands. Then his head tilted up, my head following as we stared at each other. "I was wrong to push you away, Mia. I need you; Agate Harbors needs you."

I looked back down at our hands, our fingers intertwined.

"I'm getting help," Bower said, his voice trembling. "Chloe pointed me toward some veteran organizations."

He looked at Chloe for confirmation. She nodded, watching us.

"I was going to reach out to you after you got settled into your first couple weeks of school."

I looked up at Bower. I knew him. I'd known him for over a decade. His eyes were full of hope, longing. Begging me to give him a chance.

I glanced around the room and at all the tiny cairns built around it. There had to be hundreds of rocks here. How many packages had he sent me? He'd never forgotten about me. All these years thinking he had…

Betty had put them away. Maybe she'd known what she was doing at first, trying to protect me from the hurt of our relationship ending that summer, but then she had put them away subconsciously. Who knew with how much she'd slipped over these past years.

Then I remembered—she'd told me a few weeks ago that she had something for me back at the cabin. It must have been the packages she'd wanted me to see. If I had gone with her and seen, maybe all of this would have never had happened. Bower and I could've already been well on our way to our happy ending.

But life didn't work like that. When I had met Bower, it had been when we were young, naive. Young love was ignorant of the future, ignoring all the roadblocks ahead. It was bliss. We'd experienced that together, that euphoria of finding someone who understood you completely. We'd never thought ahead, of what might happen in the future.

We hadn't known what we were doing. My mother had warned me. Young love was supposed to be something that left you heartbroken. Something you lost. Something tragic that you could never forget.

That wasn't what I had experienced. I'd never forgotten Bower, but he'd never broken my heart, not truly. He had held it for me all those years. Keeping it safe. Now it was my turn to return the favor, keep his heart safe with mine. He was holding it out for me, offering it to me. I'd be a fool not to take it. It was everything I'd ever wanted.

I leaned in toward him, our noses brushing. Bower grabbed the back of my neck, pulling me close to him. Our lips swept against one another before I opened my mouth, inviting him in. He took the invitation, crushing his lips onto mine, pulling my body against his. Our heads tilted sideways, our mouths opening, deepening the kiss.

This was it. Young love didn't have to end—it could grow into something beautiful and real.

Gill cleared his throat. I opened my eyes, surprised by the sudden interruption. I had forgotten there were other people in the room. Chloe squeaked, her hand covering her mouth, excitement glittering in her eyes.

"I'd like to reiterate the job offer I made last month," Gill said, and I let out a tearful laugh. "Agate Harbors would love to have you."

Bower gave me a peck before sliding his lips along my jaw, his mouth meeting my ear.

"Stay," he whispered. "The summer never has to end."

Epilogue

Ten Months Later, Mia

Instead of once a year, I got a fresh start each week. But instead of a new week starting every Monday, it now started every Saturday when a new group of weekly renters arrived.

I'd finished up my last year teaching first grade just last week, and I was already up at Agate Harbors. This time for good. I was no longer coming up here to go on vacation; I was coming home.

My hand hurt, but I was finally at the end of the pile of loons I was cutting out of black construction paper. That was going be our craft this week for Kids Camp. I already had bits of white paper cut out for their spots and red circles for the eyes sitting in piles on my new desk. Bower had cleared out one of the small back rooms in the lodge for my office.

Gill had made good on his offer to hire me as the activity director—I'd oversee Kids Camp and take over most of the other guest activities. Bower was ecstatic that he no longer had to call bingo. It wasn't a lot of money, but I was okay with that. I had free lodging and got to live in my favorite place.

Over the past school year, Bower and I had seen each other

whenever we could—mostly on school breaks and on the odd weekend when I'd drive up to Agate Harbors or he'd find time to drive down to the Cities. We'd been taking it slow, learning how to be with each other after years of missed moments.

I couldn't be happier.

Especially because I'd moved into his cabin. It was small, but I never wanted to be far from Bower. Most of our time was spent outside on the resort grounds, and by the time we were ready for bed, we didn't need much space.

With a final snip of my scissors, I set the loon down on top of the others. They weren't perfectly symmetrical, but the kids wouldn't care. I needed to check on the markers. There were always kids who left off the caps, and the markers dried out during the week. As a goodbye gift, the art teacher at my school had given me her stockpile of student markers from the year—many of which hadn't been used. I'd protested, but she'd insisted, telling me she had it in her budget to order new markers for the next school year.

Bower had stayed busy with the resort while I'd been finishing up my last year. Between odd jobs around Agate Harbors, he was going to therapy twice a week and met with a group of veterans once a week on Sundays.

After their first meeting, Bower had showed up followed by two pickup trucks and five guys from the group. He'd shared his trouble with the resort's weekly firework show, and the group had jumped in with an immediate solution. The beds of the trucks had been filled with acoustic foam panels, adhesive, and screws.

It had taken them a few hours to insulate our cabin from sound—this way, every Friday night Bower could retreat to our cabin and relax instead of having to hide in the shower to drown out the noise. I didn't mind the aesthetics. The panels kept the sound of the fireworks out—and the sounds we made together at night in.

I still wore my rain boots everywhere, and no one batted an eye. When I'd accepted the job and officially moved in with Bower, he'd surprised me with a stack of Agate Harbors tank tops, all of them tagless. They'd become my daily resort uniform. Between those accommodations and my weekly virtual therapy appointments, I was doing better than ever. Maybe one day I'd be able to stand barefoot on the beach with Bower's hand in mine.

Betty had remained stable over the past year, a lot less agitated. Gill and Bower had hired an in-home nurse to help keep an eye on her and keep her company while Bower worked and Gill fished. Bower's grandpa wasn't handling Betty's condition well, but we all tried to support him the best we could.

Betty seemed content, even though she no longer recognized me. She'd forgotten who I was shortly after riding in the back seat with me back to the resort. It was like she'd done what she set out to do—get Bower and me together—and now that that was done, she could relax.

As I finished putting away my art supplies, the door to the lodge swung open. I couldn't see anything but his silhouette as the sun streamed in behind him.

"Are you ready for the week?" Bower asked.

I nodded. I had everything prepped for Kids Camp.

"Come with me to the lake before the guests start arriving." Bower held out his hand, but I pushed past it, instead reaching up and wrapping my arms around his neck. I took a deep breath in through my nose. I could smell him, smell the lake.

"You mean before my family gets here?" I asked.

This week Ruby was coming up with my parents, who seemed actually excited for me to be working and living here. My parents were bringing up the rest of my things from their house and were using the trip as an excuse to stay at the resort for an extra week this summer. I was surprised Ruby was driving up with them—she hadn't complained or made any off-handed comments about dreading the ride. Maybe it was because I lived here now and she missed me...but I suspected there was someone else she was looking forward to seeing.

"Exactly," Bower said. "I need to squeeze in some more time with you while I can. I have a feeling you'll want to be with Ruby this week."

"I wouldn't be so sure she's going to have time for me."

He bent down and brushed the tip of his nose against mine. "What do you mean?"

"There's something magical about the lake... I have a feeling Ruby's about to find out."

Bower smiled, leaning in even closer, this time pressing his lips to mine.

There were only so many summers. We had to choose how we spent them wisely.

This was the first summer I'd chosen to do what made me happy, without the judgment or influence of others.

What made me happy was Agate Harbors and Bower—I was going to spend my entire summer loving both.

Lucky for me, my summer never had to end.

BOWERBIRD: Found in Australia and New Guinea, male bowerbirds collect objects like **ROCKS** and sticks to build a Bower and attract a mate.

Afterword

"Dementia has no rules," one of my beta readers commented after reading an early version of *Only So Many Summers*. It was that comment that made me dive deeper into why I wrote Betty Hanson and her journey with dementia the way I did.

There is so much we don't know about the umbrella of diseases dementia encompasses, and everyone's experience with the disease is so different. Those with dementia can display a large variety of symptoms and different amounts of lucidity. No one's story is the same, and there is so much more research to be done.

I took liberties with Betty's experience, pulling from my exposure to the disease—what I've seen as I've watched family members wrestle with the diagnosis and their subsequent battle with dementia.

As many authors do, I also spent a lot of time researching—reading about things like paradoxical lucidity and the "blips" of positive lucid moments caretakers of those with dementia see.

After reflecting on my experiences, other's experiences, and looking at the research, I asked myself the question: Would Betty have recognized Mia if this weren't a work of fiction? My answer: Maybe. For the sake of Mia and Bower's story, I really hope so.

Acknowledgments

This book is my love letter to the state I grew up in and the week I spent at Minnesota lake resorts every summer. While I never fell in love there, the memories of turtle racing, canoeing, and s'mores are forever etched into my brain.

Thank you to my parents for taking my sister and me up north every year—driving the three hours with the car so tightly packed that my sister and I had to sit, squished, thigh-to-thigh, without any electronics (it was the nineties) and only our bickering to entertain ourselves. I'm sure that ride was anything but relaxing for you.

Bringing this book to life was a group project where I was lucky enough to have the A-team working beside me.

My editor, Mandi Andrejka, is someone I feel like I've worked with forever (it's only been two years). I can't tell you how thankful I am to have found someone so compatible and collaborative. This book would be not nearly as good—as smooth—if she hadn't sprinkled her fairy dust all over it. Thank you, Mandi.

I was blessed with a group of beta readers who took the time to read and give me feedback on an early version of OSMS. Thank you Anna, Katie, and Sydney, your feedback was crucial.

A good friend of mine, Alyssa, is my personal resource concierge (seriously—you need something, she knows someone). She introduced me to WTJones, a local artist, and the rest was history. Thank you WTJones for lending this book your talent. The cover and chapter headings are gorgeous. Mel D. Designs took the art and designed a beautiful cover—thank you!

I made a post on Threads asking if anyone could sensitivity read for Mia. I needed someone with very specific knowledge regarding sensory processing disorder. Sara Brodt reached out and has been such a wonderful resource. Thank you for your time and care for Mia.

Thank you to Etta for giving me feedback on Bower and his military experience. I can't tell you how much your emails helped me out. I'm so glad we connected!

Andrea—thank you for your keen eye and help finding all those pesky formatting errors. I love having you go over the final formatted book to point out issues I've missed after I've gone cross-eyed from staring at my words for so many months.

Finally, thank you to my readers! This is the first contemporary novel I've published, and your willingness to follow me from the paranormal side of the romance genre has been amazing. I can't wait to write more stories for you.

About the Author

This is Evi's fourth novel.

Evi lives with her husband, two daughters, and a clingy cat in Minnesota.

Website: evijamesauthor.com

Also by Evi James

<u>The North Woods Series</u>

Entangled in the Woods

Shadows in the Woods

Magic in the Woods

www.ingramcontent.com/pod-product-compliance
Lightning Source LLC
Chambersburg PA
CBHW032002150726
47990CB00005B/1805